Praise For *SOMEBODY ELSE'S LIFE*

Lucid and engaging prose, incisive social insight, high wit, ironic brilliance, narrative urgency, the puzzlement and poetry of human life, above all an elegantly stocked *mind:* Morris Philipson's novelistic signature comprises all of these.
—Cynthia Ozick

Places are finely rendered—the office of a Sotheby's managing director, the Bank of Zurich, a Salamanca mansion, the Villa Serbeloni at Lake Como. . . . We move inside Cooper's chilly satisfaction as he and his lover-accomplice bring off one trick after another in the identity-switching necessary to their scam.
—Benjamin DeMott, *New York Times Book Review*

Can you be other people than you are, or have so far made yourself? That's what Stephen Cooper starts wondering while in Washington for his niece's wedding . . .

The novel recounts with convincing detail each stage of the intricate plot. . . . Despite its framework of crime and fakery, *Somebody Else's Life* is not just a commonplace thriller. . . . This is a story about authenticity.

[Philipson's] point is fundamental—that in a world where everything from politics and works of art to body parts and the qualities of the past can be created in a near-perfect facsimile of the real thing, so can, and will, one's emotional capacities, will to live, and personality.
—Paul Skenazy, *Chicago Tribune*

T0294632

Philipson has delivered a vivid intellectual adventure from which one should depart . . . significantly wiser and still wholehearted.
—*Chicago*

An entertainingly mordant psychological thriller.
—*Washington Times Magazine*

Philipson creates a sympathetic and believable protagonist in Stephen Cooper, a fifty-year-old bachelor academic who, while visiting his millionaire brother, is thunderstruck by the revelation that his tidy academic life has cloistered him from the power and beauty that money can buy.
—*Kirkus Reviews*

Somebody Else's Life is an adventure story, set round with its author's favorite themes: the dark difference between what is and what seems to be, the secret worm in the apple of virtue, the charm of money and what it buys, and the possibility of being someone else. . . . *Somebody Else's Life* holds up well as a suspense story about the perils of putting fantasy into action. . . . The book finally may be read as an extended and absorbing meditation on the loss of integrity.
—Beverly Fields, *Chicago Sun-Times*

An authentic and ingenious account of the ingeniously counterfeit in art and life.
—D. J. Enright

SOMEBODY ELSE'S LIFE

SOMEBODY ELSE'S LIFE

a novel by

MORRIS PHILIPSON

THE UNIVERSITY OF CHICAGO PRESS

Chicago and London

Grateful acknowledgment is made for permission to reprint: Lyrics from "THERE'LL BE SOME CHANGES MADE" by Billy Higgins and W. Benton Overstreet. © Copyright 1921, 1923 by Edward B. Marks Music Company. Copyright renewed. Used by permission. All rights reserved.

The University of Chicago Press, Chicago 60637
The University of Chicago Press, Ltd., London
Copyright © 1987 by Morris Philipson
All rights reserved. Originally published 1987
University of Chicago Press edition 2000
Printed in the United States of America
05 04 03 02 01 00   6 5 4 3 2 1

Library of Congress Cataloging-in-Publication Data

Philipson, Morris H., 1926–
    Somebody else's life : a novel / by Morris Philipson.
      p. cm.
    ISBN 0-226-66750-2 (alk. paper)
    1. Impostors and imposture—Fiction. 2. Philosophy teachers—Fiction. 3. Chicago (Ill.)—Fiction. 4. Art restorers—Fiction. 5. Art forgers—Fiction. I. Title.

PS3566.H475 S6 2000
813'.54—dc21

                                          99-059838
                                            CIP

♾ The paper used in this publication meets the minimum requirements of the American National Standard for Information Sciences—Permanence of Paper for Printed Library Materials, ANSI Z39.48-1992.

For my sons

NICHOLAS
and
ALEX

Remember: There is always the danger
that the other person might
mean what she says.

CHAPTER ONE

THE SEED OF DESIRE to escape from his identity was planted in Stephen Cooper's heart on the evening of April 26, 1984, although he was not aware of it at the time. A man without strong family ties, he found himself at a family reunion by the luck of a coincidence. Having spent the winter quarter of his sabbatical leave from Northwestern making a review of the current operations of Fulbright fellowships in eight European countries, he was due in Washington, D.C., for a three-day debriefing period, which ended on a date that coincided with an invitation to the wedding of his niece Katherine in Georgetown. Although he would not have gone out of his way to attend a family affair, the coincidence made it so easy that he couldn't say no. It did not occur to him that this social event might result in a turning point for his life.

It had been nearly ten years since Stephen Cooper last visited his brother, Mark, and his sister-in-law, Lillian—when his niece was thirteen years old. They were, in fact, only half-brothers. Stephen's father had been killed in an automobile accident. His mother married again a few years later, a pleasant enough man named Halsey. Mark was five years younger than Stephen. At the time of his last visit the Halseys lived in an apartment in Cathedral Towers off Wisconsin Avenue not far from the Washington Cathedral, very comfortable, upper middle class, but nothing to write home about. Besides, there was no one at home for Stephen Cooper to write to. He was a bachelor of fifty, a member of a much shrunken class of unmarried males, the bachelor uncle, who could never be mistaken for a homosexual. He was a man of many affairs.

He knew that his brother Mark had done well financially, starting out as an accountant who became a junior partner in the real-estate enterprises of some of his clients —and eventually became a senior partner in a number of large real-estate developments. He had seen from the engraved invitation that his brother and sister-in-law had a new address, but he was not prepared for the evidence that his brother had become a multimillionaire any more than he anticipated the opulence of the estate in Georgetown. It overwhelmed him. Speechless, now, he stood at the side of the swimming pool with a glass of Dom Perignon in his hand.

The house, concealed from the road behind a brick wall eight feet high, was the replica of a manor on a Virginia plantation of the eighteenth century. It was built on a knoll and surrounded by huge copper maple trees. Walking through the house and out to the terrace on the garden side of the building, one saw in the distance, beyond the pool and the Halseys' land, the magnificent gardens of Dumbarton Oaks. No other house could be seen. It was as if his brother's mansion, barely a fifteen-minute drive from the center of Washington, and still trapped in the confines of a city, was in fact isolated by miles of woods and gardens.

The wedding ceremony had taken place in front of the inner wall, at the bottom of the garden, within a border of tulips: the bride and her bridesmaids color-coordinated with the Queen Elizabeth II pink tulips punctually in bloom—the Unitarian minister reading as text the favorite poems of the bride and groom, ending with their vows of eternal friendship. The silent wishes of many members of both families shored up the determination of the young couple to keep their promises. And then for Stephen Cooper the ritual of family reunion flowed into high tide.

There were the first cousins—James, Luke, and John —whom he had not seen since some grandparent's octogenarian birthday party in deepest Ohio in the 1940s. There were second cousins and their wives, usually second wives, whom he had never met before, and their children, half-children, and stepchildren, blonds and brunettes with pale gray eyes or with great brown eyes like milk-chocolate candies.

"Oh, you must be Stephen!" the new wife of some distant relation would exclaim. "I've heard so much about you. What is it you do?"

"I'm at Northwestern University. I'm a professor of the history of philosophy."

"Isn't that nice . . ." The dying fall was not from disrespect but from remoteness, a genuine lack of interest —as if he had said, "I'm a tester for pollution in the sanitary department." He was outside of their realm and, as he gradually became aware, from their point of view, by no means in a higher realm. He was simply reminded of everything about his family that he had escaped from nearly thirty years before: all of that simple, un-self-conscious philistinism. All of these men did things that produced large incomes, which were used to buy expensive goods and services, none of which was accessible to him. They did things that resulted in red-brick mansions and swimming pools and cases of vintage champagne; they could fulfill the promise that tomorrow a group of professional gardeners would make good the damage to the lawn and forcefeed the flowering plants; professional mechanics would lubricate the chauffeured cars; and a housekeeper would arrange for the English antique table to be repaired from the damage of a cigarette burn. They were skilled but in no sense learned. They were successful only materially—having relatively little moral and absolutely no intellectual lives. Seeing himself through their eyes, he tried to grasp the idea that he was a person of no consequence in the world they inhabited.

Stephen Cooper wandered through the garden from the swimming pool—which was lined around the aquamarine water with arabesques of Spanish tiles—holding his champagne glass to his lips, before grappling, for the eighth or tenth time, with the question: "What is it you do?"

"About what?" he responded. The anonymous young person in front of him blushed; she was only trying to be sociable, as her parents had instructed her to, and he was embarrassed for having responded rudely. "I'm sorry," he added, trying to smile. "You see, I'm not married, and weddings make me very uneasy. Let's start again. Who are you?"

"I'm Denise Rawlins. I'm a cousin of Jeannette Rawlins, one of the bridesmaids. Jeannette and I and your niece were in the same class at Vassar. We're awfully good friends."

"Yes. Oh, I see. Well, I hope you will always stay that way."

The young woman looked at him with an unconcealed flash of anxiety, as if it had never occurred to her that her cousin, the bride, and she might not continue to be best friends for the rest of their lives.

Stephen Cooper gazed up beyond the leaves of the copper maple trees to the cloudless blue sky above, saying, "I'm afraid the heat must be getting to me. Or maybe it's the drinks. I think I should go inside for a little while."

"But the dancing will begin soon. . . ."

He looked up to the terrace where the tuxedoed musicians were assembling.

"Of course, the bride and groom will lead the first dance," she said. "Would you like to dance?"

Stephen Cooper was unable to answer because he felt that his jaws had been clamped shut. The bride and groom had appeared in the center of the terrace to start the first dance. Gone was the white satin dress with lace around the bride's neck and down her arms; gone were the bridegroom's dove-gray cutaway and his white bowtie. Both of them appeared in bathing suits. Briefer bikinis have never been designed. It was as if the fig leaf had been invented for this use only, and the bride and groom were reenacting a prehistoric ritual: showing their respective families and the family of this new spouse that they were such admirable physical specimens of their sex that the faith of all who supported their commitment to marriage was fully justified, for they would carry forward the responsibility of maintaining the human race. Those two spectacular, sexually charged bodies then performed the intricacies of a slow tango on the smoothly polished flagstones of the terrace, surrounded by relatives and best friends, only a few degrees short of performing the act that consummates the ceremony of marriage.

Suddenly, the newly married couple broke free from the terrace and ran down to the swimming pool, dove in —symmetrically and in harmony—splashing their way from one end to the other and back until they burst forth like living fountains, embracing while spraying the atmosphere with drops of water that glimmered in the sunlight of late afternoon. Stephen was not aware of anyone else suffering his astonishment at this unconventional behavior; he felt only that they shared an attitude of acceptance from which he was excluded. This nuptial performance concluded, the bride and groom retired to change again before appearing in their traveling costumes. The gift of a white convertible Mercedes—only one of the bride's parents' donations to the future well-being of the couple —awaited them in the driveway. It was rumored that they planned to make a tour of country inns in New England during the rest of April and most of the month of May.

It was rumored that, subsequently, the groom intended to take a master's at the Harvard School of Business Administration, before joining his father's firm of stockbrokers.

Stephen, who always tried to take the long view, asked himself whether this was not the fulfillment of the American dream. Early in the nineteenth century, the Coopers—of Scotch-Irish-English origins, origins lost in the mists of time earlier than 1800—immigrating through Baltimore—traveled overland into the frontier territory of Ohio and put down their roots. For three generations they produced farmers and then merchants, and in the beginning of the 1900s two engineers and a doctor. It was Stephen's stepfather, the lawyer, who had hoped his son would go into business and industry, for the great fortunes were no longer to be made in railroads or shipping but in automobiles or the financial alchemy of Wall Street. Stephen had rejected his stepfather's advice. He felt a higher calling—to the life of the mind, the studious meditation of the academy, the cultivation of the intellect in the service of rational thought, which, at the time of his self-commitment to that goal, he thought would satisfy as an end in itself. Here in the azure and rose-tinted twilight of his niece's wedding day, Stephen Cooper wondered whether all his years of modesty, a sort of decent moderation, living within the limitation of a comfortable but rather small academic income hadn't been a cover for fear of ambition or fear of inability to do the particularly trying things that result in great wealth, that result in estates and swimming pools and gifts of white convertible automobiles.

It was his half-brother Mark who had moved in that direction and was, now, enormously more successful at it than Stephen had appreciated before.

Younger cousins had attached a "Just Married" sign to the trunk of the white Mercedes and tied strings with tin cans on them to the rear bumper of the car. The bride and groom came down the stairway of the front hall wearing sports clothes that made them look like an ad out of a page of *Vogue,* and Stephen's niece threw her bridal bouquet into the crowded hallway. It was caught by one of her best friends at Vassar, who squealed a little yelp of surprise, grasping that promise of destiny to her bosom. As the newly married couple left under a rain of shouted good wishes, the almost invisible servants arranged the buffet tables on the terrace and all the remaining members of the wedding party were invited to dine al fresco.

Stephen Cooper wandered through the capacious house. In the dining room—where Stephen noticed that the long table accommodated twelve armchairs—the wedding gifts covered the sideboards as well as the table itself. All that investment in hope! he thought. All that silverware and crystal and linen; all those appliances, and picture frames, candlesticks, perfume—and even a set of golf clubs—turned sour in Stephen's mind. He thought of Dorothy Parker's maxim: "You can lead a whore to culture but you can't make her think." You can supply all the conditions for a new household but you can't make a marriage. Stephen figured that he never knew of a single successful marriage. He didn't believe he knew a single happy couple. His own mother had fought with her second husband throughout the childhood of his memories. He was convinced that the insight of his eighteenth or nineteenth year had been confirmed over and over again for the rest of his life: that the shared intensity of mutual passion, the lust that brings a couple together into marriage, lasts for about nine months, and that from then on the unlikelihood of any one person's caring enough about the well-being and satisfaction of another person dooms every marriage—for the next thirty or forty years—to a statistical probability of despair and then an accommodated pretense; resignation if not divorce.

It was that attitude toward relationships between men and women that determined Stephen Cooper's refusal to marry. He made it clear to every woman with whom he started an affair that he would not consider marriage. He was "not the marrying kind." Early in life he discovered that he was something special in bed, from the time that he was a junior in high school and began having sexual intercourse, he could take it "slow and easy." He could hold back, he could postpone his own orgasm until the girl or the woman he was having sex with achieved hers. It wasn't until some ten years later, when it burst upon the popular culture of the entire United States that it was a problem between men and women—men weren't sensitive enough or considerate enough to do more than take their own pleasure—that a reorientation of mentality of the masculine population of the country had to take place in recognition of the legitimate desire of the female population to find separate but equal satisfaction in their own orgasms, that Stephen came to recognize why he had been so successful with women from his earliest youth. He never wavered in his resolve to remain footloose, eternally unattached; but he did satisfy them.

In both the professional and the social world that he inhabited there was an inexhaustible supply of available females, among the faculty, the wives of his colleagues, his students, and casual acquaintances.

His sister-in-law found him contemplating the wedding presents in the dining room. "Do you approve?" she asked superciliously.

"Weddings always make me sad," Stephen replied. "There's such an outpouring of wishful thinking for such a dim probability."

"Well, I consider that very cheap cynicism," she began rapidly, "considering that you've never—"

He interrupted her, saying, "—been man enough to—"

"Oh, no, I understand you're man enough. I assume it's just that you don't choose to take the responsibility."

"I think it was Samuel Butler who said, 'Just because I drink milk doesn't mean I ought to own my own cow.' "

"And who the hell was he?"

"A bachelor. Let's begin again: I must say, your daughter and her husband make a very promising-looking new couple."

"Well, then, why should weddings make you sad?"

"Promises are so rarely kept. It's so difficult to keep them. In fact: I think there's everything in the world to keep them from being realized."

"Is that why you never . . ."

". . . took the plunge?"

"In a manner of speaking."

"I don't see why you should resent it or make me feel guilty. The world is overpopulated, you know."

"If I resent it, and I'm not saying that I do, it would only be because an unmarried man of your sort is a—how should I put it?—a danger, a threat, a spoiler; you're on the side of the forces that tend to make marriages unsuccessful."

"I hadn't thought of myself that way."

"You don't see yourself as others see you."

"Nobody does. Do you?"

"I think I see myself quite objectively: a good person living a good—responsible—life."

"I don't resent that. Why do you resent me?"

"You think you're smarter than everybody else. You think you're better. Now, whether or not you are couldn't matter less to me, but I see what it's done to my husband. You've always put him down. You've always made him feel that he lived an insignificant life." She took a deep breath. "I barely know you. I doubt that I've seen you half a dozen times in the past thirty years," she said. "But I live with you day in and day out. Because I see the effect you had on your brother; I know that he's driven himself the way he has to achieve what he has, to become what he is, because he is forever in competition with you. And he'll never allow himself to believe what he's done is good enough—and so he can never relax and enjoy it. He'll never believe he's admirable enough in your eyes. And it's your eyes that he sees himself through. Not mine! I never appointed myself as his superior, his judge, the one who would determine whether he gets a certificate of approval or not. It's you. It's something you did early in your life that's spoiled his life."

"We've gone our own ways for as long as I can remember."

"It doesn't matter what you remember. I'm talking about what he remembers." She continued: "We all started out plain and simple. And now we're rich, very rich. And you're still what you were twenty years ago: the bachelor professor. Big deal. What was so much better about your choice of lifestyle?"

"It's not a style, it's a life."

She looked through the French doors to the crowd of people on the terrace. "I must be getting back to my other guests."

"A good hostess."

She turned on him a glare of undisguised distaste. "Don't you scorn me."

He threw up both hands as a sign of unarmed innocence. "You see criticism where none is intended."

"All I see is what you are and what you stand for as far as my husband is concerned. And that's bad news. Because the truth is that being an intellectual doesn't make you any better than he is or than I am." She laughed a grim chuckle. "It just makes you poorer."

She left the room as the band on the terrace broke into the music of "Everything's Up to Date in Kansas City."

Feeling as though he'd been slapped in the face, Stephen Cooper went to the bathroom under the stairway in the front hall. He splashed cold water on his cheeks and on the back of his neck. He dried himself with a fleecy white towel on which the word "Guest" was embroidered. He ran his comb through his hair—his thinning chestnut-brown hair. After steadying himself with his hands against the hot and cold faucets, he studied those bathroom fixtures, wondering whether they could be solid gold. He looked into his pale gray eyes reflected in the mirror before him, realizing that he was profoundly tired of himself.

He wanted to escape; but to what? He still had the spring quarter off, with no teaching obligations, through the summer vacation, until the autumn quarter began. He had started a new affair with a youngish woman, a conservator at the Art Institute of Chicago. He was fancy free; but nothing caught his fancy.

Stephen Cooper had taken it for granted that through

his lifetime there had been a sense of *dislike* between him and his brother, as between him and his cousins, and he had long since relegated that to a corner of his memories where it had no power to hurt. But now he was confronted by an act of hatred. His sister-in-law hated him. Never before in his life had he thought of himself as an object of hate. Not that he was treated unfairly. But then it's not fairness one wants all the time; it's being thought well of, no matter what. It was his belief that he lived a life in which he was well thought of. His sister-in-law undermined that belief. She'd made him feel unsteady, as if something had snapped in the inner ear, and he might lose his balance if he tried to walk a straight line. He wanted to make it all right between them. He wanted to hold his brother by his shoulders, look him in the face, and say, "You are an admirable man." It was like being reduced to childhood, asking for forgiveness for some childish prank which the grownups took very seriously. No, no, it wasn't that at all. He realized that he could not ask for instant forgiveness and that, in any case, it could not be given.

They were the grownups now—his brother, their cousins, and he; they were the older generation. And they were not the kind of people who talked about their feelings, in any case. A woman like Lillian, his sister-in-law, stylishly dressed in her mother-of-the-bride mauve gown, might take the occasion of a wedding day to allow herself to become sentimental and actually express her feelings of resentment toward her husband's brother. But where had they come from? The parlor psychoanalyzing, the armchair game of amateur psychologist, the fantasies of unemployed women trying to "understand" their over-achieving husbands. If Mark had actually harbored resentment toward Stephen all their lives, he had certainly never made those feelings known to him.

Stephen straightened his shoulders, pinched the flesh along his high cheekbones until a little livelier color appeared, winked at himself in the mirror for reassurance, and left to join the other guests at dinner.

The sun set, casting a golden glow on men and women and youngsters, who found places to sit around the pool or on carved marble benches hidden at different levels of the garden, to eat their buffet dinners from china dishes balanced on their laps. The band played and the intrepid elders danced even more determinedly than the youths.

After the parfaits and the éclairs for dessert, the crowd gradually began to thin out. Stephen wandered back into the house. Throughout the long hall stood pedestals holding up ceramic bowls and vases, and glass-doored display cases containing many shelves of dishes: pottery from earthenware to porcelain, decorated with Arabic calligraphy—with high sheens, lustrous hues from black to lavender to gold. There was a bar set up in the hallway from which he took away a brandy snifter, and he walked past the library to the billiard room. It was as if he arrived according to plan. His brother Mark and his cousins James and Luke and John awaited him. They took turns at the billiard table or lounged in large overstuffed leather armchairs. If they did not talk about their private feelings, they had no reticence about their public achievements. Stephen was merely the captive audience. They knew each other intimately; they were repeating their deals, their maneuvers, remembering the stages of their winning strategies and tactics for the benefit of the outsider: the not-for-profit professor.

Stephen Cooper was aware of the physical resemblance among them. All of them were tall, with wide but sloping shoulders and slender torsos. None of them was bald, but all of them were suffering from receding hairlines above fair complexions punctuated with strong masculine noses above fairly thin lips. They were all healthy and trim. It struck Stephen that not only a generation ago but a mere decade before, this generation just before or just after reaching fifty would have become portly, if not obese, would be found smoking large Cuban cigars and drinking scotch on the rocks from wide tumblers. But all of these men had given up smoking, drank only very moderately, and exercised assiduously. They were as proud of using the Nautilus calisthenic equipment in their health clubs as they were of taking advantage of less life-prolonging exercises in conspicuous consumption. It came out that Mark had a fifty-three-foot houseboat-sort-of-yacht which he kept in Chesapeake Bay; John was a champion golf player; James owned a condominium in Aspen so that he could ski as frequently as possible throughout the winter; and Luke jogged ten miles every day.

These were the men who now recounted their "killings."

They retold their tales of triumphs in stock-market manipulations. "And now the thing to get into is not the hardware companies making the computers themselves but the suppliers who produce the mini-bits for those computers. That's where the growth is. That's where the competition is. And that's where the stock is still low. But hold on to it. Give it two to five years."

Mark talked about a real-estate deal that involved most of a county in northern Maryland—"practically the size of the state of Rhode Island"—which he'd turned around in the course of six months by selling twenty percent of it to the state of Maryland for a park, completely covering his initial investment, and then selling the rest of it off for industrial development—which happened not to be legal under the conditions of selling the state park but, what the hell? "Every politician in Maryland is up for sale."

They talked about facing down banks that threatened to investigate their holdings simply through knowing which shady deals those same bankers did not themselves want investigated.

They talked of the joy of a numbered Swiss bank account as in a much earlier period of history other true believers might have spoken of the ultimate gratification of personally owning a holy relic.

Stephen Cooper was reminded of why he was not one of them. He had become convinced early in life that big money cost too much. To become wealthy required that you be a manipulator, an operator, probably a swindler; in the end, it would cost you your soul. If you devoted all of your time and effort to making more and more money, there would be no time left in which to enjoy life. Or, rather, if making more and more money was the joy of your life, then you would surely have no soul to lose.

But then the conversation took an odd turn. Having boasted of their prowess, their cleverness, their achievements to each other, all for the purpose of informing Stephen of what he had been missing, they began quite decently to talk with pride about satisfactions in the rest of their lives. Each of them had become a world traveler. That meant there was a time when they would stay for weeks either at the Connaught Hotel in London and make guided excursions into the countryside, or at the Okura Hotel in Tokyo and do the same on that island on the opposite side of the world, but they had grown more confident and better connected along with growing wealthier, and now they stayed with friends in country houses, went birdwatching in Peru or in the Galápagos Islands. They took pride in their children's accomplishments at Vassar and Dartmouth and Stanford. They cultivated collections of objets d'art: besides Mark's Middle Eastern ceramics, there were his unique French art deco bookbindings, John's collection of fine cutlery—the knives and forks and spoons from the early eighteenth century through the Victorian period; Luke's immense selection of African sculpture, for which he had built a wing onto his home in Minneapolis.

These men, during a period of thirty years, had gone through the stages of development from philistine robber barons to aesthetes, which previously it had taken three generations to arrive at.

But none of them asked Stephen Cooper a question about himself. Not that he was unprepared. "Well, what's new in the history of philosophy?" used to be asked, and he was ready with his declaration that "Everything's new in the history of philosophy. We keep reinventing the history . . ." and he would take off from there, depending on how much he thought the audience could bear.

However, by the end of the evening of this wedding party Stephen felt it was a measure of the most unconcealed condescension toward him that neither his brother nor any one of his cousins asked him a single question about himself. They are afraid to embarrass me, he concluded. No, they were so certain that I would be embarrassed to contrast anything of my lackluster life to their sparkling lives that they protected me from my own shame. The latter thought completely disoriented Stephen Cooper. I am, he imagined, like every man, capable of seeing myself only at the center of a life in relation to which everyone else is on the margin, everyone else is removed to some distance farther and farther away from the center. It is just that my brother and my cousins feel they share *a similar center* and, for them, I am very remotely relegated to a distant margin.

He was disoriented by thinking kindly of them—as though they lived worthwhile lives, which truly put his judgment about himself in jeopardy.

A servant in a tuxedo brought bottles of cognac into the billiard room to refresh their glasses periodically. Was he a bartender hired for the evening? Or was he a butler, a permanent, live-in servant for his brother Mark? A servant! Imagine what it costs to afford a manservant in this day and age. Evidently it had not cost Mark his soul.

He was disoriented by the shiver of jealousy that ran through him when he heard a conversation about "numbered Swiss bank accounts." What was it that made the phrase not only mysteriously alluring but, for the first time in his life, desirable? That phrase "a numbered Swiss bank account" watered the seeds of envy and greed planted in the heart of Stephen Cooper that day, so they took root and began to grow, without his knowing it.

Lillian came to the door of the billiard room seeking her husband. "Mark," she said, "you really must say goodbye to some of the people who are leaving."

The cousins looked at their wristwatches and straightened up. "I ought to check on my own brood," Luke said.

James wondered: "How did it get to be so late?"

Alone in the center of the room, Stephen leaned against an edge of the billiard table. Lillian came in and closed the door behind her. "I want to apologize," she said.

In the light of the shaded lamps on the end tables, Stephen now saw the lines of worry around her eyes and around her mouth, which had been invisible in the dining room when she had stood there gilded in sunlight. The years had added ripeness and softness to her pretty, round features—and the marks of worry as well.

She approached him and took one of his hands in both of hers. "I'm sorry I spoke to you that way," she said. "I had just waved goodbye to my only child, who was placing all her chips on the gamble of this first marriage—I'm sorry, I mean on *marriage*. And, for all that I wish her well, I have my doubts. I think I was trying to keep from gagging on my doubts at the moment you said, 'Weddings always make me sad' and . . . and . . . that was just too much. I was frightened by a sense of unfairness. How unfair it was for you to even raise the possibility of sadness or sorrow or the fear of sorrow, when you . . ."

". . . have never raised a daughter, let alone given her in marriage."

"That's right. That must have been what I was feeling, and I lashed out at you. That was unkind. I'm sorry, and I do apologize."

Stephen embraced her and held her close to him appreciatively and affectionately. "That was a very civilized thing to do," he said compassionately. "I admire you. I admire Mark."

Suddenly their eyes met. "Well, then, we're all right again, aren't we?" She moved away from him slowly to sit on the arm of a small leather sofa, looking toward the distance beyond the window, as if to follow the route of a white convertible Mercedes. "They're off on the beginning of their adventure, now."

Then, more brightly, she concentrated on Stephen as though she had no other guest in the house to concern herself with, and asked, "And you, what adventures do you have in store for yourself?"

"I never think of myself as having adventures . . ." he began.

"But other people think of you that way."

"Only because I'm not married. People think that being married means settling into a routine so that you can be expectable, people can depend on the pattern of routines that you're likely to carry out. People have a fantasy about bachelors and romantic adventures; but the fact is a bachelor's routine might be even more expectable." And then he added, as an acceptance of her apology, "And dull. Probably even more dull . . ."

"Please don't ask me to think of your life as dull."

"But your life—Mark's and your life—must be filled with much more mystery and excitement than mine has ever known." The phrase "a numbered Swiss bank account" rang through his imagination.

She stood up to say, "Let's be friends." She kissed him on one cheek and he reciprocated. Then she led him back to the large living room, where the few remaining guests who were not still dancing on the terrace had settled themselves down for their last drink.

Alone in his room at the Washington Hotel, Stephen fell into despair. His brother's ultimate kindness of the evening triggered the undoing. With few guests left at the wedding party, Mark arranged that his driver should take cousin John and his wife, along with Stephen, back to their hotels. The car was a Silver Cloud Rolls-Royce; the driver wore a chauffeur's livery. Stephen said that his cousins should be dropped off first, because they were staying in a suite at the Ritz, whereas he was "closer to the White House." He hoped they drew the implication that his room was at the Hay-Adams on Lafayette Square, but in fact he was staying at Fifteenth Street and Pennsylvania Avenue—in the very much more modest Washington Hotel. He was unnaturally taciturn through the drive back to the heart of the city for the simple reason that, although he knew of the existence of Rolls-Royce cars, had seen pictures of Rolls-Royces probably since he was a child, watched movies in which Rolls-Royces played significant parts, observed actual Rolls-Royces in the streets of New York or London or Chicago, he had never before in his life ridden in a Rolls-Royce. That might have made the drive exhilarating—a high point of luxurious experience. But this Rolls-Royce belonged to his brother, whom he had never in any sense taken seriously, to whom he had always felt superior, and who now—whether with any malicious intent or not—had put Stephen in his place.

The uncertainty of where that place was began to unravel him.

In the previous four months of traveling through Europe, unpacking his bags in different hotels every week or ten days, Stephen had experienced no uncertainty of place. He had a mission, he had the competence to carry it out, and he did it with efficiency. But on the night of this happy day, the night of this wedding, this reunion, these emotional encounters and sudden expressions of feeling, Stephen Cooper felt undone.

The Washington Hotel room itself was not much larger than the lavatory under the stairs in his brother's home. There was a window, but the shade was drawn and there was no view. There was no picture on the wall; there was no cover on the bed. There were a table, a chair, a chest of drawers, and a metal rod with wire hangers instead of a closet. Stephen took off all his clothes and lay down on a cool sheet, having switched off the light and let himself slip into turmoil. Either the champagne and the cognac, which made him feel logy, or the events and the remarks of the day that bumped into each other in his mind filled him with a sense of disorder and uncertainty.

Not only was he tired of himself, he was disappointed by himself. Sometime in his mid-twenties he had made all the important decisions for the rest of his life: he would not marry, he would not raise a family, he would be a dedicated academic, he would live decently if modestly, a sort of combination of Roman stoic and late twentieth-century libertine. And here he was twenty-five years later, looking at himself through his relatives' eyes: not only "not smarter . . . but poorer." He taught the history of philosophy because he had nothing original to contribute to philosophy. There were no adventures in his life. He was dull even to himself. Having begun with the assumption that to be a realist is to be skeptical of everything, he had become a cynic with an investment of love in nothing that would carry him away. The benefit, then, of seeing everything sensibly, disinterestedly, and self-protectively was to have made no exciting or interesting mistakes. He had played it safe, so cautiously, so uninspired, so unwilling to gamble, that he had neither family nor possessions nor challenges to make him care about waking up the next morning to see himself through the wonder of another day. There was nothing to wonder at. He had never known awe.

He felt no sense of either a gaping void or abyss into which he might fall, on the one hand, or overwhelming, suffocating isolated sterility, on the other hand. He felt only hollow. Even that was not exact enough, because he did not feel a shell, an all-embracing outer form within which he was hollow; he felt hollowness as his total condition. It was as if nothing was left of him but the consciousness that his existence mattered to no one—including himself.

If he died during the night—alone, naked, in a narrow bed in an ordinary hotel in Washington, D.C.—he could be easily disposed of. His last will and testament stated that his physical remains should be cremated; all his books, whatever money remained in his accounts, and his life insurance would go to the Northwestern University library; his car and clothes and furniture to the Salvation Army. That was all there was to dispose of. His students would be taught by other professors. His current lady friend would find another gentleman friend. His relatives would shake their heads sorrowfully and say they never did know him very well. Did anyone? Well, yes, there were a few better than mere acquaintances here and there. They would find out later on, in three months, or seven months, and one would turn to another and ask, "Was he really *alone* when they found him dead in that hotel room?"

The obituary would be heartwarming: portrait of a dedicated scholar-teacher. A man whose personal life was apparently minimal because he had devoted himself to teaching, research, and writing. Remember his articles— every now and then over the past twenty years—in the *Journal of the History of Ideas?* A writer of "spartan elegance." A thinker of "laconic directness." A heartwarming obituary; but short.

His lack of satisfaction with himself struck him as boring.

He tried to think of the couple who had sworn the marriage vows to each other that afternoon, his niece Katherine and her new husband—whatever his name was. He could think of them only dancing the tango, nearly naked, and then swimming smoothly across her father's pool. With them went the future of the human race. The optimistic idea of the future of humanity, which starts in requited erotic love, ends as easily in a chauffeured Rolls-Royce as in a single room at a second-class hotel. Perhaps not "easily." Therein lay the difference between his life and the life of his brother Mark, who, for whatever his shortcomings, had earned the devotion of a wife protective enough to accuse Stephen of being the villain in her husband's psyche.

For Stephen himself: wasn't it the same unwillingness to risk the dangers of making a wife unhappy that kept him from having a wife who cared that much about his happiness?

He had reached the point where it was no longer a question of how to be happy; it didn't matter whether he was happy or not. He had reached the point where the only question was: "Why go on living?" or "*Who* was living his life?"

The sense of nothingness frightened him. He put his hands up to his face to see if his features remained, and yet when he identified his forehead, his eyelids, his nose and mouth and chin, he was barely reassured that a person remained. He felt cold sweat on the skin of his features and it terrified him to think that what he had to look forward to—all that remained—was to fall into decay, to become old and ill and senile. To waste away.

He saw the desk in his study at the university's library: a model of neatness. Each thing was in its proper place: the pencils, the pens, the stapler, the Scotch tape neatly aligned along with the yellow legal pads, the stationery for interoffice memoranda, the envelopes. Such neatness made for facility. There would be an absolute minimum of accidents, of the unforeseeable, of the fortuitous. Neatness made for all the conveniences of regularity, dependability, routine. Messiness made for adventures—uncertainty, serendipity, surprises. He had organized his life so neatly that there was no opportunity left for adventure, for taking a risk, for placing a gamble.

He knew that he had to take up with a new woman every now and then—in order to remain a bachelor; other than that he feared any new challenge.

I am jealous of my brother Mark, he suddenly told himself. For Mark to have command of such goods and services in the material world as he now can control reduces my sense of my self-worth to nothing. Now that is not reasonable, not sensible; it throws away the advantages of a lifetime of being an intelligent man with an appropriate awareness of the ways of the world and my own capacities—to be overwhelmed by jealousy. All I need is an adventure, he told himself. And if I can't find it for myself, maybe then I should write a novel. I should write an adventure story; if I can't have it, I can make believe.

But what for? What for?

He had never merely trusted to his luck. On the contrary, he had always thought that the exercise of intelligence would minimize the dangers of bad luck. Of course, he did not control the world that he lived in, but he thought that he could control the way in which he struggled with it. What he was suffering now was not an identity crisis, because he knew very well who he was and where he was within a given—narrow—social, professional, and economic class; what he suffered from was the anxiety created by seeing himself through the eyes of his sister-in-law, his brother, and cousins, in the ashen-gray light that made the class of which he was a member of dubious, if any, value.

He no longer cared for himself. He would have liked to be someone else if only he could generate enough drive to bring about a transformation. Stephen Cooper slipped away from himself into the restful escape of sleep with the perverse thought that it might be fun to rob a bank.

CHAPTER TWO

Waking in the morning to a sense of blankness for his existence, he was saved from atrophy by the habits of a lifetime. He rose, put on a bathrobe, went to the washroom, took a shower and shaved; he brushed his teeth and he brushed his hair; he dressed in a lightweight gray flannel suit, a white shirt, and a polka-dot blue necktie. He shined his shoes and he tied his shoelaces as he had learned to do as a child, cleaned his fingernails, and checked to see that he had his wallet in his breast pocket and the keys to his room, which he locked behind him. He went down to the cafeteria in the ordinary, second-class hotel and had a toasted English muffin with butter and orange marmalade along with his breakfast coffee. He was ready for the day, which he had realized all along, through these preparations, was free to him without any obligation, without any appointment or plan. He had completed his business in Washington, he was still on sabbatical, no one expected him anywhere, nor did he have any expectation for himself. He walked out of the building and along to Pennsylvania Avenue, wondering whether the world would offer him anything that he cared to respond to.

There was a poster on a billboard at the corner announcing the opening of a special exhibition of works by James McNeill Whistler in the collection of the Freer Gallery of Art. He took that in at the moment a policeman approached, and he stopped the man politely to ask where the Freer Gallery was located. The policeman gave him directions, which he then undertook to follow as if there were some purpose to be fulfilled by exposing himself to the Whistler exhibition.

He strode across the Mall, the White House behind him, the Capitol building at his far left and the Lincoln Memorial at his right—surrounded by the monuments of national life—headed toward the Freer, which he could not remember ever having heard of before.

He tried to recall what little he knew about James McNeill Whistler: an American expatriate who lived most of his life in England, right? Hadn't his father been an engineer who helped the Russians build a railroad—was it from Petersburg to Moscow? Or was it the Trans-Siberian Railroad? His most renowned painting a portrait of his mother—"Composition in Black and White." Was it really of his mother? And moody, impressionistic, plum-toned views along the Thames River in London at twilight. Something about his having been a great wit. Wasn't it to him that Oscar Wilde once said, "I wish I'd said that"? And he replied, "You will . . . you will." A late nineteenth-century aesthete—the "art for art's sake" believer, who painted a butterfly instead of writing his signature in the corner of each canvas he painted. That was as much as Stephen Cooper could remember about James McNeill Whistler.

Along with its newest neighbors in the heterogeneous architectural conglomerate that constitutes part of the vast holdings of the Smithsonian Institution, nearest to the so-called "Castle," which is the red-brick Victorian Gothic administration building, and near the ultra-modern Hirshhorn Museum, with its sunken garden for twentieth-century sculpture, is the white marble Freer Gallery of Art, a squarish building of great solidity, implying self-important security: a cross between an ancient Greek temple and nineteenth-century mausoleum in cemeteries from New England to Illinois. It was given to the Smithsonian Institution at a time when a multimillionaire could make a present of his art collection and of the building in which it was to be housed, along with the stipulation of Polonius: "Neither a borrower nor a lender be." Nothing ever leaves the Freer Gallery to travel on exhibition anywhere else, and nothing is invited to visit in it; although it will accept the gifts of permanent additions to its holdings. The Freer Gallery of Art consists almost exclusively of the art collection of Mr. Charles Lang Freer, 1856–1919. There was no Mrs. Freer.

Stephen Cooper entered the quiet halls, went up the few stairs, past the souvenir shop, past the unattended cloakroom, and began to wander through the galleries. It was so early in the day that the building appeared nearly empty. He moved silently through a room in which Japanese fans were displayed, a collection of exquisite portrayals of nature and of court life which had taken an object of simple utility—a fan to create a breeze for a privileged lady or gentleman—and turned it into an object of art by virtue of its decoration. Useless now behind cases of clear glass, each fan became a window into a historic past at great geographic distance. Stephen Cooper could not remember which one of his affluent cousins collected ancient knives, forks, and spoons as objects of art, but the thought that one of them did made him turn his back on Mr. Freer's collection of antique Japanese fans, and he moved forward into the adjoining galleries.

What seemed to be on display there was possibly the historic development of pottery, for it began with Egyptian vases and Greek urns and then presented Arabic bowls, but led to a much larger room exclusively devoted to blue-and-white Japanese pottery. There was a man in a white suit ostensibly checking on the labels of information attached to the walls near the displays who continually caught Stephen's eye with an expression of curiosity. Was he trying to pick him up? The thought only bored Stephen Cooper, who moved rapidly out of that exhibition room.

On his way to the next hall, he realized he was moving around the inner courtyard of the square building. He came upon a group of visitors being given a guided tour through the Whistler exhibition. Along the walls and on the movable partitions were the rarely seen watercolors, drawings, etchings, and sketches for paintings from Mr. Freer's private collection. The female guide who was lecturing spoke in a vivacious voice platitudes that pass for insights into the nature of art in conventional lower-school art-appreciation classes. She named certain colors to be seen: amber, burnt sienna, lavender, azure, and pearl. She spoke of forms—meaning shapes such as curved lines that were echoed in other curved lines; and straight lines that balanced with other straight lines. She was able to tell that a sketch of boats on a river was—in fact!—a sketch of boats on the Thames River as seen from the docks at Newgate. Best of all, it seemed to her, she was able to tell when a design showed *the influence of* a Japanese print that Whistler had admired. She was an oral catalog rather than a critic who could say, "Look: here is what should exalt you; this is what can fill you with wonder!"

Stephen Cooper escaped from that exhibition hall, along the corridor of the courtyard toward what appeared to be a permanent exhibition entitled "The Peacock Room," with the amused sense that he might be entering a small zoo.

At once, he felt he had entered the most extraordinary room in the world.

It was empty but for a velvet-cushioned ottoman in

the center of the space. The room gave an overwhelming impression of sublime peacock blue and shimmering gold, except for a full-length portrait, an oil painting, hanging above the mantel of the fireplace at the near end—the portrait of a lady in a kimono or a satin evening gown, a handsome dark-haired lady in that long patterned gown of soft colors accentuated by such Japanese touches as pottery in one corner and a small print in the background. But the high ceiling, from which hung down six large pendulous globes, the four walls, including the long side wall opposite the entrance, made of shuttered and paneled doors, leading to either a terrace or a balcony, were painted with images of large, stately, arrogantly strutting golden peacocks against a "spaceless" background of eternal peacock blue. Stephen Cooper felt as if he had walked inside an enormous piece of jewelry. He could not remember ever having seen anything more breathtakingly beautiful.

In a state that he was subsequently to judge as being "hypersensitive" and too vulnerable to endure so ecstatic an experience, Stephen Cooper's head became a heavy weight that sank into his collapsing, seemingly boneless body, which gave it no support, as he fainted dead away on the floor.

When he awoke, he was seated on the velvet ottoman, with the man in the white suit holding a vial of smelling salts to his nose.

"There you are," the man said. "You're Professor Cooper, aren't you?"

Stephen assumed that the man had gone through his wallet and taken the name from his driver's license or university identification card; it made him feel taken unfair advantage of.

"I can't imagine why . . ."

The man in the white suit said, "Oh, it happens more often than you would expect. From the statistics it would appear that we're second only to the Louvre in the number of incidents of—"

"Well, I never . . ."

"You're quite all right now, you see." He put the smelling-salts bottle back into one of his white pockets.

Stephen Cooper said, "I don't believe I've ever behaved like that before. I can't imagine what got into me."

The man in the white suit smiled. "The *mysterium tremendum.* That's what I was giving a lecture about at Northwestern—when we met. I thought I recognized you when I saw you a little earlier this morning but I couldn't place you."

Stephen felt a vague glimmer of recognition. For many years he did attend lectures at his university delivered by visiting academics—as if he could benefit from anything and everything, as if he wished to learn about as much as possible. Vaguely he groped for an answer to the question of how long that attitude had continued. Until yesterday . . . Then he turned his attention to the man sitting next to him: a short, slender man with a slight southern accent, balding pate haloed with a fringe of raccoonish hair, the aging face of what once must have been a pretty boy. Stephen Cooper thought of drawings by Mary Petty of middle-aged men still under the thumbs of their matriarchal mothers. He said, "Then you must be . . ."

"Peter Brewster. I'm the Deputy Curator here at the Freer. You asked one of the most interesting questions after my lecture at Northwestern. That's why I recognized you, I'm sure." He stood up. Stephen realized that not only was his suit white but his shirt was white and his necktie was white and his shoes were white. He was spotlessly white. He was the Deputy Curator of the Freer Gallery of Art but he behaved like the chief intern in an asylum or a fancy sanitarium.

Mr. Brewster kindly suggested, "Perhaps you would like a cup of coffee. Why don't you come to my office? There's always a pot brewing there."

Stephen took a deep breath and acknowledged, "I'd appreciate that." Then he followed the white man out of the Peacock Room.

In the office of the Deputy Curator of the Freer Gallery, Stephen drank the strong Jamaican coffee black, began to feel restored, and tried to remember something from the lecture that he must have heard. "Your talk was about people so conditioned by the ordinary world that when they encounter a work of art that's absolutely extraordinary they really and truly don't know how to respond to it and they . . ."

"Cave in. Yes. You remember quite rightly. I was saying that I doubt that any psychologist has given thought to that particular phenomenon and I was citing examples of it and trying to account for it by the feeling of inadequacy in the face of powers that one is totally unaccustomed to coping with."

Stephen yielded: "Well, then, that must be what just happened to me." He waved his hand toward somewhere in the direction above, where the Peacock Room must be located. Mr. Brewster's office was half underground and the windows along the outer wall were at ground level, showing the feet and half of the legs of the men and women who approached the entrance of the gallery. He sat behind his comfortable mahogany desk and Stephen sat across from him in one of the three chintz-covered chairs. They drank coffee from Limoges cups decorated with little rosebuds.

Mr. Brewster said, "You must be a very sensitive man."

Stephen offered: "Hypersensitive . . . at least, at the moment. I've never seen anything as remarkable as the Peacock Room before."

"Oh, yes, it's unique."

Stephen Cooper said: "As is each person who sees it." He wanted to take some stab to indicate to Mr. Brewster that, for whatever the Deputy Curator of the Freer Gallery of Art was about to tell him concerning Whistler's Peacock Room, the fact was that Stephen's experience of jealousy of his brother Mark just might be more important to the psychological explanation for why he fainted than anything of a historical or aesthetic nature that Mr. Brewster might launch into.

"Well, James McNeill Whistler certainly was!" Peter Brewster said. "And the Peacock Room is probably his most outrageous gesture, his most uncontrolled assertion of the freedom of the artist who takes matters into his own hands. I mean, if you consider the fact that artisans and artists were mostly anonymous for the first three thousand years of recorded history, and realize that only with the Renaissance in Italy and subsequently in France and England did the role of the artist take on importance —artists were allowed to sign their works, to be identified with their productions rather than have their patrons acknowledged as the primary source of their art—then you come to understand how merely during the past three to four hundred years the importance of the artist as person has been acknowledged. But, even toward the end of the nineteenth century, a man like Whistler was still fighting the battle with his patrons over which of the two was more important. Consider how the Peacock Room came to be. . . ."

"Do tell me. I haven't a clue."

"It's a subject one could easily warm to," Peter Brewster began. "You know that Whistler was a somewhat irascible fellow . . . ?"

"I think I do," Stephen said tentatively.

"Oh, yes, indeed he was. And he had very mixed relations with his patrons—the most important of whom were Mr. Freer, of Detroit, Michigan, and Mr. Leyland in London. One was as wealthy as the other. But Leyland, who like Freer collected Japanese blue-and-white porcelain following the lead of Whistler, was—how should I put it?—more readily accessible or available to Whistler, who also lived in London. It was in the 1880s or early 1890s that Leyland bought a mansion on Grosvenor Square and undertook to renovate it. In the course of his redecorations, he introduced a number of things that he'd bought from the Duke of Devonshire, such as the stairway in the main hall, along which he had Whistler paint the panels. And then—ah, this is the most important mistake Leyland ever made—when he wished to place the portrait called 'Princess from the Land of Porcelain' in his dining room, Whistler proposed that he alter the colors on the walls in the dining room to coordinate better with the colors in the portrait."

"That's the painting over the mantelpiece?" Stephen asked.

"Precisely. All that Leyland agreed to was Whistler's 'touching up' the colors on the four walls around the painting—for a fee that was stipulated as one hundred pounds. Leyland and his wife then went off on a holiday for the rest of that winter and Whistler had free run of the dining room, which he was to 'touch up.' "

"That is the Peacock Room?"

"Exactly. Whistler repainted all of the walls and the

ceiling during the time that Leyland was away. He called a news conference and showed the room to critics of the British press, who wrote about it in the papers. Leyland, somewhere in Capri, I think, read about what was going on in his house to his complete surprise. He came back to London not only to find that he disliked what Whistler had done—intensely—but that Whistler presented him with a bill for one thousand pounds."

"Fantastic! Did he pay?"

"No," Brewster said. "He was a man of principle. He had not asked Whistler to completely redecorate the room; he did not approve of what Whistler had done with the room; and he refused to pay anything more than the one hundred pounds that he had agreed to originally."

"Philistine."

"No," Brewster said in Leyland's defense, "at least he didn't remove or damage—let alone destroy—anything. He did not have the dining room he wished for. He was saddled with a work of art that he didn't even like, but he left it alone, and so when Whistler's other major patron —Charles Freer—offered to buy it from Leyland, the terms of sale were readily agreed to."

"But how can you remove or reconstruct that sort of room?"

"Ah, the secret is that the walls are not solid. What made it all possible not to say easy is that what appear to be walls are leather hangings, and they are placed against scaffolds, which adhere to the solid walls. Now, when Leyland planned the dining room to exhibit his collection of blue-and-white Japanese porcelain, an engineer was engaged to design the scaffolding against which the leather wallcoverings were to be placed and to design the extremely delicate, extraordinarily beautiful shelves in the corners and above the buffet where the porcelain would be exhibited—a generation before Frank Lloyd Wright began to use such delicate verticals in his designs for shelves in living rooms or dining rooms—and all that preparation had been executed prior to the application of the leather wall hanging which Whistler objected to. When he saw his painting of 'The Princess . . .' hanging in the room with the tone of leather that he disapproved of, he proposed to touch up the walls. He painted over the leather."

"I really must go back and look at the room again," Stephen said.

"Of course you will, naturally, of course . . ."

Stephen looked at him. "You live with it all the time, don't you?" he said with respectful admiration.

" 'Curator' is another word for 'caretaker,' " Peter Brewster said self-deprecatingly.

Stephen thought: Familiarity breeds indifference. I should never become familiar with this unique room. I would always be amazed by it.

Brewster was going on about ". . . that particular point of transition in which the Japanese influence produced the formative stages of *art nouveau* . . ." and Stephen Cooper looked at him, realizing that "influence" is a kind of neutral term, an impersonal attempt at explanation as though power is exerted against one's will or despite one's wishes, "artistic influence" then thought of as *being under the influence:* as being drunk. Whereas, in truth, what is meant by influence is the experience of someone loving something —some object, some gesture, some design—enough to want to assimilate it, repeat it, make it one's own through *reliving* it, that is to say, giving it new life, adapting it to one's own purposes, incorporating it. It is not that Whistler was educated to imitate Japanese art; he gave Japanese art a new lease on life by wedding it to the images of the Western world.

"Of course," Brewster was droning on, "Whistler hated his patrons and the far wall in the Peacock Room —above the buffet, where you see two large peacocks, one scattering gold coins with his claws and the other spurning him—is Whistler's 'portrait' of Leyland, the patron who had nothing but gold to cast upon the ground, and Whistler, the other glorious peacock, haughtily turning his back on him as he goes off doing his own thing."

Stephen said, "I would like to return to the room," as he stood up.

Peter Brewster also got up. "It has been a pleasure talking with you. I do hope to visit at Northwestern again sometime; but in the meanwhile, if I can be of any help to you . . ."

"You have been very kind. I am grateful to you; and I thank you."

Now that it was late morning, Stephen Cooper found he was not alone in the Peacock Room. A man seated on the ottoman contemplated the peacocks on the far wall; a mother and daughter were making a slow circular tour; a young child appeared lost in this cul-de-sac and retreated; but their presence did not disturb him. He allowed himself to drink in the beauty.

He considered the wealth of detail that seemed to coat every surface of the walls and ceiling without overdoing anything. The rhythmic repetition of a fanning, shell-like design, repeated along the walls at eye level, seemed at first to him to be waves of peacock blue foamed along the upper edge with gold—until he saw even in them the repetition of the bull's-eye design on a peacock's feather.

He no longer had the feeling of being inside a jewel or somehow both under water and yet completely safe, as in a cavern of the sea: because the space was inescapably that of a genuine room. A room to be lived in—a dining room—at the same time that it was an incomparable work of art. He calculated that the room was about twenty-five feet long and that the ceiling must be about fifteen feet high, because the lanternlike fixtures that were held in the air above him, like huge teardrops, were themselves at least twelve feet above his head.

Seating himself on the edge of the ottoman, away from the man who was staring at the painted French doors now, Stephen Cooper contemplated the portrait over the mantelpiece. Large enough to be life-size, it represented a European woman, probably Mediterranean, with a noble mane of brunette hair; she was dressed in a Japanese kimono, standing before a Japanese screen, with blue-and-white pottery behind her on one side. "Princess from the Land of Porcelain." These people were crazy about Japanese porcelain, he said to himself nearly out loud. All of the delicate tall, thin shelves in the corners and elsewhere along the walls of the room, created with the reverence and aesthetic originality that went into constructing Gothic cathedrals, were designed to house a collection of Japanese porcelain. It boggled his mind. But then he was not a collector of anything.

When he was ten or eleven years old his stepfather had tried to interest him in building a stamp collection, but the little colored squares with images of people who meant nothing to him or places he had never seen had no attraction and he left mostly blank the large album of pages marked off by rectangles of different sizes. At this moment he could almost hear, muffled deep within the recesses of his being, a strangled moan from the sense of loss in never having been a collector. Never having had enough enthusiasm for stamps, or baseball cards, or matchbooks, or shells, or geodes, or souvenirs of travels, let alone drawings or etchings or sculptures or paintings.

Which brought him back to the oil painting, the portrait, opposite him. He had lived his life in such a way that it had never once prior to this moment occurred to him that instead of the modesty of living within his modest means he might have aspired to the ownership of such a painting as "Princess from the Land of Porcelain." It reminded him of the chilling shiver of jealousy that had run through him the night before, so that he had sat on the luxuriously leather-covered cushion of the passenger seat in his brother's Rolls-Royce with his teeth clenched.

On his way to the men's room in the basement he walked through a corridor lined by mahogany bookcases with glass-paneled doors. There were also some sofas and armchairs where one could smoke. When he had come back from the restroom, Stephen Cooper sat down in one of the armchairs and leisurely lit a cigarette. On the wall near him were photographs and legends offering information about the history and construction of the Peacock Room. One showed the interesting hidden engineering feat that made it possible to suspend the pendulous lighting fixtures from the ceiling. Another referred to the fact that the tooled leather used to cover the walls of the room came out of an ancient tradition, different from the use of movable tapestries—closer to the use of wallpaper, which did not develop until a century later but had itself reached its age of highest art in the sixteenth century. The edges of the chosen pieces of leather would be beveled and glued together so as to make a seamless whole before they were further treated with different patterns of decoration.

A label to a photograph of the portrait "Princess from

the Land of Porcelain" explained that the model for the painting was the daughter of the then Consul General of Greece in London, who refused to buy it from Whistler because he didn't think it was a good likeness of her. It then went on to attest to Mr. Freer's extraordinary devotion to Whistler. He had not bought the portrait from Mr. Leyland when he was able to purchase the rest of the room, because Leyland had sold it at an earlier time; it changed hands some seven or eight times—and locations in Europe as well as England and the United States—before Freer was able to own it and return it to the Peacock Room.

The last of these "stories" that appeared on this wall in the basement stated that the leather wall covering located above the mantelpiece, behind the "Princess from the Land of Porcelain," the only section of wall covering not painted over by Whistler, had been brought to England by Catherine of Aragon among the gifts in her royal dowry, when she arrived to be married to the eldest son of the king. It then went on to say that that section of the wall covering *disappeared* between the time that the Peacock Room was dismantled on Mr. Freer's estate in Michigan and the time that it was reassembled in the Freer Gallery in Washington.

Stephen Cooper looked at the illustration above the legend and saw the image of the original gift that Catherine of Aragon had brought with her: a rich tan color with a small pattern of pomegranates repeated on it. Then he reread with fascination the information about the disappearance of that royal gift.

What could have become of it? Destroyed by accident? Lost through negligence? Stolen? The word "purloined" came into his mind, probably for thinking of the sixteenth century.

What did he remember of Catherine of Aragon? The glories and miseries of royalty—the ultimate robber barons. Daughter of Ferdinand and Isabella, she was a pawn in the game of diplomacy. Promised to become the Queen of England, she was sent as a child—what? sixteen or seventeen years of age—to a northern, foreign climate and country to marry first the eldest son who died and then his younger brother, who became Henry VIII. She gave birth to seven or eight daughters, only one of whom survived—to become Queen Mary, "Bloody Mary." But she gave birth to no son. Henry fell in love with Anne Boleyn. In order to marry her, he needed a divorce from Catherine and that resulted in a break with the papacy and the establishment of an independent church. Catherine never recognized the divorce and remained faithful to the Roman Church, although Henry kept her under house arrest—an exile within his own kingdom—and ultimately starved her to death.

What a pitiful fate for the young Spanish princess who came on a galleon that sailed up the Thames River at the beginning of the sixteenth century, bearing gifts: among them, the leather wall hanging which—or at least a remnant of which—James McNeill Whistler hid behind a painting of his. And then sometime near the beginning of the twentieth century the hanging was "purloined" or kept to this day by someone who—in all probability—had no idea of its history and its value. If it could be found, wouldn't it be worth a fortune?

Now that would be an adventure, Stephen Cooper told himself. And, although he sensed immediately and powerfully the dramatic elements involved in searching it out and finding it, he had absolutely no confidence that his tentacles, his hooks into the real world, into the way things are done and the way things happen, could possibly lead him first of all to play detective well enough to discover the current whereabouts of that priceless object and second to know how to do anything with it if, by any chance, he actually were to find it. It was only something that gave him material for his imagination to play with. He knew himself to be a teacher, a scholar, in some sense a thinker, but in no sense at all a man of the world, least of all a detective who could possibly track down the missing wall hanging and make something of it. Still, he promised himself to think about it.

He snuffed out the butt of his cigarette in an ashtray and rose from the armchair in the corridor of the basement of the Freer Gallery of Washington, devoid of any sense of value that his life had, and without any knowledge of what he might do with the rest of the time allotted to him.

CHAPTER THREE

ALICE JENSEN CHASE was a descendant of Danish farmers in Minnesota who had grown comfortable in the granary business in Duluth after the First World War and who had financed her education at the Cranbrook School of Art, the University of Pennsylvania, and at Harvard for her doctorate, enabling her to become a conservator engaged in the preservation and restoration of works of fine art on the staff of the Art Institute of Chicago. During the years between leaving Philadelphia and completing her graduate work in Cambridge, she had married, given birth to a son, and then divorced a sometime alcoholic graduate student of theology. She was now thirty-seven years old: a tall, handsome woman whose blond hair was swept up in a French bun on the top of her head; her son was enrolled in an excellent boarding school in Connecticut; and she was having an affair with Stephen Cooper.

She found it both convenient and exceedingly pleasant to sublet his apartment on Hinman Avenue in Evanston during the year that he was on sabbatical. It enabled both of them to save money; it gave her a leg up in their relationship; and it pleased her to feel she was keeping the home fires burning.

She understood authentication in museum acquisition work. She understood the physics and chemistry of brush strokes and pigments and the aging of canvas. She was an authority on the use of X-ray exploration and on the dating and aging of an enormous variety of art objects. She had reassured her superiors of the authenticity of certain dubious purchases, and she had unnerved them by the discovery of anachronisms in the nature of some recent acquisitions. She was taken very seriously and her salary was commensurate with the appreciation of the administration of the Art Institute of Chicago; it was hardly a munificent salary, being lower than Stephen Cooper's for a full professorship. She was a feminist who strongly believed that the work she was doing, if carried out by a man in her place, would have been rewarded with a considerably larger salary. She was ambitious. She was watching for the Main Chance. She was embittered by feelings of betrayal and abandonment, which was the only way she could interpret the failure of her foolish youthful marriage, and by the burden of raising their son, now sixteen years old, with which her irresponsible former husband had saddled her.

Stephen Cooper was some twelve or thirteen years older than she—a sophisticated, laidback academic man, who wrote for learned journals articles she found incomprehensible but surely impressive for being technically arcane. He was pleasant and kindly in private; he opened doors for her in a social world of Chicago and Evanston that gave her satisfaction; and he was thrilling in bed.

It had been understood between them that after he reported in Washington on his three-month review of the Fulbright program, he was to return to Europe, where he would be from May until the middle of July on Lake Como at the Villa Serbelloni, which the Rockefeller family had established as a writer's "retreat." He would concentrate on the long-projected, and only slowly progressing, history of philosophy that was to be his magnum opus, the distillation of his thirty years of grappling with the topic as a researcher and a teacher. Therefore, it came to her as a complete surprise when he telephoned from

Washington to ask if she would mind if he flew into Chicago for a visit of unspecified duration—a few days or a week—and by the fact that, while his voice sounded keenly alert and eager to be with her again, she could also hear a powerfully nervous uncertainty in his tone. Although it made her fear some disaster threatened his ability to finish writing his book, it flattered her to think that he was coming home to her to be restored and reassured.

If his plane arrived on time at O'Hare Airport, he could be at the apartment by nine or nine-thirty that evening. She did not know whether he would be hungry and want dinner or whether he would have eaten on the plane and would rather they go out for a late supper sometime afterward, but she made ready a plate of hors d'oeuvres and put a bottle of American champagne in the refrigerator. Then she showered, long and invigoratingly, and dressed with a great deal of thought: so that she would appear neither in a hostess gown, as mistress of the house, nor in jeans and a T-shirt, as if she were a temporary squatter in his apartment. In the end, she chose to greet him in a full black tweed skirt and a long-sleeved silk fuchsia blouse, both proper and provocative: for a meeting between equals. Thus she awaited his return.

As it crossed the sky above the western half of the state of Michigan, the Boeing 727 carrying Stephen Cooper began to lose altitude heading toward its destination. Stephen was a nervous passenger. For all the dangers inherent in flying, at least he was calmer while the plane flew at its cruising altitude; but as it gradually aimed downward toward the earth, he was reminded of all that could go wrong, and he thought of the impact, and the flames, and the death that would result from an accident —if anything did go wrong. He clutched the arms of the cushioned seat and closed his eyes tight, and joining his self-pity with the last stage of this flight, he told himself: "I am entering *my* decline."

This uncommon and oppressive self-concern on his part repelled him at the same time that he felt helpless to rid himself of it. He had changed his plans, as any ordinary man might have done, when he sensed danger to himself, and run for home. For him, as he knew, the danger was from within himself; and "home" meant only a comfortable but ordinary apartment that he'd lived in for ten years, and the companionship of his current lady friend.

He forced himself to open his eyes and look out the window at his left side. The plane was descending over Lake Michigan and directly toward Evanston. To the south he could see the skyscrapers rising higher and higher along Lake Shore Drive to culminate in the giants —the Hancock, the Standard Oil, the Sears buildings—at the center of the city. It was just after eight o'clock, a spring evening at the end of April, when the air was clear and the sky cloudless. The color of Lake Michigan was battleship gray; the skyscrapers appeared as silhouettes, punctuated by the gold or silver lights on floors of offices at different levels, and beyond them to the west where the sun had set there was still an aura of orange light along the far horizon.

On the many occasions over the previous twenty years when he had flown west to Chicago and seen this same view at a similar hour of the day he remembered having been exalted by the anticipation of excitement, by the sense of power that returning to Chicago engendered in him; the promise of action, liveliness, fulfillment. Perhaps it was because he himself had seen it change over twenty years. All of the great new buildings—imaginative, extraordinary architecture—had been constructed during the years that he lived there. It was like having placed his bet on a frontier town, but the frontier had not spread laterally away from where the city had taken root —it had soared skyward; it moved up, not out. And he had identified himself with that upward surge. This night he thought of that attitude as only a curious psychological delusion. It reminded him of the incident some years before when one of the members of the faculty in the biological sciences shared the Nobel Prize for Medicine and a waitress at the faculty club serving him lunch that day said, with the pride of intimacy, "Isn't it wonderful that we got a Nobel Prize?" He had not imagined that she so identified herself with the university. A waitress at the faculty club . . . Now he realized that he himself had no right to identify himself with the skyward gains of Chicago. He was no longer at the center of anything; he was a man on the periphery. He understood that at the heart of his anomie—now encircled by a corrosive feeling of jealousy—was his inability to believe he would ever finish his *History of Philosophy,* which was a reflection of his even worse conviction that it wouldn't matter to anyone, anyhow, even if he was able to finish it.

The plane flew directly over the Northwestern University campus, low enough for him to make out the concert hall near the edge of the lake, the library, the hall in which he gave his seminars. It all looked small as a toy village, as make-believe as the set for a Hollywood movie. There had been times—in the 1930s—when university campuses still imitated Gothic or Georgian buildings while Hollywood imagined them filled with twentieth-century architecture. Later, after the Second World War, universities began imitating the architecture in Hollywood movies. Stephen Cooper thought of himself as a bit player in a grade B movie, someone who could end up on the cutting-room floor, edited out of the script.

Stephen Cooper let himself into his apartment with his own key, while calling out, "Anybody home?"

When Alice stood up from the sofa in the living room and came to greet him, he was surprised—not by her being present, but by the sense of not having remembered she was such a handsome woman.

They embraced. He left his luggage in the hallway and went to the bathroom to wash up. He remembered that he hadn't done anything about fixing the leaking cold-water faucet in the sink at the same moment that he remembered the sight of the gold-plated—or were they solid gold?—faucets in one of the washrooms in his brother's home.

He heard the pop of a cork out of a champagne bottle in the kitchen. When he returned Alice was pouring the bubbling wine into glasses on an end table in the living room, her back turned to him. He took advantage of that instant of silence, that instant before conversation was to be engaged in, to quickly take in the sight of his many books on the shelves of his bookcases, the unpretentious but comfortable furniture, the soft glow of lamp lights, the promise of good cheer in Alice's welcoming gesture and in her lively presence. It was all as he might have expected—if not all that he might have hoped for. It was all the comfort of old shoes that had been fully broken in, when it suddenly dawned on him that what he wanted was a different pair of feet.

They sat down near each other on the sofa, sipped the champagne, and fell into small talk, trying to disguise their surprise at being unexpectedly together. They asked each other how things had been going. Alice responded to his questions about her son away at school: not only was he a good student and a fine athlete but he had decided he wanted to take up the euphonium—a brass instrument that Stephen had never heard of. It was described by Alice as "bigger than a breadbox but smaller than a tuba with a sound somewhere in between the two."

Gradually, they sat closer together, with their arms around each other; they snuggled, they nuzzled, and they kissed each other. After the drink and a snack and evasive answers about the wedding in Washington, and the latest gossip about people at the Art Institute—most of whom Stephen had never met but knew about through Alice's vivid stories and picturesque descriptions; after cuddling and kissing, their conversation turned to how much their bodies had missed each other and how true they had been to each other. Stephen suspected she was not very strongly charged sexually and didn't really miss it all that much; at the same time he felt fully aware of the fact that he had not had any sexual encounter during the months they had been apart, not as the faithful expression of his exclusive devotion to her, but out of caution about sexually transmitted diseases.

The conversation about their lack of sexual activity during the time of their separation from each other was itself a style of foreplay, and eventually led to their undressing each other on the sofa and then on the carpeted floor. When both were naked, they stroked and fondled and kissed each other until Alice suggested a shower, and under the running water they continued—through liquid soap and lather and laughter. After drying each other in the bathroom, Alice blindfolded Stephen with a towel around the upper half of his head and led him to bed.

They made love as though they had just awakened

and remembered they'd promised to help each other start the new day vigorously.

Everything was good about it except Stephen's realizing they were not in love with each other. That is, he assumed that Alice was not in love with him, because for all the good-companion intention to comfort and befriend him, to share news and views and general concern for each other's well-being, there was no edge to it; there was no dread of loss; there was no fear of ruin. When one is in love—romantically in love, possessed by concern for the other—one lives in constant need of the other and the loss of the other would be the ruin of one's own life. Stephen felt no such fear or need on Alice's part. While he lay back in bed propped up against the pillows smoking a cigarette, Alice brought in their champagne from the living room and curled up against his legs, facing him. He had reached the point of pursuing this negative judgment about Alice to the point where it turned back on himself and he saw that he realized all these things about her, or rather assumed his interpretation of her feelings was correct, because it simply mirrored the nature of his feelings toward her. I like her, he figured; and I take pleasure in her, and I will do what I can to give her pleasure. That is as far as it goes, he told himself, in order to keep from suffering. Truly loving someone makes you run the risk of suffering miserably if you disappoint or if you are disappointed. Theirs was a modern relationship meant to maximize mutual pleasure and minimize individual dangers, an absence-of-marriage of convenience. That thought struck him as clever, and in an earlier life a little example of such wit might have cheered him up considerably. But in his present state of self-pity he merely shrugged his shoulders.

Alice asked, "What are you thinking about?"

He responded by beginning to sing in a mock torch singer's voice:

Nobody wants you when you're old and gray . . .
I'm gonna change my way of livin',
And if that ain't enough,
I'm gonna change the way
I strut my stuff . . .
Nobody wants you when you're old and gray;
There'll be some changes made today,
There'll be some changes made.

She laughed. "Is that what you came home to do? Like packing up a different set of suits for the rest of your time in Europe?"

"No. I don't think it's as easy as that, but I have to do something to . . . get started again."

"I thought you were running on all six cylinders."

He wanted to tell her that he had come back heartsick, empty, purposeless. That the experience of his brother's success left him feeling impoverished, with his self-confidence shriveled and his life made pointless. If he had loved her, he might have been able to beg her forgiveness in advance and then burden her with all of this sorrow; or even if he believed that she loved him, whether he loved her or not, he might have taken advantage of that longing for his happiness to tell her all of these feelings. He began to say: "There is nothing like being on your own for a while . . ." and thought he might actually confess, "to confirm your own insignificance." But he didn't say that at all. Instead, he said, "There's nothing like being on your own for a while to make you unsure about which you long for more, a glass of champagne after a good screw or a good screw before a glass of champagne."

Alice chuckled. "If I didn't think of you as a man with no sense of humor, I'd think of you as a very funny fellow."

She asked if he was hungry and wanted to go out and he agreed as how it might be pleasant to stroll over to the Yesterday Restaurant and have a midnight supper. They dressed casually, putting back on the clothes that they had taken off each other. He had avoided exposing his soul; he had avoided showing Alice how vulnerable he was. He had put back on his conventional social skin. Therefore, when she began asking how he had found things in Europe during the winter, it was easy for him to continue being his usual low-key, objective, disinterested, sometimes imaginative, sometimes cynical self.

"Jogging!" he answered. "That's what I think happened to Europe since I was there last a few years ago. Jogging everywhere. Just like here. Joggers—male and female; young, middle, and old—in sexy shorts or baggy sweatpants and bright-colored sweatshirts with radios strapped to their butts and earphones plugged into their ears, plodding away, jog, jog, jog, on the streets and through the parks of every major city west of the Iron Curtain." He was fully dressed now and ran his fingers through his hair. "I wonder if they jog east of the Iron Curtain?"

The fuchsia blouse and the tweed skirt and the nylon stockings and the high-heeled shoes were all in place, enveloping Alice in a cloud of dangerless attractiveness. "Well, then, I suppose jogging is the latest contribution to the Americanization of Europe."

He thought about that for a moment and said quite seriously, "I believe it's only the cities that have been Americanized. You know—you can fly from one city to another and in certain ways not know whether you're in London or Stockholm or Amsterdam or Paris or Madrid, and so on. Because there is so much alike among them as far as 'Americanization' goes.

"But this time I didn't only fly; and having rented a car and driven a great deal of the time, I was very much aware of those worlds that are barely Americanized at all. For example, there are villages in Tuscany or Lombardy where life is lived almost exactly as it was lived in the thirteenth or fourteenth centuries. In Switzerland and in Germany there are similar pockets of medieval life, or life of the early Renaissance—as in France and Spain and certainly Portugal as well."

Alice asked, "You mean there are people who live lives unaffected by the fact that they live in the twentieth century?"

"Exactly. Because they aren't living in the twentieth century. In those hill towns or in the backwater villages or even in an isolated ancient city like Saragossa, there may be some use of radios, electricity, telephones, and there are automobiles or trucks that come and go, but other than those few inventions, people are untouched by the twentieth century. I mean: the ideas of the twentieth century, the ideas we live by. Their ideas were formed anywhere from five hundred to a thousand years ago; that's what they live by!"

"My God," Alice exclaimed, "you sound positively exalted by the thought of such little rock pools of ancient life. Life untouched by recent civilization."

"Well, that isn't a very fair way of putting it. They're living under their own styles of civilization."

"Whereas I think that civilization stops at a town where you can't buy the *New York Times*."

Stephen laughed comfortably; one of the advantages

of not being in love is that it doesn't matter if the spouse-substitute doesn't understand everything you say or doesn't have sympathy with your every thought and feeling.

"You know—although I've never thought about this before—it seems to me that the only way to escape from our kind of life, but on this earth and during this lifetime, would be to pull up all roots from the here and now and go live in one of those rock pools of a different kind."

Alice watched Stephen tie his shoelaces. "Not Fiji, or Tahiti, or some primitive island off the coast of Borneo?" She was smiling skeptically.

"No," he replied slowly. "That's not the same thing at a different time. Civilization in those places has always been primitive in the same way. Exotic way. Too exotic. Escaping to places like that wouldn't give you any sense of living at an earlier time; it would be more like going to live on Venus or Mars. Too different. And too remote from touchstones of today." He paused before asking, "Have I ever told you about the Lago d'Orta?"

"Not that I remember."

"Oh, you'd remember if I'd talked about it. It's a small lake in the north of Italy practically due north of Milan —about an hour's drive; untouched by the tourist trade. While all the other lakes in northern Italy, like Maggiore, Como, and Minore, have been stampeded to death by the tourists of the world, Orta remains off the beaten path. There are the remnants of a church on the island that go back to the fourth century, and the island town in the middle of the lake, built in the fourteenth century, remains today more or less what it was when it was first constructed, as a refuge from the invasions from the north —the way Venice was originally founded." He looked up at Alice, his hands resting on his knees, and sighed. "I can imagine escaping into the fourteenth century by living in a villa on the side of the lake looking at the village on the island in the middle of Lago d'Orta," he said, smiling, "and then driving an hour or so into Milan, occasionally, to pick up the *New York Times*."

Together they wandered along the deserted streets at this late hour, walking the few blocks from his apartment on Hinman to the Yesterday Restaurant.

By contrast to the empty streets, the restaurant was filled with people, nearly every booth and table occupied by a group of students; waiters and waitresses hurried about. Alice and Stephen were seated in one of the dimly lit, raised booths. She ordered Swedish pancakes with lingonberry jam. He wanted a western omelet and beer.

They had not been seated in the booth five minutes before they heard the surprised voice of a student saying: "Mr. Cooper!—but you're not supposed to be here." It sounded more like an accusation than an expression of disbelief.

Stephen recognized Daniel Weaver, one of his doctoral candidates. "And you're supposed to be working on your dissertation."

"Well, I also eat sometimes. I didn't expect you'd be back until next fall."

"I had to come back for a few things . . ." He interrupted himself and introduced his student to Alice and then continued, "But I'll be leaving soon."

"Well, it really would be wonderful if I could talk with you for a while."

"I'll be leaving again in a few days."

"How about tomorrow?"

Stephen looked at Alice with an odd grin implying pleasure in the thought of someone needing him—an implication she was not receptive to; she had no way of knowing he was sending her such a message.

"How would it be if we met here for lunch tomorrow, say about twelve-thirty?"

"It will be breakfast for me, Mr. Cooper. But I'll be here. I'll be here! Thanks for the invitation." He turned away from them, without acknowledging Alice, socially without grace, a pleasant enough looking fellow in his middle twenties, dark-haired, dressed in a heavy Norwegian sweater and khaki Levi slacks.

When the student was gone, Alice frowned, saying, "They're so graceless, so gauche. Do they ever grow up?"

Glibly Stephen answered, "When they start looking for a job. Money is the root of all social graces."

She laughed. "There you go again. Anything for a laugh—no matter how perverse."

"Thinking of money," he began brightly on a new tack, "I had an idea just the other day that I doubt would ever have come to my mind if I hadn't known you."

"What's it about?"

"Forgery."

"You thought about that because you know me?"

"Because you are a conservator—someone who knows how to restore and repair works of art; who knows the genuine from the meretricious."

"Oh, meretricious! I like that. You mean fakes, right?"

"It's a long story but—you wouldn't want me to make a long story short, would you?"

And so over Swedish pancakes and lingonberry jam, over his western omelet and beer, without any emotional charge revealing his state of mind at the time, Stephen described his experience of Whistler's Peacock Room in the Freer Gallery, the information that he'd garnered about its background from the man in the white suit, Mr. Brewster; and the line of thought that had evolved in his imagination from the time that he was struck by the information that the leather wall hanging of Catherine of Aragon had "disappeared" to the idea of writing a novel about a confidence game, a scam, a scheme to make a fortune by palming off a counterfeit of the missing object as the genuine article. "Of course, whether I should actually try to write it or not depends on you."

Alice asked, "In what way?"

"It would depend on your telling me whether it is feasible. I mean, from the technical side—would it be possible to fake such a four-hundred-year-old object? And from the practical point of view, as far as selling works of art, either to museums or to private individuals or some kind of institution, could it be done?"

She was obviously thinking about it seriously, silently, nodding her head thoughtfully and looking at him across the table in that small restaurant booth but actually absorbed by calculations of ways and means. Before too long she spoke, saying only, "Yes, I'm pretty sure it could be done. I don't have a very clear idea yet of how difficult it might be or where peculiar obstacles might occur, but let's say simply in theory, yes, it could be done. Such an object could be replicated; and, one way or another, I think a buyer could be—how should I put it?—"

"Taken in?"

"Yes. By the way, I don't think you know: the Art Institute is sending me to Washington for two weeks' worth of work at the National Gallery in about a month's time. I'll go to the Freer while I'm there—look at the things you told me about—and see what I come up with."

He smiled, wondering: could this actually engage my interest enough to make me feel alive again? What he said to Alice was "I'd be very grateful to you."

"Is that all?" she asked.

"All of what?" he asked with surprise.

"All that I'd get out of it? I mean, if I go to the trouble, do all the work of calculating how this might be pulled off, so that you can write a novel about it, is your gratitude going to be my share of the benefit from it?" She was neither frowning nor smiling. There was nothing supercilious in what she said or how she was saying it. She simply spoke to him as an equal, or equal partner.

He struck the palm of his right hand against his forehead and nearly shouted, "I've behaved like a fool. Forgive me." Then he declared: "How's this for a proposition. If you supply me with information that makes this scheme practicable and I write a novel based on it that gets published—and maybe made into a movie—"

"—and is sold for translation in lots of other languages, and appears in paperback editions—"

"—then you and I will share in all the income from all the commercial success of the book in equal amounts, right down the middle, fifty-fifty, half and half, on every dollar that is made out of it."

"That," she agreed, "is a proposition I can't refuse."

They went back to his apartment as potential collaborators.

Over a cup of coffee in bed the next morning, Stephen proposed that they have dinner "on top of the world"— that is to say, on the ninety-sixth floor of the Hancock Building. Alice would leave work at the Art Institute at five and meet Stephen at the Images Bar there. The day started with a flawlessly blue sky, promising perfect weather for the last day of April.

Stephen went up to the bar punctually at five to wait for her. He seated himself in one of the bucket-shaped low black leather armchairs, ordered a margarita, and stared out at the view—east across Lake Michigan and south to Indiana.

This was not the tallest building in the world; the

Sears Tower was. But, as far as he knew, there was no restaurant in the world located at a higher level than the ninety-sixth floor in the Hancock. On clear days, such as this one continued to be, it was possible to see for fifty miles. He felt sure that that slightly wavering pencil line along the distant horizon of the lake was the west coast of the state of Michigan; he could easily make out the chimneys of steel mills to the south, in Gary. Both were suffused with the light of the sun setting behind him. Below, as far as he could see at that angle to the southwest, beyond tall buildings—steel and glass office buildings, stone and glass apartment buildings with swimming pools on their roofs—spread the city of Chicago, neighborhood after neighborhood. But awareness of the proximity of millions of people could do nothing to ease his loneliness.

When he was a child growing up in Ohio and made visits to a farm his father owned and let out to a tenant, he would climb to the top of the barn and sit on the peak of the roof, feeling that he was indeed on top of the world, where he could see for eight or ten miles—the pastures and the woods, the cornfields and meadows, with no feelings of being alone in the world at all. In those days he knew the security of being surrounded by his family and friends as closely and warmly as he was comforted by his clothes. But, in his decades of adult life, he had played it so *safe* that here he was on top of the world but out of touch with it.

"Oh, my, you look unhappy . . ."

Stephen found Alice standing before him. "Black thoughts," he said, standing up, embracing her, pulling a chair close to his at the little table so she could sit next to him and share the view.

"But it's such a beautiful day!" She herself radiated a

sense of well-being. She stroked the blond hair about her head, took a deep sigh that somehow increased the shapeliness of all her curves; she reached out and stroked his cheek with a cool palm. "You just have to snap yourself out of it," she said.

What helpful, practical advice, Stephen thought sarcastically; is that the way she talks to her teenaged son? What he said was, "I'd like to. I just haven't found the snap yet." He knew that what made for the convenience of their relationship was the assumption that they were not important enough to each other for either to burden the other with essentially private worries. They could not afford to bare their souls to each other; dealing with soul worries was considered too high a price to pay for an otherwise convenient relationship.

Dealing with just the surface of life was sometimes burdensome enough. He was brought back to their common surface and tried to smile as he asked, "And how was your day?"

"Productive. Satisfying. I got through almost a square half-inch in cleaning a painting that hasn't been cleaned in three hundred years. A Watteau!"

"How many square inches do you have to go?"

She laughed. "I haven't figured it out. One half-inch at a time . . ."

"You'll go far."

"It's a small Watteau."

A waitress, wearing a black skirt slit up to her hip, brought the vodka and tonic Alice had ordered and both of them sipped their drinks. Then she asked, "Did the student you met at noon give you a hard time?"

"Very." His sigh then had the tinge of a moan. "He threw in the towel, or, rather, he threw it at me. He's giving up his dissertation, giving up trying to get a doctorate. He said he was so glad I had materialized unexpectedly so that he could talk it out in person instead of having to write me a long explanation. I think I would have preferred reading a long explanation."

"Not everyone who starts can finish the race."

Where did she pick up such conventional wisdom, he wondered, at the movies? Is there real solace in such truisms? "He gave up—he says—because he discovered that the emperor has no clothes. That philosophy is only a word game that gives satisfaction to people who like words—the arrangements of words, *like flower arrangements*—more than they like things or events or feelings; whereas he now knows he'd prefer to be in touch with the real world. He's going into computers."

"He'll ride the wave of the future."

"Maybe. I won't be involved in his future."

Alice looked at him now with more consideration. "You feel rejected? That's taking it all too personally."

"I don't think so," he said with a false chuckle. "I'm just taking it personally." It was exactly that—the sense in which it was personal—that he could not talk to her about. He knew he would not repeat the student's argument to her—even if she were prepared to make him think he had not failed the student as a poor teacher might have failed him. What was most personal was the fear that both philosophy and teaching had failed Stephen. He could barely admit that to himself, let alone express it to her. Suddenly he blurted out: "I really must do something novel to 'snap out of it.'"

"Well, a villa on Lake Como sounds pretty elegantly novel to me."

Trying not to sound dreary, he said, "I'll be working on my book."

"Don't you want to say, 'How I wish you could be there with me'?"

"How I wish you could be there with me."

"That's nice," she said, finishing off her drink, "whether it's true or not."

"People can't do very much for each other, can they?" he said seriously.

She did not take the remark to heart; instead, she suggested, "A gentleman could take a lady out to dinner. Isn't that what you invited me here for?"

The interlude was over soon enough. There was one overnight flight from Chicago to Milan, once a week, on Thursdays on Alitalia. Stephen Cooper was on the flight that left Thursday, May 3. The jumbo jet was crowded. As he aimed toward his window seat in smoking, Stephen was jostled by American tourists and American business-men, by Italian tourists going home, and by Japanese photographers taking pictures of each other as they aimed toward their seats. For the previous few months in Europe, Stephen had the impression that there was no place in Europe without some Japanese tourists visiting it. It had occurred to him that perhaps they were subsidized by the government: that a sizable percentage of the popu-lation of Japan is sent abroad and kept on the move, on some rational plan of rotation, so that there would always be some degree of relief for that overpopulated island.

Finding his place, he slipped his briefcase under the seat in front of him and lowered himself into the narrow cushioned seat that he would be belted into for the next ten hours or so. The man who sat down next to him—of medium build and with Mediterranean features, as likely to be an Egyptian as an Italian—held on to an object between his knees that looked like a soft leather covering over a trombone. They fell into a halting conversation in which the man, who said he lived in Nevada, explained that he was returning to his native village in northern Greece for the first time in a dozen years and was taking with him a gift that would be greatly valued by his family remaining there: a rifle for hunting—in a country where people fed themselves not only by what they farmed but by wild beasts they could capture or kill. Stephen wondered whether there was any truth in what the man said. Can you bring a rifle onto a passenger plane flying an international route? People lie all the time, he reminded himself; they make up stories to make themselves feel better or to make others feel worse, or simply to enjoy the novelty of not being limited to telling the truth.

Stephen turned away from him with an uneasy feeling of uncertainty and gazed out the window at the activities around the plane being prepared to leave. He felt uncertain about everything.

His student—now his former student—had brought down his judgment against philosophy because it remained only contemplative: it did not determine actions, it did not "produce" anything other than slight adjustments in states of mind. What passes for knowledge always ends in the fuzziness of uncertainty rather than in wisdom. It was wisdom and peace and salvation that the boy was after and that Stephen had to agree the study of philosophy would not achieve for him, as it did not for anyone.

He was tired of thinking! He wanted to turn his mind off—to experience whatever was happening then and there: the smell of the tweed suit of the Greek sitting next to him, the rattle of the service truck pulling away from the plane on the cement runway underneath, the gardenia smell of the too-sweet perfume from the woman concealed in the seat before him; or to let whatever images the mind threw up haphazardly to confront him, to calm him or to unnerve him.

The plane rolled away from the airport buildings and moved into place for its takeoff. It smoothly gathered speed and smoothly lifted off and steadily rose away from the earth. Within a matter of a few minutes, the plane was up above Lake Michigan in the darkness and all the lights of the city, grand or gaudy, lay back on the earth behind him.

He closed his eyes and willed himself to visualize Whistler's Peacock Room again, but try as he might, by making the memory play with words like "peacock blue," no vision of the room appeared to him. Thoughts of Washington and the Freer Gallery and the ordinary, second-class hotel brought instead to his mind the hours spent in his brother's house during his niece's wedding. It was the tantalizing idea of *all that money can buy* which suffused his mind. It was the sense of his own being out of it that had undercut or devalued his sense of himself. Could it be possible, he asked himself, that out of envy for his brother's lot he had been robbed of his own happiness? But to what extent had it been genuine happiness? he wondered. Was he robbed of the delusion of happiness that he didn't know better than to live with until then? Even a delusion of that sort is desirable in a world in which most people are unhappy; he had thought that his modesty and his caution had guarded him against the sufferings of unhappiness. The essence of his way of life had been his investment in thinking and teaching.

And then there was the student who only a few days before, at noon at the Yesterday Restaurant, had pulled the rug out from under him. "I can't go on with philosophy," he said. "I don't want to give up my life to become nothing but a mind. This kind of thinking," he had said, "this pretense of pursuing truth, is all in an effort to become impersonal. So that what one discovers and believes is true anyone else can discover. The whole method, the whole effort of pursuing thought in this disinterested, objective way, is to cease to be a person with interests, who is subjective. And it's all a sham, anyhow. Because each philosopher pursues what in the end comes to be judged as personal and subjective—what satisfies him and nobody else because no one else will ever consist of exactly the same combination of elements that need to be satisfied. So what passes for logical argument is only a cover for the exercise of personal power that's been transferred from the realm of action, in which power matters because it results in money or sex or the things that money can buy . . ."

It had been a desperate interview—much more a monologue on the part of his student than a dialogue he could engage in, because he had lost conviction in the reasons he would have brought to persuade the student that he was wrong. That the exercise of speculative thought is its own reward struck Stephen Cooper even now as so paltry a reward that, no longer believing in it himself, he could not countenance the fraud of trying to persuade someone else to believe in it.

On the contrary, he found himself believing in the powers that he did not possess—"all that money can buy." He could believe in his brother's mansion, with its gardens, his Rolls-Royce, and the gifts heaped upon his niece to launch her married life. Stephen Cooper had to admit to himself that—as never before—he longed for "all that money could buy."

He imagined that he could make a great deal of money by writing a successful novel. He had the germ of an idea for it, which turned on one piece of information: that the leather wall hanging Catherine of Aragon brought with her when she left Spain with the promise of becoming the next Queen of England had "disappeared." He was reassured by Alice's initial response that such an object could be replicated—could be faked! And he told himself he would turn his attention for the rest of the flight across the Atlantic Ocean to what he would have to figure out, for the purposes of the novel: how to pull off such a confidence trick: a scam.

Assuming that the replica could be created, first of all, and secondly that a support system of authentication could be created, the primary concern would be how to zero in on a potential buyer. Who would have interest in the object and enough money to pay for it at as high a level as could appropriately be asked for it?

It seemed to Stephen that there were three obvious and immediate answers: first was the King of Spain, who must consider himself the heir of Ferdinand and Isabella, who sent their daughter off to England and who could recover this remnant of that tragic life and restore it to the Kingdom of Spain; second was the Queen of England, who, being herself a successor to the throne from which poor Catherine of Aragon had been removed, and who might wish to suppress the memory of the unkind actions of her predecessor, might buy the leather in order to keep it hidden away in some royal vault rather than have it made public and renew thoughts about the reasons for the break between the English and the Roman Catholic Church; third, there was the Pope, in whose Vatican Museum this one relic might be made public as a reminder of the shameful reason for the separation of the English nation from the Roman Catholic Church.

The first question was how to reach each of them—to stimulate their interests and to see how far they would go; another thought was how to play one against the other, if possible, in order to raise the stakes.

But he could not go on thinking about maneuvering

and manipulating; the faucets in his brother's bathroom got in the way. They couldn't be solid gold, could they? The thought of Alice, responsible for raising a son who was away at a boarding school in New England, got in the way. The thought of his student who rejected all of the frustrations of "the life of the mind" got in his way.

It is not true—he told himself—that there is a radical split between thought and action and that thinking doesn't lead to actions that matter. The person who lives the life of the mind also has to make a living for himself and, in that sense, thought and action are never divorced from each other. But he realized that the essential connection is made, day in and day out, by the relationship between the assumptions one holds regarding how someone ought to behave and the judgments one makes about behavior, all the time. Those ideals are a procrustean bed in which we torture the impressions we have of each person against what we expect of each person: because we come up with the idea of what each person we deal with might be at his or her best, and against that idea we measure his or her accomplishments, and therefore come up with the actual value of each against the imaginary best of each. Everybody does it for everybody else and therefore we are always in conflict.

In other words, most people do not see what they are looking at most of the time. What they look at is what another person is at the moment; but what they see is what they want the other person to be—and therefore there is constant criticism that the other person is not what one expects or desires of him or her. That is bad enough. But what Stephen Cooper realized was that he felt that way about himself now. He looked at himself and felt nothing but dissatisfaction for not being a man of the world, a man of wealth, a man with a numbered

Swiss bank account, a man who owned a Rolls-Royce. He thought that writing a successful novel about a historical art scam could lift him out of his self-condemnation and raise him to a level of satisfaction he had not known before, and that thought came to obsess him.

The plane landed in Milan early the next morning. More or less like a sleepwalker, he moved through the mob of Italians, Americans, and Japanese who reclaimed their luggage and scattered away from the terminal into buses and taxis and private cars. He maneuvered himself to the appropriate train; he got off at the appropriate station, at Lake Como; and delivered himself to the Villa Serbelloni, where he was handsomely ushered into the bedroom-drawing-room suite, where he could do his own thing in Spartan luxury. The scholar as "temporary king."

By the end of the afternoon—after taking a nap—Stephen had hung his clothes in the closet or laid them out in drawers of the dresser, lined up his shoes in the shoebag hung on the inside of the closet door, placed his books along the back edge of the desk and his notebooks in a neat parade across the work table, and removed the cover from the typewriter in front of the window. Whatever was happening to him, he could not escape from a lifetime of being methodically efficient. He took a solitary walk on the grounds of the villa along gravel paths between wide velvety green lawns and banks of lush flowers. Then he returned to his suite to shower and dress for dinner. He had been informed in advance of proper attire; everyone dressed for dinner at the Villa Serbelloni.

The director of the villa and his wife were host and hostess to the scholar-guests. There was so much polish to their surface appearance, their live-and-let-live manners, their mastery of understatement, that Stephen assumed they were only two-dimensional. His fellow guests were more readily recognizable to him. He was thoroughly familiar with the middle-aged to aging members of the intellectual establishment. They fell into only two categories: the ones who radiated the arrogance of their self-esteem, and would not deign to discuss the projects on which they worked, unwilling to waste their time, certain that those who could understand the complexity of what they were pursuing were very few and far between. The other class of the erudite were those who feared to discuss the projects they were pursuing out of their thoroughgoing conviction that anyone else could do it better than they, or they were forever fearful that it wasn't worth doing at all.

The dinner was excellent, the wine superb.

After dinner, in the splendidly appointed long sitting room modestly referred to as the common room, where large windows made available the view of the lake and the Swiss mountains beyond, they were treated to the spectacle of a dramatic thunderstorm. The sky had gone all peach-colored before bruising black-and-blue clouds invaded it, and then jagged streaks of lightning struck at great length toward the mountains in the distance, brightening everything briefly with a theatrical silver glow. Then the downpour came and the thunder continued banging directly above them as if a giant were stamping on the roof of the building. The whole performance did not last more than half an hour, after which the sky offered a flawless view of stars in the growing darkness. Stephen, who had no intention of cultivating the acquaintance of anyone else staying at the villa, avoided conversation in the common room, sipped his espresso and chewed on the lemon rind, isolated in an armchair in a corner. As soon as the first guests got up to return to their rooms—one of the arrogant scholars with an alcoholic wife, and one of the insecure scholars with a hen-pecking wife—Stephen Cooper bade goodnight to the host and hostess and retired to his suite.

He switched on the lamps, took off his clothes, wrapped a bathrobe around him, and walked over to the work table, where he flipped through a few of the pages at the end of his last pad of notes. On a page by itself stood the following sentence in his handwriting: "Ours is a civilization that is winding down."

He thought of his student's condemning judgment that what passes for philosophy is always only autobiography. Stephen looked for one of the pens he had put in the drawer of the desk and came back to the notebook, striking out the words "ours is" and writing over them "I am," so that the sentence read, "I am a civilization that is winding down."

He knew that he would not write his history of philosophy. It was not destined to be. Changing his mind had become too ingrained a habit.

He went to bed hoping that he would dream of all that money can buy, without despising the thought.

Stephen sent a letter to Chicago.

My dear Alice:

Yes, of course it is all very beautiful and very comfortable; but it really doesn't matter—although it would matter a lot more if you were here with me! —because I am getting nowhere on my history of philosophy. I walk around the grounds here and look at the gardens or, beyond them, at the lakes; or, beyond them, at the mountains, and I suppose the other people here imagine that what I am doing is thinking. Since I imagine that they are thinking, therefore, I imagine they think I am thinking. And there are times when I think that I am thinking. But I am not thinking about that book.

I am still thinking about breaking out and doing something entirely novel. No pun intended. I know you once said that "anyone can write a novel—and usually does." By which you meant to put down all the badly written junk or, for that matter, all the well-written junk. But I have something intriguing to write about. And I need the change. Not only the small change but the big change.

So I've taken the plunge. I've started my research. I have been in touch (in Milan) with the cultural attaché of the British Consulate, and with the Consul General of Spain himself.

With the British (my first try) I was very nervous about the whole thing and risked only a telephone call. I had no trouble getting through, and found myself listening to the voice of what I assumed was a middle-aged lady sounding somewhat put upon. I didn't even have the grace to introduce myself or identify myself in any way; I just barreled right in with the question of whom I should get in touch with in the Queen's Household with regard to an artistic and historical object that might be appropriate either for the Queen's Picture Gallery at Buckingham Palace or the Royal Collection at Windsor—you know, the one that includes drawings by Leonardo da Vinci.

In a staccato soprano voice the cultural attaché said, "Oh, you're a potential donor, aren't you?" I bumblingly began to explain *No,* on the contrary, I have an object of interest that I think that the Queen's buyer might wish to purchase for . . . and before I could complete the sentence the cultural attaché interrupted *laughingly* to share her amusement with me about how amazing is the number of calls she gets from people who think they have something the Queen might *buy* from them! "But you are a potential donor, are you not?" she repeated in no uncertain terms, so it was obvious there would be no further conversation unless I played it her way. Actually, I marveled at her finesse in both treating lightly the thought that anyone would approach the Queen to sell her something, and at the same time expressing contempt at the idea. So she protectively went on her way, telling me that if I'd like to donate something to the Royal Collection at Windsor I should get in touch with the Keeper of the Queen's Archives, the Right Honorable Sir Philip Moore, in the Round Tower at Windsor Castle; or, if it would be more appropriate to make the gift to the Royal Library, then I should get in touch with Sir Robin Mackworth-Young, the Librarian. But, if the gift would be most appropriate for Buckingham Palace, then I should get in touch with the Lord Chamberlain's Office in St. James's Palace, London, SW1.

She never once asked me what the object was or why I wanted to "give it as a gift" to the Queen, but in the end turned me off with a sudden expression of appreciation at my thoughtfulness at wishing to become such a "generous donor."

I thought it all very funny when it was over and I discovered that it was really quite harmless and easy to pull off, and it did result in my having the names of three people whom I can write to—if I wish to do so.

Well, then, emboldened by the discovery that I could survive a telephone call, I decided to try making an appointment at the Spanish Consulate. The telephone receptionist informed me that they have no cultural attaché or, rather, that the Consul

General performed those functions as well; she merely asked me for my name and "affiliation"; and made an appointment for me to meet with Sr. Castillo the following week. So yesterday I went into Milan first thing in the morning to keep my appointment at 11 A.M. and found my way to the twelfth floor of a Milan-sized skyscraper. The building is one of those descendants of the Bauhaus style, made of steel and glass, which can be found today anywhere in the world; but inside the suite of rooms rented by the government of Spain the furniture and decorations immediately stamp it with a Spanish personality.

Behind the Consul's large mahogany desk, on legs carved like spiral staircases, there hangs a tapestry of velvet incrusted with a coat of arms embroidered with gold thread—a bas-relief of fabrics and colors. Pictures of the King and Queen of Spain, in costumes appropriate to various seasons of the year, adorned the wall, overshadowing maps, hand-colored and illustrated with vignettes, from the period when Spanish navigators discovered most of the Western Hemisphere and the coast of southern Africa. I sat on a burgundy-colored plush sofa, with a table on each side bearing a lamp in the shape of a Spanish galleon. And on the wall behind me were crossed swords of Toledo steel with those typical inlaid gold and black designs. Thus, despite the sense of being in a concrete, steel, and glass box, all the significant "signs of life" were genuinely Spanish.

The Consul General was an amiable, relaxed, worldly, polished fellow—easily identifiable as one type of Spaniard, rather tall and lean, with a fine head of white hair and pale gray eyes, which I took to be his own; but a set of perfect white teeth, which I assumed were not. When he discovered that I was American, he said he found it most agreeable to have the opportunity to converse in English. He spoke an excellent British English, which he said he had not learned until he was in his forties, but then he had spent ten years in London.

I began by telling him that I am a professor of philosophy, but instead of using the old ploy of having "a friend" who has come into possession of an object he's interested in selling to the King of Spain, I, more honestly, put to him that I also write fiction and am working on a novel in which such a situation takes place.

"Oh, I understand perfectly," he interrupted. "Imaginative literature is the great escape from the mental labors that one performs most of the time. I myself am a poet. An epic poet. That is to say, I have written a number of epic poems, and—" standing up from the sofa where he had been sitting next to me he moved swiftly to a cabinet near his desk, opened a file drawer, and brought back with him a snap binder that must have contained at least three hundred typewritten pages. When he was seated next to me again he not only held the binder open in his hands but riffled through the pages to show me what the columns of verse looked like. My fear that he would read aloud for an hour or two was never realized, fortunately. I think I deflected him from that by saying something about how many French authors had been members of the diplomatic corps. Even Saint-John Perse, who won the Nobel Prize, and Paul Claudel, who wrote plays to be performed in Paris while he was Ambassador to Japan.

"But those are writers," Sr. Castillo remarked, "simply to put you to sleep. That they are

considered successful, let alone important, is just the
result of propaganda. French critical propaganda.
They are very good at making up reputations. Or do
I mean to say making believe reputations? Ah, I
know what I mean: making reputations that are
make-believe." He smiled appreciatively at his
cleverness, while he took the binder full of his epic
poems back to his file cabinet.

When he returned to the sofa he looked
sympathetically at me and asked, "Now, what is it
that you propose to sell to the King of Spain?—in a
novel, of course?"

"Well, actually, it is a piece of leather . . ."

He suppressed a laugh, converting it into a snort,
and smilingly repeated the phrase: "A piece of
leather . . ."

I continued: "A sixteenth-century work of art
with extraordinarily important historical
associations."

"Yes? What would that be?"

I then explained the background and the nature
of the work to him.

He looked thoughtful for a long moment and
then said, "Well, something of that sort proposed to
the King himself would quite naturally and officially
be turned over to one of the King's advisors for the
Prado Collection or any of a dozen other museums,
but I doubt very seriously that they would
recommend purchase. Do you know, it's terribly
important for the King to keep his money in Spain. I
really can't imagine how payment could be
authorized to purchase an object either for the
King's personal collection or for the state that would
mean spending the money outside of Spain."

I suppose I expressed my first reaction of

disappointment with something dismal like the hollow sound "Oh?"

"Of course, to the common man an object of that sort would have no significance."

"For all its historical associations?"

He made fun of that. "My dear fellow, the younger generation—even at the universities—say, Madrid or Salamanca, for example—are more likely to know who Michael Jackson is than Catherine of Aragon."

"But they wouldn't be in a position to buy such an object—"

"And those who are—the museum curators, aristocrats, industrialists—well, I don't know that any would have an interest in that sort of thing. They would be attracted by paintings—a Goya, an El Greco—or jewels, or sacred objects, but 'a piece of leather' "—he chuckled—"wall coverings and door coverings made of sixteenth-century leather are *everywhere* in Spain."

So, at the practical level, I came away with the information that a letter could go to the King of Spain and in all likelihood he would turn it over to a curator in one of the state museums and I would probably never receive a response. Besides that, I can still hear the gentle mockery of the Consul's voice as he repeated the phrase "a piece of leather" with increasing disbelief and ironic amusement, as if I literally had proposed selling coals to Newcastle.

Back at the Villa Serbelloni I slumped into an armchair in the lounge before dinner, weighing the disappointment of that interview. Charming as Sr. Castillo had been, I realized that he had left me with nothing but an acute sense of improbability for such a sale. Still, perhaps, that was his job—simply to dissuade anyone from trying to get money out of Spain, for whatever reason. All he wanted was to retire and to write his epic poems. I was stuck on the hope that the way to manipulate this deal was to get the Queen of England, or the King of Spain, and the Pope, to start bidding against each other for the treasure.

It was at that point that the hostess at the villa appeared suddenly before me. "You look very deep in thought," she said. "It seems to be an occupational hazard here."

I looked into her placidly experienced face, wanting to shake her up, and blurted out: "I was wondering how I could arrange to sell a work of some historical interest to the Vatican Museum."

Only too pleased to be of help, she calmly said, "In that case you must approach Mr. Persegati—Walter Persegati. He's quite a good friend. He's visited here many times. You know, he was behind that extraordinary traveling exhibition of the Vatican Museum's—the one that was in New York and Chicago and so on. He's the Secretary-General of the museum. If you wish to get in touch with him," she said, "don't hesitate to use our name."

There you have it! Two days' worth of work—if you call this work—and I have the first round of the names of people to get in touch with. Now all we need to work out is how to replicate "a piece of leather" and authenticate it—that's all!

A warm hug and a deep kiss.

Stephen

Two days later he received a letter from Alice, which obviously had crossed his in the mail. Actually, it was a postcard enclosed in an airmail envelope. The image on one side was a view of Whistler's Peacock Room in the

Freer. The message on the other side read: "I've been to Washington and learned what I could about your whim. I can tell you off the bat that it *is possible* to do what you have imagined! Conspiratorially yours, A."

Four days after that Stephen received a cable from Alice, which contained a rather cryptic message: "Received your letter regarding research in Milan. Do not think you should use your own name and affiliation. Letter follows. Ciao, Alice."

Why not? he wondered. And he continued to wonder for the next few days while no letter followed.

During the last week of May, according to the "revolving door" system at the villa, a few additional scholars arrived as guests, including an English economist of renown, Sir Basil Milford. As was his wont, Stephen wondered: what do I know of "renown"? What do I know of "economics"? Sir Basil is spoken of with respect, in acknowledgment of his achievements, by his peers and his superiors—the authorities—presumably on the assumption that only they can assess what he has done and evaluate it properly. All within a hermetic group speaking a secret language. Thus, he has A Good Name. But in what language? What is it he has done? What does an economist do? There was some talk by the host at dinner before he arrived that Sir Basil was world famous for his "models" of growth industries in capitalist, communist, and mixed economies. The idea of models of growth brought to Stephen's mind only images of endomorphs, mesomorphs, and ectomorphs—of body types and personality types—all discredited. But, whatever an economist does, Stephen imagined, he must be interested in money, must know something about finance and banking;

and Stephen would be on the lookout for a time to ask him some questions.

When he arrived, Sir Basil Milford turned out to be a large model of roundness, of circles. His bald-headed pink face was perfectly round. He appeared to have no neck. His barrel chest was truly round—from side to side and from front to back. His rimless eyeglasses were sparkling, flawless circles. The fingers of both of his hands, curled back toward his palms, two loosely held fists, dangled like pink-hued grapefruits from the ends of his jacket sleeves. The only straight line about him was the pinstripe in his Oxford gray suit, the uniform of a City man. When not smiling impersonally, his face modeled curiosity through thin lips rounded to silently ask, "Oh?"

The morning after being introduced, Stephen found himself alone with Sir Basil in the lounge. They sipped coffee, read the *Times* (London), and surreptitiously eyed each other. Finally, Stephen caught his eye and smiled. He lowered his newspaper. Sir Basil lowered his, thereby signaling his willingness to be interrupted.

"If you wouldn't mind," Stephen began, "may I ask you a question?"

"Not at all." Sir Basil cleared his throat.

"A very naïve question, I'm afraid."

"That's the only pleasant sort of question to deal with," he pontificated.

Stephen explained that he was being sidetracked from his work on a history of philosophy by the nagging allure of writing "a sort of adventure story" that revolved around the desire to establish a numbered Swiss bank account. "But," he confessed, "I really don't know what gives a numbered Swiss bank account its mystique—its special attraction. In fact, I just don't know what gives it the importance it has. Why is it so desirable?"

"Anonymity," the great man declared, ready to raise his newspaper again as a shield.

It was not in Stephen's nature, despite the fact that he had taught courses in logic, to point out to a layman the tautological nature of defining a bank account with a number rather than a name as having the advantage of no name. Instead, by honestly displaying his innocence and simple-mindedness, he led Sir Basil into a conversation by asking, "What is gained by that?"

"Secrecy," the renowned economist replied. "And," he continued, "you probably know, in Chinese calligraphy the ideograph for a secret is something that is known only by one person. But, as far as the Swiss account is concerned, the secret is known only by two—the banker and the depositor. Or by a third party, if the deposit is made by someone other than the person who owns the account."

"What is the benefit of such secrecy?" Stephen asked.

Now Sir Basil spoke as kindly as he might to a backward grandchild. "You see," he began, "there are people who might wish to evade taxes and there are others who might seek to avoid international exchange controls. They might even smuggle suitcases full of some foreign currency—which it might be illegal for them to export—into Switzerland, for the purpose of keeping it secret. Do you see now?"

"Their own governments would not be able to identify them with those funds?"

"It is as if that money didn't exist, as if that person didn't have it. It is 'unreported.'"

"It really is illegal!" Stephen was unable to conceal his amazement.

"From the point of view of certain Western governments and in the light of their tax laws. But—to be blunt about it—such accounts are made use of by the officials of governments of countries in much of the rest of the world." He added, "As they come and go."

"The countries?"

"No. The officials."

"Why does the Swiss government tolerate it?"

Sir Basil took his time before answering that question. First his response was, "The self-righteousness of Swiss morality is based on being financially successful—stable, sound, and safe." Then he added: "Banking makes Switzerland a very, very wealthy country. This is possible because Swiss law makes legal in its own country what is illegal only in other countries."

Stephen was warming to the disclosures. "You mean that the Swiss government allows a banker to keep secret from a foreign government the name of an account owner and the amount of his deposits despite the fact that the depositor—or the owner—might be a citizen of a country which, for tax purposes, requires that information from banks in his own country?"

"Precisely. Besides, the Swiss government requires exactly that of Swiss citizens and Swiss banks. No Swiss citizen may have a numbered Swiss bank account."

Both men laughed out loud at that.

"Where do the Swiss hide their money?" Stephen asked.

"In their mattresses, I suspect."

They put their newspapers aside, took more coffee from the buffet, and continued in a relaxed, casual manner, seated again in comfortable armchairs.

"Is there a fairly high minimum amount," Stephen wondered, "needed in order to open such an account? A hundred thousand dollars or more?"

"Oh, I don't think it's that high. Yes, a minimum requirement, but I believe more modest than that."

"And then, how does someone living in another country arrange to have access to those funds?"

"Well, you telephone your Swiss banker and instruct him to transfer the amount you stipulate into an account in your own country. Or there's the alternative of traveling to Switzerland, withdrawing the desired amount, and carrying it on your person."

"What's to keep one from tapping into someone else's account? If it's all done by numbers? I mean, how is the banker certain that he's turning over funds to the right party?"

"Oh, a very elaborate system of identification is established when the account is opened. Just as with an ordinary checking or savings account one has a bank identification card and a few pieces of 'special' information to be checked—such as your mother's maiden name or the date of your dog's birth—there are more complex but comparable 'personal' identification techniques." He paused to contemplate the excellence of Swiss efficiency. "Ingenious devices of facilitation . . ."

Stephen spent the rest of the beautiful warm spring day, solitary, in a maze of fanciful speculations about identity and means of identification. He remembered the night in the Washington Hotel when his sense of himself was annihilated, when he felt that he was Nothing. Still, he didn't die of it. The momentum of a lifetime of habits started him up the next morning as if he continued to be identical with what he had been before, whereas no one but he knew his identity was lost to himself. Only he experienced it as no longer possessing the value he had given it previously. It used to be that his identity explained his habits; now the persistence of those habits disguised the loss of that center of value, his identity for himself.

A photograph, fingerprints, your mother's maiden name, the description of your pet parakeet when you were thirteen, might be used by others to narrow down the chances that you are indeed the person you claim to be, but that is the most superficial of claims. The subjective, the interior knowledge of whether you are what you "lay claim to" is constantly reconfirmed or readjusted through reflections of how the rest of the world values you compared or contrasted with how you value yourself. And when you have lost value to yourself? What is your identity then?

This line of thought distressed and finally heavily oppressed Stephen. He grew restless, at loose ends, drifting, unmoored. He reached out for straws. He could be identified as "Alice's lover." Why hadn't he heard from her? Perhaps her letter was lost in the mail. Half of the mail to Italy these days doesn't get delivered, he told himself. And it was meant to be an important letter, something crucial to the plan for his novel.

He looked at his watch. It was ten o'clock in the evening in northern Italy. Seven hours ahead of Chicago. It would be three in the afternoon there. He went back to his room and asked the switchboard operator to place a call to Alice's office number at the Art Institute of Chicago. He didn't stipulate "person to person."

A colleague of Alice's—a Miss McInerney—answered the phone. "I'm sorry. She isn't here."

"Hello. This is Stephen Cooper. Do you remember me? We've met."

"Yes. You're supposed to be in Italy."

"I am in Italy. I'm calling from Italy."

"It doesn't sound it. I thought you were right here."

"Modern technology makes the big difference. Can you tell me when Alice will be back?"

"Well, no." Miss McInerney's voice became nervously hesitant. "She's away. On sort of 'leave.'"

"What? *Away?* Where? What are you talking about?"

"Then you don't know."

"She hadn't told me anything about taking a leave. She's staying in my apartment."

"Alice had to go east."

"Why? What's going on?"

Miss McInerney's long pause was maddening. Stephen suggested, "Perhaps she's been trying to reach me. It's very difficult to contact me here." Gently he tried to persuade her: "Won't you tell me where she is, so I can telephone her?"

"I really don't know if I should. . . ." After a silence, she added softly, "It's so pathetic."

"What is? *Please* tell me." He was wheedling.

In a whisper that was perfectly audible six thousand miles away, Miss McInerney said, "Alice went east because her son died."

Stephen shouted, "I don't believe it!"

"Well, nobody *wants* to believe it; that's *why* people say, 'I don't believe it.'" She was chastising him for doubting her word.

"But how? He was healthy. What happened?—an automobile accident?"

"No. Sadder, much sadder."

He wanted to choke her. Suppressing his anger, he very calmly asked, "Did Alice leave you a number she could be reached at?"

"Her son committed suicide," she whispered to him.

Now Stephen was silent.

Miss McInerney asked, "Are you there, Mr. Cooper?"

"Yes," he answered through the clutch in his throat. "That is terrible."

"Awful. Awful! I thought Alice was going to drop dead when she heard the news."

"You were with her?"

"She got the phone call here at the office."

"Who called?"

"The headmaster at her son's school."

"When was that?"

"Four days ago." She now became practical with explicit details. "Alice said there was to be a memorial service at the school two days after that—she didn't know what else to do—she would fly from Boston," she whispered, "with the remains. Then go back to her mother's in Duluth. She didn't . . . ." Miss McInerney sobbed, "she didn't know what she'd do with the boy's body, but her grandparents were buried in Minnesota."

"I understand. I see. Please, Miss McInerney, please, try not to cry. Be kind to yourself. Be calm. I'm obliged to you for telling me this. This terrible news. But if you'd stay on for just another minute . . . are you there?"

"Yes, Mr. Cooper."

"Do you know how I can reach Alice in Duluth?"

"I do." She read him a phone number and listened as he repeated it to her. Once it was confirmed, he expressed his gratitude in controlled, polite clichés. Then, as soon as the conversation was over and the receiver returned to the cradle of the telephone, he broke out weeping, tears pouring down his face, tears of shock and sorrow for Alice and her son. He lowered his face to both of his hands, weeping. Tears of compassion for humanity, pathetic self-consuming humanity. He had never wanted to suffer on its behalf.

CHAPTER FOUR

At the villa serbelloni, Stephen introduced Alice as his wife. The host and hostess were graciously understanding; the other guests were graciously indifferent. Alice looked frail, bone weary, possibly a recovering drug addict or insomniac. It was better for them not to ask, not to pry. Everyone was considerate of everyone else's privacy. They were left alone.

"My life is over," Alice said calmly when Stephen reached her on the phone at her mother's home. "I don't know why I don't kill myself."

It was a long, slow, painful telephone conversation. She apologized for not getting in touch with him. She was too broken, too distraught. Then she wept with gratitude for his having tracked her down. She had left New England with her son in a casket, in some reversion to type, an unexpected need to return to the land where she had grown up, to return her son's body to that land—only to be told, by the minister of the church where her ancestors were buried, that a suicide could not be given a grave in their cemetery. Infuriated by this ultimate frustration, she ordered his body cremated. She saw his life become a handful of ashes. She spoke of ashes scattered over the huge spiky evergreens at the edge of the Great Lake. She wished she were dead.

Slowly, sympathetic, coaxing, cajoling, Stephen urged her to join him in Italy. "You're on leave from the Art Institute. They'll understand, no matter how long you stay away. You must have a change, a rest. You have to be with someone who cares about you. You ought to be with me. I'll take care of you."

He did not remember, afterward, how far he had gone. Had he told Alice that he loved her? needed her? He doubted that. But he offered her a sheltered escape from everything she was familiar with, escape from the regular, daily routine and whatever signs or symbols might remind her of her son—of the loss of her only child. Eventually, she agreed, more out of resistance to resuming her accustomed life than out of anticipation of pleasure in being with him or of being in Italy; but she did agree. Three phone calls and seventy-two hours later she arrived at the airport in Milan.

Stephen waited at the gate to welcome her. It was early morning. Fog delayed the arrival by more than an hour. He drank unnumberable coffees; he smoked an unbroken sequence of cigarettes. He was keen to be ready for her—friend and refuge—prepared to greet her, offer her succor, peace, rest, quiet, beauty, everything that would relieve her, help to repair her. It was all in the abstract for him. The loss of a child—or worse, an only child—was not a personal disaster he could easily grasp, imagine, out of fear for himself, for he was childless and distanced from the parenthood of others; but he contemplated it in the abstract as one safe and sound might try to conceive of exile or disgrace or amputation. And yet he missed her.

The jumbo jet finally arrived. He stood in the aisle opposite the gate through which all of the passengers would deplane; he watched each of them appear and fall into the arm of others waiting or walk briskly with determination down the wide corridor toward the luggage claim station. He did not recognize her and continued to watch others appear. She was smaller than he remembered. She stood before him and asked—her tone of voice, actually, was uncertain—"Stephen?" for he was not taking her in. Her face was colorless, waxen, without makeup. Her blond hair was hanging uncombed, long, and lusterless, down to the collar of a trenchcoat he was not familiar with. They fell into each other's arms. She wept. He caressed her; he stroked her back; he wiped her eyes; he took her hand luggage and urged her to rest against him as they meandered slowly out through the airport.

Alice was then, and for the next few days, like a sleepwalker. It amazed him that she had been able to make the trip at all. Perhaps her last investment of energy in ordinary practical affairs had brought her through the stages of buying the ticket, taking a taxi to the airport, getting on the plane, and collapsing into a seat. Beyond that she had given herself over to grief and despair. She delivered herself to him, not as a tourist looking forward to the pleasures of a vacation; she was nearly destroyed. They were not husband and wife suffering a common catastrophe, but lovers, so-called. It was only she who was in need of restorative treatment and care. He had not realized how prepared he was to supply that for her. But, as it turned out, he was able to satisfy the need.

Stephen was kindness itself. He protected her; he made her rest in the bower he created for her; he listened to her silences. He listened when she chose to speak. He left her alone or was silent when all she could bear was silence.

He slept in the double bed; she insisted on sleeping on the sofa. He watched her fall asleep. He listened to her breathing until it gradually calmed down.

In the days that followed, the story she had to tell— of how and why her son committed suicide—came to be told in fragments, desultorily, at her own pace, according to Alice's needs. They would be walking together in silence along one of the gravel paths when suddenly she said, "It was by carbon monoxide. He locked the garage and turned on the engine of the station wagon. The car radio was on. It was still playing when he was found—about a day later."

During lunch the next afternoon, she explained that her son was a favorite of the headmaster, who asked him to house-sit while he and his wife spent a weekend in New York. They set off in a sporty Karmann Ghia, leaving the station wagon in the garage—in case her son needed it!

While they sat on a bench in the garden overlooking the confluence of the lakes beyond Serbelloni, out of the silence of their communion, suddenly she told him, "There was a message; difficult to consider it a suicide note. A note. Not addressed to anyone. Just a sentence—two sentences—written in his hand on an envelope. On the floor of the front seat of the station wagon. You know what it said?" Alice recited it from memory. " 'I don't see any meaning in life. I don't think life is worth living.' I shit you not. Those were the very words. I kept the envelope. It's somewhere; in one of my bags." She wept softly. Then, overcome with rage, she spit out: "The dumbbell. The jackass. How dare he? A teenager. Who was he to judge the meaning of life? But to throw it away like that —oh, my God! How dare he?" she repeated. Then she whispered, "The message wasn't even addressed to me. It wasn't a message for anybody. He wasn't in touch with anyone. . . ."

Stephen kept his mouth shut. He said none of the things that came to mind. He had been struggling with the questions of the meaning of life throughout his adult career. There are ways to answer that assume the analogy of translation, as with a word from one language into another. If you hear the word "Achtung" and ask what it *means,* the answer is "Attention!" Or—more often on the analogy with banking or financial investment, the meaning of life amounts to the possible return on an investment. "I've gone to all this trouble—now what's it worth to me?" To those who feel life is not worth the trouble— "it's more trouble than it's worth"—there is no meaning, no adequate return on the investment. In contrast, life is said to have meaning when one feels that it's worth the trouble one takes. It is a performance, an exchange, a gamble full of risks with danger as well as delight at every turn; but only if one cannot roll with the punch does one give up—choose to withdraw totally. Only if one has no belief that any gamble will pay off.

There are those people for whom the meaning of life is found in an afterlife—this investment, that return; and those for whom it is the immediate experience of each event here and now; those for whom it is beyond consideration, because the danger of living is so great that the evaluation of life never has the quality of a reward. In any case, when one judges that life has no meaning, it implies that the return on the investment of energy and hope is not worth the effort.

A few days later, Alice explained that the headmaster of the school had taken her for a walk on the school grounds, and ever so gently revealed that, when her son had declared his love for the headmaster's wife, it was necessary for her to point out their differences in age, the fact that she was happily married, and to assure him that he would find the love of his life later on—which served the purpose adequately most of the time—because, you must understand, this happened rather often. But in the case of her son, it mattered not at all. He persisted in "pleading his suit." The headmaster actually used that expression. Alice was unsure whether she hated him more for implying her son wasn't a fast learner or despised him for denigrating her son's feelings. Moreover, the head-master's wife was—she moaned—"An ordinary, plain woman, *older* than I! How humiliating!"

Stephen held her hand; he nodded and he frowned; but he did not argue with her or try to change her mind about anything. He consoled her by agreeing and by sup-porting even her hatreds.

On another day, she added: "Let me tell you some-thing worse. I hadn't seen my former husband for about fourteen years. He showed up at the memorial service. He didn't come to the court hearing for the divorce proceed-ings; but he came to the memorial service. The darling man. Guess what: a born-again Christian! Holier than thou! So touching, so healthy and clean-looking, like a great big G.I. Joe doll. And you know what surprise he had in store for me? What act of penance? You'll never believe it. He'd maintained a life-insurance policy on our son from the time he was about two years old. Isn't that sweet? A life-insurance policy. Not to guarantee his life, but to pay out money if he died. And it's made out to me. Can you imagine? Two hundred thousand dollars coming to me, because the poor boy died before he was thirty. Thirty!" she shouted. "He was sixteen!

"Normal people take out insurance on themselves so their children will have the benefit of the money when the parents die. This son of a bitch never paid one cent in child support; but all the while he was maintaining a life-insurance policy worth two hundred thousand to give himself some feeling, some trivial, self-indulgent sense, of doing something worthwhile for me. How perverse can you get?" she asked. And answered: "The goddamn fool!"

Her conclusion from that line of thought made perfect sense. She said, "I think life drives people mad."

The meaning of life, Stephen thought, is like the meaning of a piece of music, for the theme is played out through a give and take in the world, and differs for each one of us as a march differs from a symphony, as a hymn of joy differs from a dirge. Thus, each one of us is a different meaning of life. Only how we value it for ourselves determines whether we go on living or not. Alice's son had made his choice from the "negative value balance." Stephen had come close. He no longer valued his life; but he had thought of "refinancing" it rather than destroying it.

Alice continued later that evening: "I'm serious about being driven mad. I myself experienced it once. It comes when you're so disappointed in life—when something so unfair dumps upon your whole life—when you see yourself as having played fair all the while only to be treated so badly that you feel nothing but 'Where did it get me? Nowhere!' And, since good luck or bad luck comes just as arbitrarily to people of integrity as to those who have always played it unfair—well, then, bad luck having driven you crazy, you say, to hell with the fairness or even sanity. Then you deliberately go out and break the rules. I know. I did it once."

There in the balmy air of evening in the ancient villa in northern Italy, Alice confessed that she became a thief once, briefly, until she was brought to her senses. In her impulsive and passionate youth she had married a handsome, good-natured young man only to discover him irresponsible and undependable. He could not cope with her pregnancy, he could not bear the idea of becoming a father. He escaped into alcoholism and infantilism. He ran away. Alice imagined that the threat of a divorce would turn him around and they would make a good life for themselves and their son together. She was crushed—as only the foolishly innocent and optimistic are—by the joy with which he accepted the conditions of the divorce, the happy relief with which he escaped.

She was on her own. She accepted a position at the Art Institute of Chicago, moved to the city new to her, found an apartment, arranged for a babysitter, launched herself alone and friendless into a world that she felt had treated her with cruel unfairness. She had wanted to live on good terms with everyone else. Now, she wanted only to get even. She began by stealing food in supermarkets, paying for only half of what she walked out with. She stole books, and records, and jewelry, scarves, hats, and gloves, and even useless decorations—like a solid silver penguin two inches high, from a tray of bibelots in Tiffany's. In the end she attempted to steal a dress from I. Magnin but was caught.

Alice casually wandered through the floors of the elegant store on upper Michigan Avenue, looking indifferently at furs and evening gowns, beaded purses and silk-covered shoes; but she alighted in the department that sold afternoon dresses starting at a thousand dollars each. She was wearing a loose-fitting dress with a hood halfway down her back. She remembered it was sand-colored with decorations around the collar and cuffs in fuchsia. She tried on one silk or satin dress after another. They remained on hangers in the changing room while she brought back another to try on. The salesladies gave her her head, only admiring each outfit when she appeared on the floor to stare at herself in a three-sided full-length mirror. Finally she stood there wearing a beautifully draped dress of French silk jersey in midnight blue; it accentuated her long neck and narrow waist. It made her feel invulnerable. Back in the changing room she slipped the larger dress over it and then, throwing her topcoat over one arm, she picked up her handbag and sauntered out to the showroom, waving a hand in thanks and good-bye to the salesladies, saying only, "Not today." She was waiting for an elevator when a floorwalker or a detective —with a white carnation in his buttonhole—stopped her and required that she accompany him to the manager's office. Alice never did know how they found out. Was there a television viewer scanning the dressing rooms? Had the salesladies recognized instantly that one of the dresses was missing? She was asked for identification and for the name of her husband or her employer. It was that which humiliated her: the sense that—in the eyes of the rest of the world—her identification was dependent on other people. For Alice, it was the discovery that she had shamed herself which was intensely more important than feeling guilty to others, and that turned her around. She could afford to pay off the price of the dress and she wrote a check to prove that. She realized she was, in fact, on her own and able to take care of herself—uprightly and fairly —rather than needing to get even by breaking the rules. You can never get even for bad luck, only try to live well despite it. And yet Alice was telling the story now to illustrate her point that life does drive one mad.

Stephen wanted to take her on an excursion. The early summer weather was superb. One morning the sky was that extraordinary color one sees only in tourmalines from Brazil—bluer than a pale aquamarine, the clearest, most delicate pale blue. He rented a car in the town of Como and they drove through the foothills of the Alps west to his hidden treasure, the town at the edge of the lake and the medieval village on the island in Lago d'Orta. They ate a midday meal on the terrace of a trattoria, outdoors under a canopy of grape leaves. He stared across the water to the island as if paying homage to a religious relic: the beauty of the past preserved intact.

Alice wore a sweater and skirt and sandals. Her golden hair was swept up high on her head. She was looking much better. Stephen thought to himself, She is beginning to recover from her grief, at the very moment when, staring as he thought she was at the village on the island, she said, "Who will take care of me in my old age?" Thinking only of the loss of her son, she could not even see what she was looking at.

Stephen did not try to distract her; he hoped only to support her long enough for her to be healed. Each time he saw evidence of how much she was suffering he felt that his capacity for compassion increased. How great could it grow? How far would he go to bring her into a state of contentment again if not of happiness, to help restore her and repair her? Not that the conditions of her life could ever be fully recovered; her son could not be brought back to life. There are, in this world, only natural happiness and natural beauty, or imitations, replicas, substitutes; the genuine article or the copy; that which is authentic or the ways to fake it. With Alice's irreparable loss, how complex would the substitutes have to be to approximate "getting even"?

She did stand to get two hundred thousand dollars from her son's insurance.

The turning point came out of Alice without thought or speech; during the night, silently, she came from the sofa into Stephen's bed and slept with him. In the morning, without any word exchanged, they made love. It was as if her body had commanded her to go on living. Stephen was so relieved he asked her to marry him then and there, and she responded immediately, "Of course." He could not have known then that she imagined being restored only in terms of revenge. But the world had treated her with the most vicious unfairness possible, and she would respond to it in kind.

With their passports and other forms of written identification in hand, they presented themselves to the cultural attaché in the American Consulate in Milan and were directed to a Protestant minister, who performed the ceremony of their wedding. Back at the Villa Serbelloni, at dinner the next evening, Stephen could not resist whispering to the director's wife, the hostess, "She really is my wife."

With a gracious smile, the lady replied, "I never doubted it for a moment." There are some degrees of polish that do not admit of any possible crack.

Late that night, unable to sleep, Stephen and Alice sat side by side on the sofa in his suite, facing the open large window, watching the stars blinking at them from inestimable distances, sipping cognac, occasionally sighing—at rest.

"You know," he began, "after your note from Washington, and the cable, I never did receive the letter you promised to send."

"Just as well. It could be used as evidence against us."

"In court?" he asked disingenuously.

"Well, it was all about how to be a successful criminal."

"Really? Why?"

"Because you had written me that when you phoned the British Consul here, or when you visited the Spanish

Consul General, you gave your real name, identified yourself as a professor at Northwestern, or words to that effect."

"Well, I was doing research for a novel."

"That's what was wrong. If you want to use it in a novel. You weren't thinking it through as the real criminal would have done. You wouldn't have given your name or any other clue that could enable anyone *ever* to track you down, if you had taken it seriously. You were putting distance between yourself and the criminal problem you were trying to solve by telling yourself—and telling them —you were doing research for a novel. I don't think someone working on a plan to sell a fake sixteenth-century work of art, or object of historic value, would have gone about it that way. He would always be careful to pretend to be someone else."

He nodded agreement.

"Because—assuming that the scam goes through—if, at some later date, the fraud is discovered—there should be no way for the buyer ever to locate you."

He nodded understanding.

"You were thinking of it only as a fiction. I was thinking of how, *in fact,* it could be possible. Otherwise, the novel wouldn't be convincing."

"Or the scheme won't work."

"Both," she agreed.

Stephen detected a new hardness in Alice's tone of voice. "I haven't got very far in imagining how to play the King of Spain and the Queen of England off against the Pope." Stephen delivered this mouthful with undisguised relish.

"You're indulging yourself. Don't take offense. It's just that the richest are the least likely to part with a lot of money, and in any case the most difficult to convince of authenticity. The piece of leather has been missing for over fifty years. If you tried to make a legitimate sale there would be all the complications of selling something that was stolen from Mr. Freer. You'd never get away with it to the Vatican or Windsor or the Prado." She chuckled: "They really are legitimate."

"So it has to be sold as stolen goods?"

"Well, it has to be sold to someone accustomed to buying illegitimately or without the usual public certifications."

"Are there such people?"

Alice laughed out loud, it seemed to him for the first time since she had arrived in Italy. "Of course, my darling," she crooned, stroking the side of his face kindly with the cool palm of her hand. "The world is full of them. The secret sharers. The ones who know that they can have something—own it!—only if they don't display it. Only if it is hidden, for their eyes only, because if they try to identify themselves with such possessions—to lend such objects to exhibitions, for example—their ownership would be disputed by the legitimate ones. There is a whole, busy underworld in which works of art change from one illegitimate pair of hands to another. It's more like kidnapping and blackmail than like the world of connoisseurs and collectors."

"Are most of the works authentic? The real things?"

"I think so. It's the owners who are phony." She was in her element now; she knew what she was talking about. "A few years ago, when I was in Rome with friends, I was taken to the home of a banker—down in an elevator to the basement gallery, where his son showed us paintings the way any aristocrat's brat might show one through a wine cellar, assuming the guests had no more idea of the value of the bottles than he has, and I recognized Fragonard, Memling, Frans Hals: a stupendous treasure of 'missing' paintings. His father must have overheard the conversation. I think there was an intercom system throughout the house, and he came rushing down after us. As soon as he realized that we knew what we were looking at he invited us out of the house. It was quite graceless. But then we could have gone to the police. I suppose no one does. So the trafficking goes on. I think of that particular Roman as having his private Fort Knox in his own basement."

Stephen concluded, "For the purposes of the novel, then, we must think of a buyer—not open and aboveboard—who is prepared to buy something without a thoroughly certified pedigree, who will take the work at face value and not look closely at the provenance. Right? Someone who wants the work more than the authentication."

"Yes," she replied. "Even for the purposes of a novel."

"What do you mean by that?"

"Darling—" Alice began, "husband, dear one—why is it you want to write such a novel?"

"To make a lot of money."

"How much could that be?"

"I don't know for sure."

"Try to guess."

Stephen pondered, calculated, trying to remember gossip he had heard from colleagues who, under one circumstance or another, had gained some success in publishing popular books. "I'd imagine an advance of *at best* fifty thousand dollars; then, if the book sold well in hard cover, twenty-five thousand more. Half of the advance for a paperback reprint could amount to *at best* a hundred thousand; that makes about a hundred and seventy-five. For movie or television rights: say, two hundred thousand. For licenses to foreign-language translations . . ."

"Around the world . . ."

"Say another hundred thousand. So, at first blush, approximately—almost—half a million dollars; and then maybe further added income from sales."

"All that trouble," Alice said sadly, "for just half a million dollars."

"Just half a million," Stephen echoed, with disbelief.

"When," she explained, "you could have a million if you did it for real, rather than write a novel."

Then there was silence.

Alice broke it by saying, "Now that we're married, neither one of us has to testify against the other in court. Besides: it's a victimless crime. The buyer—knowingly—is as guilty as the seller. I figure they cancel out each other's culpability. Good money simply passes into better hands."

"Better?" Stephen asked.

"From those who are merely rich to those who can make something."

"You indicated that you could make a . . . passable . . . replica of the leather hanging."

"I believe I can. And your account of the conversation with the Spanish Consul General makes me feel certain."

"Does it? Why?"

"Because he kept saying: 'Spain is full of such pieces of leather.' Sixteenth-century leather. Wall hangings and door coverings."

"Yes . . ."

"So what is needed is for me to find such a piece of leather that's plain and treat it the way Catherine of Aragon's gift was decorated. I know it can be done. I know how to do it. And now it's obvious how to begin. Go to Spain to find such a piece to make use of."

Stephen was not so much stupefied as unprepared, and then simply full of admiration. Alice had the know-how it would take and the motive for seeing it through. Stephen had nothing else to live for: here was a chance to feel alive again and to satisfy the desire to command a million dollars.

CHAPTER FIVE

A t the villa serbelloni, beyond the lounge in the main building, was situated a small card room. Two circles of eighteenth-century Gobelin tapestry mirrored each other on the walls and were echoed upward from a similar circular rug on the floor—full of pinks and lemon yellows. Stephen said, "If you want to make it look French, tie ribbon bows all over it." Three tables were permanently set up for chess, backgammon, and bridge. The sunlit room was rarely occupied during the daylight hours. Alice and Stephen secreted themselves there the next morning, seated near the large window at the end of the room facing an end of the terrace. Across the bridge table they looked at each other, from thronelike chairs, playing idly with a deck of cards, holding some in one hand and throwing out others, so that, if anyone passed on the terrace and looked in, it would appear as if they were playing gin rummy.

Stephen said, "Let's start again from the beginning. You say the wall hanging can be replicated. But even before we've talked about what kind of documentation we'd need for authenticating—I forget the word . . ."

"Provenance."

"Right. But assuming we'll work that out somehow—why did you leap to the conclusion that we should not look for a legitimate buyer, especially an institution like the Vatican or—"

Alice interrupted: "I think we'll save not only time but trouble if we aim for a shady deal to begin with, where the buyer can't look too closely to find out whether there's something fishy on our part."

"How do you mean, 'can't look too closely'?"

"Let me put it this way," she began. "There's an elaborate network of people who want to own things that shouldn't be in their possession. They command the financial power and the right connections enabling them to get hold of such things. Don't ask me to explain the psychology of someone who has such a private power that only he knows that he has it, but, believe me, there are such people. They even go so far as to commission thefts to get things for them."

Stephen scooped up a group of playing cards and threw them down again, as if to confess his naïveté, saying, "Thefts? From where? Other secret collectors, museums . . . ?"

"All of the above, and palaces, and churches—especially churches. Of course it can't be done without the complicity of the clergy. But there are endless thefts—thefts of priceless church property, such as a gold crucifix coated with precious jewels, reliquaries, icons, even tapestries—that can't possibly be explained without implicating the clergy that should have been responsible. Instances, for example, when the prelate is not at the place where he's supposed to be, or there is rotten security on occasion, when otherwise security is very sound. The collector who's commissioned the theft has an agent who somehow gets to the responsible clergyman, who receives his reward in—how should we put it?—appropriate goods or services. And then the objects disappear into private hands. They're either never seen again or are shown occasionally only to the collector's most intimate friends; or, now that I think of it, are used to 'trade up' for something else but equally shady, because the trading is not public.

You can't try to auction a purloined crucifix at Sotheby's or Christie's."

"Even with false documents of authentication?"

"Well, I suppose it would be much harder, because legitimate buyers in a public auction can press the hardest for verification of documents." Alice had spoken slowly and was now thinking it over as not entirely out of the question but she added uncertainly, "We will have to find an answer to the question of how to prepare some kind of documentation." Then she laughed, in low, sharp sounds. "If we can fake the leather, we can fake the papers as well!"

"How do we *find* our collector in disguise, our illegitimate buyer for our illegitimate treasure?"

Alice took all of the playing cards in her hands, shuffled the deck, and began to divide them equally between Stephen and herself. "One for you, one for me . . ." she said. Then she thought out loud, "First we disguise ourselves. We never want to deal with anyone in person, or through the mail, or over the telephone, in such a way that they can identify us in real life. We have to get the word out to the possible agents and contacts of our secret collector and set it up in such a way that we can be got in touch with only indirectly, through a false name and address."

"What agents?"

"We can let it be known at the great auction houses —perhaps under the table. We can sound out dealers or museum officials. I mean, after all, there are dealers who are probably as busy in their backroom offices as they are in their public galleries. And then museum officials— Let's say an assistant director, who will get something out of it, might be more than happy to act as go-between."

"Get like *what* out of it?"

"Favors—or commissions. It might be either a legitimate one such as a gift of money or some other work of art for the museum or whatever institution the person works for, or it might be illegitimate, simply self-serving, a personal commission of a boxful of money." They smiled at each other.

Stephen nodded. "That's okay, as long as the commission doesn't come from us."

"Oh, I imagine the go-between might try that, too."

Stephen mulled over the thought: "Treasures really do disappear, don't they?"

"It didn't start with the Nazis plundering Europe in the forties. You know, the term 'loot' is one of the few words in the English language that the British took out of India along with what it stands for." Alice smiled at her next thought. "For all we know, some of the neolithic cave paintings originally came from other cavemen's walls." They both laughed hard. She lifted her head and looked up at the eighteenth-century tapestries on the walls. "There's the fact that the last Medici ruler of Florence was one of the first great collectors of Meissen porcelain and snuffboxes. An inventory of his collection in the middle of the eighteenth century can still be read in the archives of the Pitti Palace. But not one of the objects is to be seen. They must have disappeared about two hundred years ago. Nobody knows whether they were destroyed or stolen or given away."

Stephen's thoughts were elsewhere. Suddenly he blurted out: "Could we use your connection with the Art Institute?"

"How? I don't want to be identified."

"Well, not you personally. The imaginary person you'll become when we have our disguises. What if it came to be known somehow—to the network of underground agents and go-betweens—that the Art Institute was given a treasure that it's unable to exhibit because it's ownership might be questioned. In this case, there's a leather wall hanging that might be claimed by the Freer Gallery in Washington. Let's say the Art Institute doesn't want to turn it over to the Freer, but would rather dispose of it privately to an unidentified buyer."

"What's the advantage of relating this to the Art Institute? Should the check be made out to the museum?"

"Certainly not. It would have to be made out to us, acting as agents of the Art Institute."

Alice then added to this scenario. "What if the Art Institute did not want to simply turn it over to the Freer Gallery because there was some reason to contest its ownership?" She took a deep breath and rose to the occasion. "What if there is a document in the handwriting of Mr. Freer indicating that it was given as a gift to someone whose grandchildren decided to turn it over to the Art Institute?"

"Why wasn't it made public at the time the gift was given?"

"Because the curator who was entrusted with it was sworn to ten years of silence." Alice laughed. "And then he died, and it was found in his office only afterward."

"Is that possible?"

"I think it happens more often than anyone would imagine. For example, Harold Joachim died recently. Who knows what treasures will be uncovered in his cabinets and desk drawers and closets?"

"Who was he?"

"A great curator of prints and drawings; a world-renowned authority. And he isn't around to contest anything that would be said about him now. So it's possible to imagine a situation in which the givers—after ten years

—may be assumed to be dead; and it is known that the receiver is dead, and if possession is nine-tenths of the law, then it belongs to the Art Institute—which doesn't want to display it because it might lead to a court battle with the Freer Gallery—so the Art Institute wants to sell it, but not on the open market."

Alice shivered momentarily. "Too close to home," she said. "We'd have to use a pseudonym. How could I get messages at the Art Institute under a false name?"

"All we'd have to do is rent a post-office box. The false name and that address would stand for the agent representing the Art Institute—as a shield. The Art Institute doesn't want to be implicated! But we want an association with it to create the assurance of authenticity that the shady buyer would be taken in by, or better still, make a lunge for."

Alice shook her head sadly at the same time that she smiled. "Poor, nice, old Harold Joachim . . ."

"The nicest touch of all," Stephen began his reverie, "will be that when the final show and tell takes place, the buyer, or at least his agent, can come to see the object on view at the Art Institute of Chicago—which is as respectable as any institution can be and simply wants to disembarrass itself of an authentic—but disputed—possession."

"Security has become awfully tight since those Cézanne drawings were stolen from the Art Institute."

"But you have your well-established security clearance. And you might learn how to smile at the guards more with your open, trustworthy face."

"Well, we'll cross that bridge when we come to it."

Stephen asked, "How would you like us to disguise ourselves? And what names shall we take?" He had become jolly and playful.

"Why not one name? The kind that could be a man's or a woman's—like Leslie or Jean or Evelyn?"

"I like Leslie," he said. "As in Leslie Howard."

"Or Leslie Caron," she countered.

"Now for a family name—for our nest egg."

"Nest? Egg?"

"No one's called Egg."

"How about Egmont. You know—Goethe's play, Beethoven's overture."

"I don't remember anything about him."

Alice laughed out loud. "Your history of philosophy doesn't include the history of Europe? Egmont was practically a contemporary of Catherine of Aragon and Henry VIII. He was one of those great nobles of the Netherlands in the service of Philip II of Spain, but a Catholic who protested against the King's persecution of the Protestants. Philip ordered his head chopped off. The name's absolutely ideal for Catherine's gift. And what could be more appropriately aristocratic-sounding than having someone named Leslie Egmont represent the Art Institute of Chicago?"

The wife of the director of the villa—the perfect hostess—gave them directions to a shop in the town of Como where costumes and masks were offered for rent or for sale. It was only a question of some elements of facial makeup for disguises that Alice had in mind.

By the end of the long conversation of the morning in the card room, Stephen and Alice had leaped beyond the problems of replicating the wall hanging, forging documents of authentication, latching into a network of agents and dealers for underground buyers without solving any of them, to arrive at the question of how to disguise themselves—each of them as Leslie Egmont—should the time eventually arrive when they would have to meet a potential buyer or his representative face to face. Alice's contention was that "It ought to be very simple for us, because we're both so nice-looking." Stephen guffawed; he had always thought of himself as perfectly ordinary—plain. "You see, we have no easily described peculiarities," Alice continued. "We have nice faces with even features, unblemished skin, conventional coloring. We look like so many other people that it would be hard to describe anything identifying us as individuals. The only things people find easy to describe are oddities. All we have to do is become a little odd. Only that will be memorable."

It was such oddities they went to look for in the late afternoon. There was nothing modest about the costume shop in Como. The riches of its collection of cloaks and mantles, silks and brocades, promised the possibility of disguising an entire village if that was called for. There was a whole room with periwigs for men and women. Outfits as diverse as Roman togas and feathered costumes of regal Hawaiians were available. There were baskets of walking sticks with handles of ivory, carved into the shapes of gargoyles or elephant heads or salamanders, or large globes of semiprecious stones; some of the canes concealed razor-sharp swords or daggers.

The vast assemblage of items for transformation and make-believe fed Stephen's mind with speculations on the differences between societies in which there are regular occasions on which to appear in public, among people you are familiar with, while enjoying the temporary escape from yourself disguised as someone else, and his own society, in which there was no such opportunity. He himself had not worn a mask or a transforming costume of any sort since a Halloween night when he was twelve years old. He had never been to a Mardi Gras in Italy or Brazil, a celebration of Fasching in Germany, or even an elaborate costume ball in England. The only person he had ever known who had publicly displayed himself in a completely transforming disguise was a former student who was mistakenly arrested in Chicago for soliciting as a prostitute when he was trying to be served a drink at a bar while dressed as an attractive young woman. It was not awareness that Alice and he were calculating a criminal action that was clear in his mind while wandering through the rooms of the costume shop in Como so much as the thought that at home any kind of make-believe dress-up is considered a perversion. Resentment at the paucity of opportunities in his past life to have such fun spurred him on.

Of course Alice's guess had been right: there was a whole room devoted to makeup in the charge of a middle-aged lady, portly and effervescent, prepared to give them advice and instructions. They tried on bulbous noses, enlarged ears, shaggy eyebrows, Afro wigs. In the end, as Alice had predicted, they settled for a minimum of simple elements that would be memorable.

Alice's neatly elegant straight blond hair curved like a turban above her head but was completely concealed by a wig of auburn-brunette feathery curls, pert as an adolescent on permanent vacation. A much darker lipstick, lavishly applied, created a rather fishlike distortion of her mouth. She chose a pair of rose-tinted eyeglasses in round steel frames and a clip-on nose ring—such as ladies wear in India—with a paste imitation of a diamond. Concentrating on the surprise of it, one forgot the rest of her face.

Stephen was perfectly fitted with a wig of silver-white hair and a brisk salt-and-pepper mustache brushed up from the part in the middle, looking very much like a pukka-sahib British colonel's. He chose an oddly square-shaped pair of spectacles, blue-tinted sunglasses in a frame of darker blue plastic. But his favorite touch was a trio of unattractive, spongy moles, small and wrinkled as raisins, which were applied to his left cheek in a triangle —one near his ear, one on the cheekbone, and one just above the jawline. They were fixed with a dab of the same adhesive that kept the mustache securely in place. The glue came in a bottle like old-fashioned mucilage, with a brush attached to the underside of the screw-on cap.

Despite not knowing when they would have occasion for either of them to use the disguises they came away with, they were delighted that this ingenious and not-at-all-expensive investment helped make them feel prepared for the future.

And so it was with a sense of possessing a secret talisman that would act as a guardian for each of them— a sort of bulletproof vest for their souls—that they prepared to leave the Villa Serbelloni and to undertake the next steps in preparation for carrying out their plan, each with the protective fantasy that it was "Leslie Egmont" who would be acting on their behalf. Stephen made an apologetic excuse to the director of the villa for leaving earlier than his scheduled time—and hoped he had concealed the joy he took in abandoning his unachievable writing project. Even without the disguises wrapped up in their luggage, the sixteen days that they had spent together in northern Italy had contributed to transforming them. Each of them was en route to becoming someone else.

Stephen accompanied Alice to the gate at the airport of Milan, where she left on a plane to Madrid; an hour later, he was on a plane that took off for Zürich.

CHAPTER SIX

STEPHEN COOPER COULD NOT ESCAPE the persistent thought that Zürich was the center of the world's laundry for dirty monies. All the currencies of the world poured in—checks and coins and paper money and gold bullion —soiled by all the unsavory things that the ruthless or the unimaginably clever, the cold-blooded or the immaculately clean-handed enterpreneurial prestidigitators cajole out of their fellow human beings, with whom they have lost all sympathy—all that tainted money flows through every conceivable streamlined conduit into this utopian city to be scrubbed clean and properly repackaged, disguising all crime.

Zürich was unbearably clean. It struck Stephen that the streets, cobblestoned or macadamized, the sidewalks of decorative cement, never knew the burden of a particle of dust; and surely the Swiss had discovered mutant species of domesticated animals, for there was no evidence that a dog or a cat ever eliminated anything in any public place.

Zürich, Stephen realized, is Shangri-La in reality. No hidden valley in Tibet, no fictional fantasy such as that in *Lost Horizons*, need be imagined when Zürich is here on earth. No twentieth-century bomb ever exploded a single building in any of the cantons. There was a plaque on an undisturbed restaurant that had been open to the public for over three hundred years, commemorating the fact that Goethe had dined there. The curtains over the windows in the café where James Joyce had sat out the First

World War were real lace. And the bank buildings of glass and steel were the true temples of worship of all this security and serenity. The bandits of the world came here for their financial face lifts, as they went elsewhere for their physical health resorts. All of these machinations made it more nearly possible to approach eternal life than ever before, other than through the thought of Shangri-La.

From his hotel room overlooking the lake, Stephen telephoned the Bank of Zürich and made an appointment with an investment counselor. It made him feel like a black army sergeant—now dictator of an African country about the size of the state of California—who might well have occupied the same hotel room and made a similar phone call to arrange for the security of his financial future. Stephen felt that he was entering into the world of adult make-believe—in which bloodied money and stolen money are transformed into flawless money—into a world in which it is proved that crime does pay.

Early the next morning, Stephen gave himself ample time to walk in a leisurely manner from his hotel to the Bank of Zürich, where he had an appointment at 10 A.M. There were, of course, both Swiss and tourists on the streets that he walked along; there were young girls in dirndls with their hair in elaborate braids, and children in Lederhosen; there were youths in American blue jeans and slender young ladies wearing visored velvet caps and jodhpurs en route to stables; but most of all there were simple and direct housewives in gabardine raincoats and businessmen in black suits with white shirts—carrying out ordinary, second-class lives. Stephen Cooper was unacquainted with any living citizen in all of Switzerland. He was an absolute stranger. The fact consoled him for not having put on his disguise. There was no need to be disguised, for there was no possibility of recognition. No one knew him, knew of him, or would come to know him. He felt disembodied, a phantom. He was passing through their world, making use of it; he was emboldened by the thought of himself as invisible.

Stephen maintained that attitude throughout his interview at the Bank of Zürich. He presented himself as Leslie Egmont. He was there to arrange for the establishment of a numbered Swiss bank account, planning to make a deposit within a month or so of $200,000, as Alice had agreed with him to do when she received the insurance money coming to her. He indicated that he could not give the bank a post-office box number until he returned to Chicago but that he would do so within ten days. The banker who undertook to fill out the form lying on the clean desk between the two of them indicated that there would be no difficulty whatsoever with deposits once the number of the account had been established but that for purposes of withdrawal of funds from the account a rather elaborate system of information would have to be established. Stephen was prepared. In a gleeful—not to say silly—evening before they had left the Villa Serbelloni, Alice and he had concocted a series of identifying characteristics that would be unique to Leslie Egmont. It was to be made known only to the confidentiality of the Bank of Zürich that Leslie Egmont was an illegitimate child of the late Duke of Kent. Naturally, this was unknown to the present Duke of Kent. Egmont was described as living on Goethe Street in Chicago and as an accomplished virtuoso of Beethoven's piano pieces. His pet French poodle was named Fluffy; he dined on porcelain designed for him by the Nymphenburg porcelain works in Munich; and he had an excessive sweet tooth for marzipan from East Germany. Such singularly telling personal details were invaluable for identification. They, in company with the uniqueness of the number of the otherwise unidentifiable bank account, would make possible withdrawals, whereas no one else could possibly interfere inappropriately with such negotiations.

It was a very gentlemanly interview. Propriety and decorum were promised on both sides; they would be to the advantage of all involved. "Leslie Egmont" left with the personal card of the banker, who was to be reached in confidence at any time during business hours and who would be happy to see to the satisfactory handling of each of his new client's needs.

All of the conditions for the proper laundering of monies coming from Leslie Egmont were now arranged for in general; the particulars were to follow. Stephen stood up and bowed; the Swiss banker stood up and bowed. They shook hands. They were happy in their intention to make proper use of each other.

Stephen flew away from Zürich the next morning, having chosen British Airways in an attempt to regain contact with real life. Like Shangri-La, Switzerland loathes outsiders. That seemed reasonable, natural, to Stephen, who recognized that every in-group loathes any outsider. But he had reached the point of no return; there was no in-group of which he was a member, anymore.

He would go on from Zürich to London in order to sound out possibilities at Sotheby's. As he looked down from the plane during the flight over France, he was reminded that the majority of the world's space is not occupied by cities but by farms and woodland, and the loneliness of people who live on the land is thought to be very different from the loneliness of people who live in cities. Farmers, shepherds, gamekeepers, and foresters imagine how rich and satisfying the great variety of human contact would be in cities; whereas the people who live in cities have suffered the shock of realizing how rare genuine human contact is. For them the great number of people known to them, as well as those with whom they are unacquainted, become the sheep and oxen and foxes and trees that they wander among alone. Country people innocently believe that if they lived in cities they would come to be known in all of their variety by the variety of people they'd come to know; whereas people who live in cities bear the burden of knowing that does not happen. Stephen was aware that none of the people he was acquainted with knew his potential variety—and he was about to make it even more difficult for them in the future. He remembered that in one pocket of his jacket there was evidence of his identity as Stephen Cooper: his passport, his driver's license, traveler's checks, his university identification card, and so on; but on the other side of his jacket there were the forms from the Bank of Zürich listing information that identified Leslie Egmont. He was a fish out of water, a human being in a man-made imitation of a bird flying some ten thousand feet above the surface of green that made up the lush farms of eastern Burgundy—trying to remember what was left of himself.

He was married to Alice now. What did he know of marriage? He had always imagined that it was his value as a human being that he would contribute to a marriage agreement; it was what he had held back for all those years in which he determinedly remained a bachelor. It was not what he felt he had sworn to share with Alice when he asked her to marry him. By then he was hollowed out and offered her only what she could imagine he consisted of when, out of compassion for her, he wanted to ease her suffering. He had not truly thought about it, let alone thought it through, until he was on the flight between Zürich and London, when he realized that he had surreptitiously lured Alice into acting out of compassion for him. At least she had appeared to recognize how much she needed support and sympathy given lovingly; while he had gained her sympathy and support without ever letting her know how desperately he was in need of it for himself.

And so they became a couple. The phrase "both of you" came instantly to mind in thinking of any couple. When giving invitations, one asks, hopefully, whether "both of you will be able to come." The words always implied for Stephen an image of fusion, of Siamese twins, of welding, of bonding together. "Both of you" implied a unification quite different from the distinction of separateness in the phrase "each of you." It did not at all obliterate some degree of individuality, but it called to mind the supposition that the man and woman in a couple formed a combination, a compound that in its uniqueness was—at least in theory and occasionally in practice—an enrichment of both individuals. It did not torment Stephen to wonder whether Alice and he, married, a couple, would be better for being "both of you" than they had been recently in their isolated selves; he considered the thought as dispassionately as he would have any interesting intellectual question until a chill ran through him that —because his detachment was dispassionate—implied it was most unlikely anything as mysterious as passion might be generated from either of them into the wondrousness of "both."

It was twilight when the plane arrived at Heathrow in London, and dark by the time the airport bus deposited him at the terminal in Kensington. Streetlights had come on, and monumental buildings were lighted up; in the early summer atmosphere the great metropolis showed all the trappings of a festival center. He took a taxi to a large Victorian hotel on Russell Square, near the British Museum, out of habit. He liked to think of himself at home in London because he had spent one year of postdoctoral study at Cambridge University in the early 1950s and made six or eight occasional visits since then; but he did not press himself to try to list the number of people he could get in touch with who just might remember his name.

Stephen unpacked his bags in the silence of the hotel room and wondered what he would do with himself for the evening. It was dinnertime. That would be the wrong hour to try to telephone Cambridge, although he felt strongly that his old tutor in philosophy, who certainly had connections in the art gallery and museum world in London, would be helpful in making contact for him with someone at Sotheby's. He decided to phone him either later that evening or the next morning.

He wanted to walk. London is a marvelous city to walk around. He would enjoy the public display on such an early summer's night. But he suddenly realized he wanted his pleasure spiced, he wanted the taste for it sharpened, by the excitement of going out disguised. He sat at the lady's vanity table in his hotel room and fitted the silver-haired wig tightly onto his head. The unevenly cut hairs fell along his forehead, concealing the line of the false scalp. They sounded the note of perpetual adolescent casualness. He uncapped the jar of adhesive and brushed the gluey material across his upper lip to affix the bristly mustache, and then he arranged the three raisin-like moles in the triangle on his left cheek. The square blue-tinted eyeglasses gently muted the harsh light in his small room and he stood up to look at himself in the full-length mirror on the wardrobe door—introducing himself to Leslie Egmont.

He was tired of himself; he was exhausted by himself; but he consoled himself again with the feeling that Stephen Cooper had disappeared. His place was taken by a somewhat carefree but older man named Leslie Egmont, unknown to everyone in the world.

As he walked out of the hotel, he felt surrounded by a luminous aura, which he could not keep from imagining that others could see—as if in the middle of his life he had been reborn, given a second coming, and been set free among ordinary mortals. He walked through the lime-green lawn of Russell Square with its enormously tall trees overhead, striding toward Great Russell Street, and then along Tottenham Court Road, through Leicester Square, and on to Piccadilly Circus. It was there, suddenly conscious of the great number of people milling about, that he realized it was thirty years since he had first come to London and walked among a crowd in Piccadilly Circus. It seemed to him that not a single person in the crowd on this night had been born thirty years before. There were only youths in their twenties with even younger girls. A new generation of humanity had been spawned, toward whom he felt no responsibility. And by the same token they felt no relation with him. This thought made Stephen feel all the more invisible. And yet he caught sight of himself, time after time, in the mirrors or the dark reflecting glass of shop windows—not stealthily, since there was nothing for him to conceal; but rather with fascination. He would stop and stare at a reflection he knew was not of himself but of Leslie Egmont. He thought this must be exactly what it feels like to enjoy participating in a costume ball. Here the ballroom was all of Piccadilly Circus, all of London for that matter. Could a whole life become a masquerade? he wondered.

Just beyond the railing that curves along the sidewalk, keeping the waves of people out of the streets that run in and out of the circle, stood a tobacconist's shop from the eighteenth century, with two bow windows with many panes of bull's-eye glass lighted up. Surprisingly enough, the shop was open at this late hour. There were canisters of tobacco and pipes and souvenirs of London on display. And an invitation to use international credit cards was affixed to the door. Stephen entered, relaxed, and replied to an offer of help that he'd just like to look around, finally settling his attention on a tray of meerschaum pipes. He recalled Alice's statement that what people remember and are able to describe are the oddities of appearance. Now, wouldn't a meerschaum pipe add to the peculiarities of Mr. Egmont?—when Stephen Cooper had never smoked a pipe in his entire adult life. There had been a six-month period during his senior year in high school when he pretentiously attempted to smoke a pipe, but it never "took." Stephen decided to buy such a pipe for Leslie's sake. The chalk-white bowls with amber stems (clouded amber stems like Pernod and water) were shaped into heads of old seafaring Britons, Middle Eastern sultans, African chieftains, and wise old men. Stephen chose one carved like a sailor. He bought a packet of aromatic tobacco and reached for his wallet containing credit cards. But he changed his mind and took some pound notes out of his pants pocket instead.

He walked leisurely out of the shop back into Piccadilly Circus, smoking the pipe and suppressing the tendency to cough every few breaths.

Then something happened that challenged his sense of invisibility, threw the fear of the law into him, and shattered the enjoyment of his make-believe.

Because the open entrance that led downstairs to the Underground station was brightly lighted up, the walls just beside that opening were thrown into shadows. Stephen stood against the sidewalk railing across from the entrance watching the crowd of people come and go. For no particular reason, he noticed two men in the shadow as they struck up a conversation. The younger one, perhaps still a teenager, in blue jeans and a plaid shirt unbuttoned most of the way down his hairless chest, had asked a well-dressed middle-aged man if he could bum a cigarette. Without haste, smiling, the older man brought a silver cigarette case out of the side pocket of his jacket and offered one to the youth, who, then, must have asked for a light as well; he moved even closer to the older man while he waited for the lighter to appear and be snapped on.

Stephen saw that, in the split second during which the youth leaned forward for the flame to touch the end of the cigarette, he thrust his free hand into the breast pocket of the older man, snatching his wallet out, tossed the cigarette into the street, and began to run like hell. The middle-aged man immediately bellowed out: "Stop!—Thief! —Police!" He lurched toward Stephen, punched his shoulder, saying, "You saw it, come along!"—and began running after the youth, who by then had escaped beyond the Cupid fountain in the center of the circle and was racing toward a dark alley on the far side of the Regent Palace Hotel.

By the time the older man and Stephen had reached the fountain, they could see that a policeman had grabbed the boy and was holding him firmly in place. The older man turned to Stephen without slowing down his running gait and announced, "You're a witness," continuing to run ahead. Stephen turned aboutface and ran in the direction of Haymarket with all the sudden desperation of one who was most in need of escaping from the police. As soon as he reached Jermyn Street he turned right and resumed a normal walking speed in order to avoid attracting attention. But his heart was beating to break through his chest, and his skin felt frosted. He was terrified by the unanswerable question he had never had need to put to himself before: "What would happen if, being required to bear witness to this incident by the police, he had need to identify himself with his passport, his driver's license, and his bank card, each of which had a photograph of Stephen Cooper on it, when his face was disguised so that he could pass as Leslie Egmont?" It is one thing to make believe you are someone else for your own amusement—to wander about in as numerous a crowd as fill the streets of Central London in early summer—invisible to yourself in the mirror of your own past life; but visible as someone else to everyone else. It is another thing to try to pass yourself off before the law as that someone else.

He had reached the corner of Jermyn Street, where the rear windows of Fortnum & Mason lighted the end of the block, and then crossed the street to the windows of Alfred Dunhill. The pipes on display there reminded him of the purchases now in his pocket, and while he stood at the corner trying to calm himself, he filled his new pipe for the second time and gradually began to smoke it. Then he followed the street along to the side entrance of the Ritz Hotel, went into the bar, and ordered a double scotch and soda.

He reassured himself that he had escaped from a brush with the law that could have raised questions of identity and disguise that he had never thought about before. It was a *first-time* experience charged with all the electricity of danger—risk, hope, anxiety, and excitement

—that characterizes every first-time experience of bend-
ing a rule or breaking a law: like the first time a man
makes love to a woman he is not married to. Will he be
found out? Will there be retribution?

He tried to calm himself with the thought that surely,
if he had had to bear witness in the instance of the pick-
pocket, he could hardly have broken a law by appearing
in public in disguise. He was reassured about that in itself
but he had to admit: the fear with which he had been
filled must have come from instinctual realization that he
was cultivating this disguise for the purpose of breaking
a number of laws eventually. And if he could not accommodate to that danger—the fear of the consequences of
being discovered—then he did not have what it takes to
see through to completion the plan that Alice and he had
concocted.

Thinking of Alice, he looked at his wristwatch—
nearly midnight—and wondered if Madrid and London
were in the same time zone. In any case, he would not risk
waking her in her hotel room at that hour. They had not
intended to try to reach each other by telephone while
they were still in Europe.

In the moment of recovering his calm, Stephen looked
beyond the bartender to the small mirrors along the wall
in the bar of the Ritz Hotel to see himself reflected there
and to remind himself in the cold cynicism of cheerless
truth as he had come to recognize it: he had nothing to
lose. Three or four seats away from him, an Indian sat on
a similar chair. They caught each other's eyes in the mirror. He could have been from Bombay or Madras or Calcutta, or he could have been from some remote village in
Kashmir—it didn't matter at all to Stephen, recognizing
that the Indian had been coopted by the British as much
as Stephen had. Both of them wore neat replicas of the

kind of men's suits established by the fashionable tailors of Savile Row, neat shirts, neat ties, and behaved according to the rules of neat decorum by which the British had throughout the past hundred and fifty years spread civilization throughout the world. It didn't matter to Stephen whether the man from India liked that kind of civilization any more or less than Stephen did; nor did it matter that since the end of the Second World War the British were in retreat, forced to give up one territory after another—including India. What mattered was that they had left their mark. And no such standard of presumed excellence —to say nothing of superiority—presented itself as any reasonable form of competition to them. The British may have declined; but no one else had superseded them. The Americans, on the one hand, and the Russians, on the other, were either laughable or contemptible. The former were compassionate but incompetent; the latter were heartless and incompetent. He studied his reflection in the mirror and that of the anglicized Indian.

Stephen had recognized the nullity of his life, and sought for something dangerous to make him feel alive again—a challenge to rise to, one that would reward him with things, the kind of expensive things that he had never owned before. But, looking at the reflection of the Indian in the mirror of the bar, he was reminded of the opposite extreme: an anthropologist at Northwestern had once told him about a sect he had studied briefly in India whose purpose was to divest each of its believers of all sense of attachment to worldly goods. They were mendicants who owned nothing, and they were committed to non-attachment to the extent that they never slept two nights in the same place, they owned nothing, and they asked for nothing. They would cease to exist if their form of passive begging did not prove the rest of the world would not abandon them, would not let them die of starvation and destitution. But their claim on the goods of the rest of the world was so minimal that they could expect to move from one instance of generosity to another, no matter how slight, so as to keep them at least barely alive. That was how Stephen Cooper willed to see himself at the moment: at most barely alive. But willing to take a great risk for some possible great material reward.

He began to undo his disguise. He placed the square-framed, blue-tinted spectacles in the breast pocket of his jacket. He tore off the three moles and dropped them into the pocket of his shirt, along with the pukka-sahib mustache. As he removed these forms of deception, he kept his eyes in the mirror on the eyes of the Indian, who showed no response whatsoever. To that extent, he imagined, the man from Calcutta or Madras or Bombay had become so British that he demonstrated neither surprise nor dismay, let alone shock; he showed no response at all. This was the ultimate example of the lesson of British tolerance and respect for privacy—that a man may change his public image from one instant to the next without raising a murmur of dismay on the part of the believer in the mother of Parliaments, the teacher of tolerance, the accepter of eccentric or idiosyncratic individual lives.

Even the bartender did not raise an eyebrow. He filled Stephen's second order with aplomb, although Stephen obviously did not look the same as he had when he made the first request for a double scotch and soda. The bartender could not have read Stephen's mind, but what Stephen was thinking—to follow his subjective recognition that he had nothing to lose—was that he no longer loved his life, nor did he anticipate respecting it in the morning. He was, on the contrary, so separated from his life that it really didn't matter to him whether he woke up or not the next morning.

In actual fact, Stephen woke up the next morning in his hotel room feeling enormously refreshed and re-empowered, indifferent to the world from which he was now disengaged, and prepared to carry out a scheme that mattered only to Alice and to himself, but not to the self he used to be, only the self he might yet become. And it was in his future service that he felt himself employed. For that purpose he felt prepared to make use of anyone he had known in a previous life, and he arrived in England with the express intention of getting in touch with James Crow, who had been his tutor in philosophy, his mentor in the year that he had studied at Cambridge some thirty years earlier. Crow had gone on to become Fellow in Philosophy at Peterhouse. For at least two decades the agnostic professor at Cambridge and the atheist professor at Northwestern had exchanged annual reports at Christmastime.

Seated at his small desk in the hotel room that morning, Stephen tried to put through a telephone call to Mr. Crow at Peterhouse, only to be told there was no number listed in his name. He then tried the porter's lodge. He listened as the telephone operator asked to be connected with Mr. Crow, only to hear the patronizing voice of one of the servants of the college explaining that James Crow was no longer with them. Stephen asked if that meant he had died. The answer was no, but that he lived now in a retirement apartment somewhat to the northeast of Cambridge and that, yes, there was a telephone number there at which he could be reached.

It annoyed Stephen to recognize that Crow must now be in his late seventies at least. He had not seen him in thirty years and could not think of him as other than a man in the prime of life, a source of endless brilliant conversation, carried on more often than not peripatetically, for he loved to walk, to stroll, to hike, and to examine thoughts, ideas, principles, accepted wisdom, and the most dramatically engaging ideas at the same time that he kept his body in motion. In the end he produced nothing. The system did not require that he publish, once he had received the ultimate accolade of a Chair, and he felt no obligation to put into print what he would only change his mind about in a year or a year and a half. He had been given the grace of the English belief in the life of the mind, which allows for those who ask challenging questions and need not wait for an answer. He wallowed in that ultimate luxury, life in an ivory tower, which freed him to think thoughts that might never have practical consequences, because the British conception of academic thought accepted the unpredictable gamble that some pirouettes of rationality might be merely entertaining or self-indulgent, since it could not be determined in advance which exercises of the mind would result in useful consequences. It is the intellectual equivalent of their political philosophy: muddling through.

Now James Crow was retired, and Stephen put through a call to the telephone number he had been given. He wondered whether Crow had taken into his retirement the large, unusual, and valuable library of books that he had built up in the early years of his career. Had he achieved the reward of a life devoted to philosophical meditation: wisdom and peace? Is that a possibility for a disciple of Wittgenstein's as Crow had styled himself? Probably not. How can wisdom come to one whose first principle is that certainty can never be attained, one for whom the crucial and all-determining source of satisfaction is in his delight in doubting? Crow's only certainty was the belief that there is nothing that could not be thrown into new doubt. And yet he had been a worldly man who enjoyed knowing people in many walks of life, and therefore Stephen assumed that he would know someone at Sotheby's.

When the phone was finally answered, Stephen heard a woman's voice. He gave his name and asked if he might speak with Professor Crow. The voice hesitated but finally suggested that the caller might not be aware of how ill the professor was. Stephen suddenly imagined a frail old man, wrapped in blankets, immobilized in a wheelchair. But what the lady somewhat indirectly but most discreetly communicated was that the professor had "memory lapses" and could not always be expected to carry on a conversation, especially over the telephone. Stephen then repeated his name and asked if she would let him know whether Mr. Crow would be willing to talk with him, giving her the bare facts of their relationship some thirty years earlier and suggesting that she remind him of their many years' annual correspondence.

He waited for a considerable time before the phone was picked up again, but it was the lady's voice he heard once more. No, she said, the professor did not recall a Stephen Cooper of Northwestern University. Nevertheless, she added with a sigh, is there something specific he wished to know or was there some message he wished to leave?

Stephen realized that he could hear the recording of a symphony by Mozart playing in the background and thought: this is what the peace and wisdom of James Crow's retirement amounts to—a senile mind drifting along on the waves of timeless music, in the care of a daily no doubt. The woman's voice repeated her questions and asked if he was still at the other end of the line.

Despite the expectation of being frustrated, Stephen blurted out that he had called to ask whether Mr. Crow knew anyone at Sotheby's in London to whom he could be given an introduction.

During the interval, while he waited for a response, he heard the Mozart with increasing irritation. Is that doom, he wondered, the best one could hope for in his dotage?

The answer that finally came through the voice of Professor Crow's attendant said that yes, there was once many years ago a bright student in aesthetics and art history who had to go into trade and went down from Cambridge to a job in training at Sotheby's as an appraiser. But Mr. Crow could not remember what had become of him since then. His name was Reginald Carver.

Having been given that much of what he had called for, Stephen thanked the woman, repeated his name and affiliation, and hoped that his respectful regards would be accepted by Professor Crow if, at some time in the future, his memory allowed him recognition.

Stephen then ate breakfast in his hotel room, shaved, and dressed for the day, overcoming his feelings of sorrow for the aged Mr. Crow and thanking him in spirit for a name to use as a wedge at Sotheby's.

"Is there a Mr. Reginald Carver on the staff?" Stephen asked when he reached the switchboard receptionist at the phone number at Sotheby's.

"Is there?" she echoed with ironic surprise. "Is there ever," she exclaimed. "He's the managing director!"

"Yes, of course . . ." Stephen bluffed that he had known all along. "What I mean is to ask whether Mr. Carver is in, and if I may speak with him." Isn't that just like James Crow, Stephen thought; if he were asked today whether he knew Queen Elizabeth, he would probably reply by asking whether you meant Elizabeth the First or Elizabeth the Second.

"Who shall I say is calling?" the receptionist asked.

"Mr. Leslie Egmont." Even as he said the lie, Stephen remembered the excitement of fear and the sense of danger with which he had run from Piccadilly Circus down Haymarket the night before; and this time he was not so unprepared for another first-time experience.

When she spoke to him again, the receptionist said that Mr. Carver was not acquainted with the name and wondered if Mr. Egmont would give an indication of his affiliation and what business he was on.

Stephen said he would be glad to; that he was a consultant to the Art Institute of Chicago on a confidential mission regarding a valuable object; and, moreover, he had been a pupil of James Crow at Cambridge some years ago and he came with a personal introduction from Mr. Crow to Mr. Carver.

Fortunately, there was neither Mozart nor Muzak on the telephone line while he waited for the receptionist again.

He supposed that he would never know whether it was Crow's name or the idea of a consultant to the Art Institute of Chicago that did the trick, but when the voice came back it was to invite Mr. Egmont to call on Mr. Carver in his office at four o'clock in the afternoon of the next day.

For the following twenty-four hours Stephen behaved like an ordinary tourist enjoying London by himself. He wandered in and out of the buildings of the Inns of Court and enjoyed the fragrance of budding almond trees in Lincoln's Inn Fields. He took a taxi to Westminster Abbey and paid his respects to the tombs of heroes; and then wandered through the galleries of the Tate. He ate dinner at an elegant oyster bar; a basket full of quails' eggs was set before him on the bar, whereas in America it would have been a bowl of assorted nuts. That evening he watched a ballet at Sadler's Wells. The next morning he went wandering through the zoo in Regent's Park. "He wondered as he wandered . . ."

Early in the afternoon he was back in his hotel room rehearsing in his mind how he would present himself to Mr. Reginald Carver, dressing for the occasion, and applying the facial characteristics of Leslie Egmont.

When the taxi driver pulled up in front of the address on Bond Street—the address that Stephen had copied out of the London telephone directory and handed to the driver on a slip of paper—he was disconcerted by the inappropriate look of the façade of the building. There appeared to be two entrances in the white wall, with a newspaper stand where journals, magazines, as well as scandal sheets were sold; it looked to Stephen like a converted nineteenth-century stable. How British, Stephen thought, to conceal this auction house of the art treasures of the world behind a surface on the sidewalk that looks more appropriate as the entrance to an arcade of greengrocers' stalls and butcher shops.

He was somewhat early for his appointment and spent the waiting time in the public rooms of Sotheby's, where Persian artworks to go on auction the following week were displayed in glass cases. Both delicate and monumental pottery, vases, dishes, bowls in vigorously contrasted colors reminded him of his brother Mark's collection; they were decorated only with calligraphy—probably quotations of lines from the Koran. There was a section of individually framed Persian miniatures—probably pages detached from a book, no longer in sequence. There was a display case for jewelry alone: necklaces and rings and earrings and brooches and stickpins. All of which are beyond me at the moment, Stephen thought to himself, but not necessarily beyond my means forever. It steeled his resolve to carry out his mission.

At four o'clock he presented himself at the information desk and waited there until Mr. Carver's assistant arrived to lead the way to his office. True to his impression of how the building must have been transformed from something else earlier, the route to Mr. Carver's office was labyrinthine. He followed the assistant up one flight of stairs, through the maze of short corridors to a further flight of stairs, up to the suite of rooms where he was introduced to the managing director of Sotheby's.

For all of Stephen's trepidations, he was amazed only to discover that he was not nervous at all. He had taken the plunge and imagined that he was not present. Leslie Egmont was acting on his behalf. No one would ever know.

During the hour and twenty minutes he spent with Reginald Carver, the business he had come to transact was carried out in no more than fifteen minutes and that after the first hour. The earlier period of time was spent in making tea and getting acquainted. Mr. Carver's offices had the air of a stage set for a theatrical version of stories out of Dickens's *Pickwick Papers*. The cabinets that lined both walls, some of which jutted into the room as freestanding islands, contained collections—Mr. Carter explained—of rare books, rare china, catalogs of previous auctions, account books that must go back through a century, and miscellaneous bric-a-brac.

The furniture was a haphazard collection of different styles. A tea service was set out on a table obviously just wheeled into place between a low overstuffed armchair on which Stephen was invited to seat himself, and the Renaissance chair in dark wood that looked like upward-curving semicircles set on a base of downward-curving semicircles where Mr. Carver sat. He served the tea, offering cucumber sandwiches and deviled-ham sandwiches and, later, pound cake and raspberry jam.

Naturally, they talked of James Crow and their years at Cambridge, which had missed overlapping with each other by just one year.

"The curious thing about Crow," Mr. Carver began, "is that, while he had never bothered to learn much about art history, he raised all of the most important questions about aesthetics. He was especially interested in coming back again and again to wondering how we can understand the idea of an artist's 'creation' of something, whether in a tradition or as the most extreme example of originality. And then on the other side he was a marvel at raising questions about judgment or evaluation: what it is that happens to the experience of one who 'loves' the art object?"

"I didn't know that side of Crow. I came to study theory of knowledge with him."

"Well, I daresay you got an equal dose of his doubting medicine. You know what I mean—that sense that, as there is so much ill-defined or misleading in any element of feeling or thought, it is almost impossible to discover what is authentic." The managing director of Sotheby's laughed a self-deprecating chuckle and then added, "Superior training for an art appraiser."

In light of those last remarks, Stephen might have trembled at the likelihood of gaining satisfaction in pursuit of the purpose he had come here to fulfill; but Leslie Egmont felt no such qualm.

Reginald Carver was a tall, thin man handsomely

turned out as a dandy. He was nearly bald, but what hair he had retained a boyish ginger hue, and his roseate complexion seemed radiant with well-being. His amiability warmed through telling Stephen anecdotes of pleasurable visits to the Art Institute of Chicago, and that, naturally, led to the topic of what had brought this American visitor to his office.

Leslie Egmont carried it off. Between efforts at keeping his meerschaum pipe lighted, he told the story of the leather wall hanging as he had now formulated and memorized it—from the fantasy that it had been part of the holdings of the Duke of Devonshire, which were bought by Mr. Leyland for his house in London; that it had been sold along with the other part of the Peacock Room to Mr. Freer; that it had disappeared between the time the room was dismantled in Michigan and reassembled in Washington. Beyond that, what he said in cautious, often elliptical language, was that this valuable leather piece was discovered in the office of Harold Joachim after his death.

"I knew him quite well, some years ago," Mr. Carver said with admiration and sorrow.

Stephen continued the story, hedging about the reason why the gift to the Art Institute was to be kept secret for ten years; implying that there was some written evidence that Mr. Freer had made a gift of the leather to the parents or grandparents of the people who turned it over to the Art Institute; but also deftly implying that there was no desire on the part of the Art Institute of Chicago to come into a confrontation with the Freer Gallery about it. At long last, he came to the "Therefore," which enabled him to put to the managing director of Sotheby's the question for which he had come to London. There were two sides to it. One was whether Sotheby's would undertake to sell it publicly at auction, if the documents were authenticated and certified in such a way as to fully legitimize the claim of ownership on the part of the Art Institute of Chicago. The other was to consider what sort of purchase price the sale might bring.

Mr. Carver had no hesitation about the first half of the question. On behalf of Sotheby's he said that they would take great delight in "putting it up." But he took his time over the second part of the question, thinking out loud about the difficulty of comparing it with other objects of historical as well as artistic value because of the remarkable uniqueness of this gift from Catherine of Aragon to Henry VIII. Still, in the end, he came to the conclusion it could be proposed that the floor for the bidding might be three-quarters of a million dollars. He suggested that, depending upon the economic climate at the time, the degree of competitiveness of bidding that might be anticipated among the likely buyers, and the availability of their funds at such an unforeseeable date in the future, it might just run as high as a million and a half. But, after saying that, he became more conservative again, and concluded that, in all likelihood it would go for between $800,000 and $1,200,000.

Stephen Cooper expressed his profound gratitude for the interview and for Mr. Carver's optimism. He did not get up or prepare to leave; but he gave up trying to smoke the pipe. He continued the conversation first by asking what commission Sotheby's would take on such a sale. He granted that the answer of twenty percent seemed quite appropriate.

"Would you be kind enough to put that in writing?" Stephen asked. "A little something I can take back to my principals in Chicago . . ."

Mr. Carver said, "Certainly." He got up from his Renaissance chair, walked over to a clean-topped desk, and pressed a lever along the side of it, which made part of the top sink and raised up in its place the typewriter that had been concealed. He brought a piece of Sotheby's stationery out of a drawer alongside the typewriter and inserted it into the machine. He asked how the statement should be addressed, and Stephen suggested, "To the Trustees of the Art Institute of Chicago."

Between them they concocted the text, which read as follows:

> Regarding the decorated leather wall hanging,
> originally a gift from Catherine of Aragon to Henry
> VIII of England, subsequently a possession of the
> Duke of Devonshire, Mr. Leyland, and Mr. Freer,
> and now belonging to the Art Institute of Chicago:
>   If all the necessary documents of authentication
> and ownership are properly, legitimately certified,
> Sotheby's would be happy to undertake
> representation for a public auction of that valuable
> object, anticipating a starting bid of three quarters of
> a million dollars. For that service we would bill you
> a charge equivalent to twenty percent of the selling
> price.
>   Sincerely and cordially yours,

Mr. Carver rolled the letter out of the machine, signed it with a felt-tipped pen, and folded it into an envelope, which he then handed to Stephen Cooper.

Stephen was very much obliged. "I particularly appreciate the fact that you typed the letter yourself, Mr. Carver." This was his diplomatic way of introducing the necessity for complete confidentiality in this matter, which gracefully led to his suggesting the possibility that not all of the necessary documents might be satisfactorily certified, in which event it might not be possible to present the object in public auction. The implication that the Art Institute, solely through the agency of its consultant Mr. Leslie Egmont, might then have to become responsible for selling it privately, while still considering the twenty percent fee not inappropriate, was somehow expressed through innuendo and indirection that resulted in a vigorous affirmative nod of Mr. Carver's head. He repeated, "I understand, yes, I do understand. . . . But in that event," he added, "the buyer will pay the fee."

A delighted Stephen Cooper was left with no doubt that Mr. Carver certainly did understand.

Stephen said that he was in process of moving and would send a new address at which he could be reached soon after his return to Chicago. While they stood near the door, shaking hands, about to bid each other farewell, he looked back toward the desk at which Mr. Carver had written the letter. "By the way," Stephen asked in a tone of merely idle curiosity, "what kind of typewriter is that?"

"An Olivetti electric M-15. I've had it about ten years. Very serviceable." Stephen made a note of that as soon as he was outside the building.

CHAPTER SEVEN

"How did you make out in Spain?" The question Stephen put to Alice took days to answer, because she tended to described an incident or tell an anecdote in great detail; and, in the long run, her stories did not come to their completion until the middle of August, when, at O'Hare Airport, the two of them picked up a sizable package held for "Leslie Egmont" in the customs office.

During the week that Stephen was alone at his apartment waiting for her, he received one cable that said only, "Spain is full of pieces of leather. Love, Alice." He took it for a very good sign. And so he waited both patiently and optimistically for her return. Although she looked slightly haggard after the long trip and said, "Darling, I think I must have put on ten pounds. I don't believe I'll ever be able to eat olive oil again. Do you know Spaniards cook even a fried egg for breakfast in olive oil!" she sounded content, so even before she had told him anything of what she had accomplished in Spain, he knew that the conclusion would be satisfactory. She must have got what she went there for.

On arriving at the airport in Madrid, instead of asking a taxi driver to take her to any hotel she directed him to the Prado, the Museo del Prado, and when they arrived at the entrance she asked him to find her the nearest *pensione,* a room and board, a little hotel, something unpretentious but as close to the museum as possible. The arrangement worked out very happily, and it meant she was on the doorstep of the great institution the moment it opened the next morning. She asked for the person in charge of their conservation office—in fact, the equivalent position to that of her own boss at the Art Institute of Chicago—and she was presented to him as Leslie Egmont, a consultant to the Art Institute of Chicago. There was no moment during the time she spent in Spain when she was called upon to show documentary evidence that she was Leslie Egmont; and by the same token whenever there was need to present her passport or ticket or other identification it was under circumstances when reference to the name of Leslie Egmont did not occur.

The conservator, Señor Morillo, was a man in his forties who spoke English with a pleasant Texan twang because he had spent one year of postgraduate work in the great photography collection at the Houston Museum of Fine Arts. He had lanky black hair and burning black eyes and a pencil mustache that might someday become an imitation of Salvador Dali's—but at present was merely two curves that graced his upper lip and pointed up toward each cheek. He had become a conservator only after returning from Houston and—fortunately—that one year had left him indebted to and sympathetic with Americans; she couldn't have asked for a warmer welcome.

She told him what she was interested in buying and indicated that there would be a commission in it for him. He found it difficult to continue the conversation in his office, and insisted on taking her to a very long, elaborate, and filling luncheon. She had forgotten how large a city Madrid is, and how swift the traffic. But it delighted her that policemen urging cars to move along through intersections would shout, "Vamoose!" at drivers. Just like in cowboy movies.

In the course of the afternoon Señor Morillo made

numerous phone calls in her presence back at his office and some after she had returned to her *pensione,* but he reported on all of them during a very late, long, slow, and elaborate dinner that evening. While it was true that he had been unable to locate any institution or private party in the city of Madrid itself where there was for sale a leather wall hanging (which he preferred to speak of as a "doorway insulator") coming from the sixteenth century and of the approximate dimensions that Alice was looking for, he already had determined that there were leads to such possibilities to the south, and to the north in Segovia, Salamanca, and Ávila. He was prepared to equip Alice with names, addresses, telephone numbers, and letters of introduction—but of course that would have to be taken care of in the office the next day, preferably between a long and elaborate lunch and a late and expensive dinner.

"Obviously," Stephen concluded, "he was infatuated with you." It pained him to realize that he did not experience the emotion of jealousy. He almost wondered what it would feel like. He had to think of his brother's Rolls-Royce gliding through Washington, D.C., in order to be reminded of what feelings that passion promised.

Alice agreed. "Yes, he was quite taken with me."

"And so?"

"Didn't I tell you he was a gentleman? He respected my pledge of fidelity." She held up her left hand to show Stephen the wedding ring. He remembered then their having bought it together in Milan.

"Despite that," she said, laughing, "he could not have been more accommodating. On the third day of our acquaintance he gave me this letter of introduction." Alice brought out of her black envelope-shaped pocketbook a piece of paper, folded twice; she opened it up and laid it out on the coffee table in front of the sofa in the living room, where they sat side by side. It was a piece of stationery on watermarked paper with the letterhead heavily engraved, in classic scroll-like type, with the name of the Museo del Prado, its address, the symbol of the patronage of the King of Spain. In the central panel between the two folds had been typed in Spanish a statement of information about Leslie Egmont in order to introduce her. "To Whom It May Concern." And in the lowest of the three panels Señor Morillo had inscribed his signature with a flourish over his typewritten name and title.

Unable to restrain herself from leaping to the final triumph of her Spanish tour, Alice then brought out of her handbag a second piece of paper, similarly folded— but this was a plain sheet, not stationery with the embossed letterhead. In the central panel were simply two sentences. "I asked the good man for one final favor," she explained. "I asked if he would translate a sentence for me. So he rolled a sheet of paper into his typewriter and I dictated what you see typed here in English: 'This is the gift that Catherine of Aragon took with her when she sailed for England to marry the next King of England.' And there you see," she said, pointing to the same sentence in Spanish typed below the double space, "he was good enough to translate it for me. He never asked *why*, either."

Alice then placed the page of museum stationery over half of the blank paper with its two typewritten sentences in the middle. "We have only to slit both pages along the two folds and substitute the 'translation' for the letter of introduction—and make Xerox copies—in order to have certification of authenticity on the letterhead of the Museo del Prado with the signature below of the chief conservator, Señor Morillo."

Stephen exploded with admiration. "You are a genius!" He leaped up from the sofa and applauded; he got down on his knees and kissed both of her hands; he lay on the floor like a puppy on his back, with his arms and legs waggling in delighted appreciation.

He was then about to tell her of his own ingenuity and his scheme regarding the letter signed by the managing director of Sotheby's, but he decided this should be Alice's night of victory and he would reveal that treasure later on.

Therefore, Alice continued that night to tell at least an outline of the events in Segovia, Salamanca, and Ávila. She rented a car, a small Italian Fiat, and drove herself fearlessly about the north of Spain. The sky was flawlessly blue, the weather was mildly warm, and the fields were the pistachio green of early summer. She peppered her narrative with vivid recollections of events along the way—such as the frequency with which drivers would stop in the road and leap out of their cars to take a leak in full view with exhibitionist glee while she drove past them; and both times when she had locked herself out of her car how a crowd of children gathered to watch a policeman with a coathanger unlock the car door, with a chorus of advice and encouragement as at any professionally skilled public performance. In Segovia she had dined one evening at a table on the terrace in front of a restaurant built close against the side of a Roman aqueduct. She was alone, and while waiting for the food to be served, she ran her trained eye up the wall of heavy stones that created a huge arch and then followed the line down along the other side, only to discover that in the shadows at the base of the arch a man and woman were making love. It occurred to her that this Roman aqueduct had stood there for two thousand years, and she boggled her mind with the thought that if those shadows had been used, say, once a month, for the purpose of secreting such erotic activity, then she was looking at a site on which intercourse had taken place twenty-four thousand times! They laughed out loud over that one, but it was Alice's way of telling Stephen that she had missed him.

In Segovia she had seen a leather wall hanging that was hopelessly dried out and cracked, brittle from lack of humidity, but she went through the motions of testing it to determine its age. She had brought a vial of uric acid with her from Madrid in what looked like a perfume bottle, whose stopper continued into a glass needle. When she scratched in a line along the rear side of the leather piece a brown foaming reaction resulted that would have occurred only in a piece of leather over three hundred years old.

The family offering the wall hanging for sale were down-at-the-heels aristocrats in a decaying mansion on the central square of the city. She amused Stephen by describing members of the family as characters like those in *Wuthering Heights* or those in *Cold Comfort Farm*. The rooms she was shown were half bare, which she took to mean that they were living now by selling off the furniture, tapestries, and other valuables that had been gathered over generations of the family's past. There was something slatternly about the people, just as there was a sense of decay about everything in the building. Besides, they began by asking for $15,000, which naturally made her laugh and start to haggle, by suggesting that $3,000 or $4,000 might be more appropriate. But she didn't pursue the bargaining very long, as the leather seemed to her so dried out as to make it impossible to impose the design that she would have to impress upon it.

Alice drove away from Segovia in an attitude of indifference, remembering that "Spain is full of pieces of leather." But her experience in Ávila began to make her uneasy about the likelihood of finding exactly what was needed.

In that strange fortressed town of gray stones, still looking today exactly as it did when El Greco painted it before the end of the sixteenth century, she presented Señor Morillo's letter of introduction at a handsomely furnished town house, where the only person she met was the no-nonsense merchant-type head of the family and a maid who brought in one thimble-sized crystal glass of sherry for her. Clearly, this was to be a business transaction of trivial proportions for a wheeler-dealer who was accustomed to "trading up" on the possessions of a house he had obviously bought rather than inherited, in contrast to the large-scale commercial operations—whatever they were—that he was ordinarily accustomed to. But the large leather wall hanging, which she authenticated as being well over three hundred years old, although in good condition, would have been impossible for their purposes because it was completely dominated by the image of a winged horse beaten into the tanned skin with that combination of colors favored in Toledo, black and gold. Alice thought the piece garish in any case, and the merchant was asking $20,000 for it.

She left Ávila literally and figuratively under heavy clouds; but later on the sunlit beauty of Salamanca delivered on all that it promised. There, on a great square, on two sides of which were many buildings of the University of Salamanca and at one end an enormous cathedral—all of which seemed carved out of golden-hued stones—the address to which she had been directed was a mansion at the far end opposite the cathedral. This was obviously the home of an old and prosperous aristocratic family. Alice was invited to lunch. The husband and wife in their early forties and their two teenaged sons spoke British English. When they talked of their love for America and Americans, they meant their experiences of Colombia, Argentina, and Chile. They were completely at ease describing winter ski trips to the Alps in Austria and summer vacations on the Canary Islands, while their two maids in black-and-white uniforms served lunch—in the comfortable distance of knowing that neither of the girls understood English. But they shuddered at the idea that Leslie Egmont lived in Chicago, which they thought of only in terms of 1930s gangster movies.

This family, as remote from the Spanish Civil War as the robber barons of the 1890s were removed from the suffering of the American Civil War, was house proud and they had good reason to be. They gave her a guided tour through the mansion. The outer walls of the building —three feet wide—created a fortress; the interior decorations and furnishings preserved a sense of family dignity and significance that had been sustained through centuries. Now the younger generation, under a new king and a new form of government, were affluent and free enough to move toward the twenty-first century. They were renovating and redecorating the grand house. The dining room, for example, was dominated by a new table imported from Italy, on which the design of a variety of fruits spilled out from a cornucopia, created by the inlays of different-colored marbles—peach, apple green, russet, and carnelian—against a mottled beige background. The twelve chairs that surrounded the table, with ample space around each, were frames of heavy brass, upholstered with petit point from India. In the sitting room on the second floor, there were huge comfortable sofas covered in dove-gray leather from Brazil and long low tables of glass raised on thin tubes of stainless steel.

Each room that Alice saw had its own fireplace; but the most ambitious project of the current renovation was to install central heating into the mansion. Because of this innovation, the owners had decided to dispose of such leather door coverings as had kept out the drafts. They therefore made available for purchase the ample section of leather that she sensed immediately would not only be large enough for the purposes envisaged but could even offer a little extra, so that if carbon fourteen dating was needed to determine that it was in fact from the sixteenth century, part of it could be used for that purpose.

When she learned that they were asking only $4,000 for the piece, she did not even attempt to bargain. She left with them a deposit of $1,000 in cash—so that no check need be signed, as no check could have been signed by her with the name of Leslie Egmont on it. When the time came to send the remainder of the balance due, it could be transferred directly into the owner's account in Madrid from Leslie Egmont's numbered bank account in Zürich. By then the insurance money would have been deposited there.

When they concluded the negotiation it was twilight; the family and she had got on so well that they persuaded her to stay overnight and not drive back to Madrid in the dark. During dinner one of the sons asked her whether she had any children. Alice simply stated as a fact to Stephen that she had answered, "No," without a second thought. While he did not comment, he wondered whether that meant she would never speak of the death of her son to anyone again; had she numbed herself against the feelings that would naturally affect her whenever the boy would be mentioned?

Alice continued the outline of her Spanish story by

saying that during the last day in Madrid she had insisted on taking Señor Morillo out to lunch. It was an experience, she concluded, that smacked much more of the illicit —the immoral, or even possibly illegal—than she would have felt if she'd had an affair with him in private. There is no sense in which any of the objectives of the women's liberation movement had yet been established in the kingdom of Spain. Intuitively she knew that Señor Morillo, having yielded to her persistent request that he be her guest for lunch in a restaurant—in a public place —felt that he was behaving in an unmanly way, risking the wrath of his gods by disregarding the rules of conduct of his class and his culture. So much for one year's postgraduate work in Texas.

It was late that afternoon that she asked him for the translation of a sentence that she thought would be invaluable in the future.

By the end of the story of her trip she wondered aloud about how much identification as Leslie Egmont would be needed to collect the leather wall hanging when it arrived at the U.S. customs office in O'Hare Airport.

Stephen replied that he was about to establish a post-office box in that name and then send some letters to himself so he could show them; he would have a calling card engraved; but he thought it would be a nice touch to have a passport for Leslie Egmont—with a passport picture of him taken in his disguise. How difficult might it be to come by a false passport in Chicago in the summer of 1984?

CHAPTER EIGHT

N ONE OF THE FACTS ABOUT LIFE in Chicago is common knowledge. Actually, what happens most of the time is that summer begins with a heat wave in the middle of June—weather of about a hundred degrees with equal humidity for three or four days; and similarly that amount of inhuman suffering occurs again usually over a weekend at the beginning of September. But the well-kept secret about the conditions of life in Chicago is that from the beginning of July to the end of August the weather can be agreeably warm, dry and clear rather than oppressively humid, so many people who have the means and can choose to go away from the city remain there throughout the summer and, instead, vacation during the overcast, snowbound, and arctic winters in resorts of Florida, Mexico, or islands in the Caribbean.

Stephen and Alice had missed the heat wave in June while they were in Europe. The midsummer weather of the rest of that season ranged from intolerable to balmy-pleasurable. That was the season during which they began to present themselves as husband and wife in public; that is to say, in private. They went to dinner parties at the homes of friends and acquaintances. They made rendezvous with other couples for cocktails before going to see a movie together. They met others for a late supper after a play or a concert. It was now a question of whether "both of them" could make a date.

On the first round of his meeting her friends and her meeting his friends they were cordial and forthcoming.

They meant to get to know the other people as they wished to present themselves. They were middle class, skilled or professional people: located somewhere along the coast of the lake from Evanston down along Sheridan Road, on the North Side, in Lincoln Park, on the Gold Coast, south to Hyde Park on the north-south vertical axis that is the territory of cultivated life in the city. The more fortunate of their acquaintances had views of the lake and turned their backs on the rest of the city. The newly married Mr. and Mrs. Stephen Cooper met with people like Thomas and Sarah Crane, who had a grand apartment overlooking the Lincoln Park Zoo and the marina, because Sarah had been a friend of Alice's since college days. She was now an editor at the Chicago *Tribune,* responsible for their regular columns (and extra occasional articles as well) on food and restaurants. Her husband was the marketing manager of a large advertising firm. Both Mr. and Mrs. Crane drank lemonade, although they supplied the Coopers with vodka and tonic. Most of the conversation consisted of the Coopers reporting on life at the Villa Serbelloni; Tom Crane complaining about the absurdity of having to create a market for a deodorant that no one was in need of; Sarah complaining about the pressures of working for a daily newspaper which by now, through the advantages of the word processor, made a new edition of the news possible every ten minutes. Their offer of intimacy consisted in sharing their gripes, as if to know someone else's dissatisfactions is to know him or her best.

They met such people as Stephen's immediate superior in the hierarchy of Northwestern University, the chairman of the department, Professor Eric Johnson, and his wife, Loretta, who gave a party in their honor in the small garden of their small house in Winnetka. The other guests were the members of the Philosophy Department who were in residence that summer, and their spouses. On this occasion Alice discovered that people in any one academic department of the university were totally unacquainted with everybody in any other academic department of the same university. Still, everyone seemed cordial and genuinely happy for Stephen that at long, long last he had found the right woman for him and taken the vows of matrimony. But, after the second and third rounds of drinks, by which time the men and women who wandered between the birch trees and the banks of rhododendrons on the grassy lawn of the chairman's back yard had exhausted their small talk of admiration for the flowers and the climate and the hospitality, the predictions of regret began to be heard.

It was one thing to welcome Stephen into the fraternity of married men with the hospitable implication that he, too, had the good fortune of finding his mate, although even that was tinged with the suggestion that he had gotten away for years without fulfilling his duty as a responsible adult. But it was quite another to begin suggesting that he would learn soon enough how high a price he would have to pay for becoming respectable. Words like *accommodation* and *compromise* and *frustration* and *incompatible* began to rise into the conversation as if, after having been congratulated for receiving an appointment to teach for a year at a university in some tropical paradise —like Samoa or the Seychelles Islands—conversation had turned to the torturous nature of the tropical diseases to which he would be exposed.

At times like that, Stephen deflected Alice's attention by asking her cryptically some question about the leather wall hanging so that no one overhearing him could imagine what they were talking about. She would become reflective and eventually respond with a phrase like "organic materials." Meanwhile, they had moved from the group of people in the party who might have overheard his question referring to how the design she planned to create on the leather could not be dated as recently applied. It was in the presence of another group of people that she answered "by avoiding synthetics and using only organic materials."

The contrast—simultaneously—of comments that wished them well as a newly married couple and those that wished them well-warned of all the drawbacks, dangers and difficulties to be encountered in marriage was most sharply experienced by them during the evening they spent with a curator of art from the Cleveland Museum and his wife, who were visiting Chicago that July, Allan and Lois Levine. Alice had gone to graduate school with both of them and they had remained friends ever since. The Levines were very tall, thin people who seemed to pull themselves up to their full height whenever the thought occurred to one that the other might be taking an unfair advantage. Regarding the glories and miseries of marriage an equal appreciation of both was usually demonstrated by a husband as well as a wife; but Lois and Allan seemed to divide those attitudes between them: he was optimistic and spoke only of the ways in which marriage enhanced, fulfilled, and satisfied a person; she was a pessimist who spoke of nothing but the limitations, the inevitable conflicts and the weariness of endless battle. She made it sound as though getting married was launching a thirty years' war. "You see only the bright side of things," Lois accused Allan in their presence. "It's as if you were blind in half of your psyche."

"Seeing only the dark side of things," he replied, "isn't exactly being well-rounded, either, now is it?" Suddenly he coughed. Then Allan spoke of his hopefulness about the future of their teenaged children. Lois named only her fears concerning their development. They mentioned Alice's son so briefly, in such conventional expressions of sympathy and condolence, that Stephen could hardly believe Alice and they had been acquainted for two decades.

Allan complained of catching a summer cold, saying that he had been coughing all day and now his head was stuffed up, and suggested he and his wife call it an evening and go back to their hotel. The four of them were standing together near the door of the apartment when Allan threw his head back, squeezed his eyes closed, breathed in a huge lungful of air, and let fire a horrendous sneeze—which blew his teeth out of his mouth. It flung the partial plate—his uppers—five feet away from where he stood into the living room. It came to rest there, a horseshoe of grayish-white artificial teeth embedded in a shallow arch of pink plastic. No one said anything—as if they had been subjected to an obscene performance that left them literally speechless. Allan strode forward, picked up the partial plate, and reaffixed it in his mouth before turning around and facing them again.

The words of farewell that the four exchanged were spoken as if there had been no interruption whatsoever, as though nothing unpleasant or remarkable had happened.

Stephen and Alice were silent while they cleaned up the dining room. It was only when they were alone in the kitchen to wash up, and the Levines had been safely out of the building for five minutes, that Stephen said, "People aren't much good for each other, are they?"

"It was *too* embarrassing."

"It was human, it was normal."

Alice replied, "Abnormal."

"What's wrong with us? We couldn't even laugh—
that would have cleared the air."

"Or cry? Would that have helped him?"

"Well, this way he was left just feeling like a freak."

"It was *he* who lost self-control."

"Can we put up with each other only when we're at
our best?"

"Yes, that's what I think it comes to."

This was the first argument, if it could be called that,
between Alice and Stephen since they were married. It
left him dissatisfied as much with himself as it did with
her, because he could not put his finger on why they felt
so different about the identical experience. He wished
that someone—someone else if not he—had been able to
show compassion, whether it meant laughing or crying.
But all he was left with was the sense that competitiveness overwhelms cooperation; rather than being ready to
help someone out, what comes to the fore all of the time
is the question of who will be the winner in any situation.
He was suddenly reminded of his sister-in-law's having
said to him, "You're not better . . . just poorer."

Endless jockeying for power. Is it so with every husband and wife? he wondered. With almost every husband
and wife?

The more they saw of each other's friends the more
readily they saw—through the performance of how they
wished to appear to others—into the inescapable ways in
which they appeared to each other at their worst.

Alice and Stephen invited Sarah and Thomas Crane
for dinner on the first of August. By the time that date
arrived, the Coopers felt they had something to celebrate,
for the insurance check delivered to Alice had been
deposited in the numbered bank account in Zürich and

$3,000 of that sum had then been transferred to the bank account of the family in Salamanca. Despite the fact that the post-office box had not yet been leased, a cable signed "Leslie Egmont" had been sent to Salamanca with instructions simply to ship the leather wall hanging to that name care of General Delivery at O'Hare Airport's import customs office.

Stephen bought a case of Moët et Chandon champagne and put four bottles on ice. As if that would not be enough, he arranged a complete bar on the coffee table in the living room. But Alice reminded him that, when they were at the Cranes' apartment, their hosts drank only lemonade. She saw to it that soda water and soft drinks were added to the collection of bottles awaiting their guests.

It was an awkward and ultimately unpleasant evening. Stephen had wanted to be celebratory but of course he realized nothing could be said about the imminent arrival from Spain of the piece of leather. Still, he was in high spirits, and he credited it to the sixth weekly anniversary of their wedding.

The Cranes looked freshly scrubbed, pink, and determinedly youthful. But Sarah seemed taken aback by the display of alcoholic beverages as the centerpiece of the living room. She insisted on pouring soda water quickly for both Tom and herself.

They had brought with them a wedding or house-warming gift, which Alice made a great ceremony of opening: admiring each inch of the satin ribbon as she unwound it and of the imitation Chinese paper that she was careful to smooth out and preserve after she had unwrapped the box. She separated one layer of tissue paper from another as she slowly approached the revelation of its contents. The gift turned out to be a deep candy dish of sterling silver made in the shape of a pomegranate. Sarah explained, "It's not just that I'm the Food Editor at the *Tribune*—you must think of its appropriateness for a marriage."

Alice said softly, "I have."

"It's an ancient symbol, with associations for royal fertility and fecundity."

Thomas Crane explained: "All those seeds, you know. All those juicy red succulent seeds . . ."

Alice and he seemed properly appreciative but Stephen could tell from the degree of cool politeness with which his wife now expressed herself to her old friends that she felt any reference to Stephen and her having children in the future was not only gauche but impertinent. Sarah could not know whether Alice was still fertile; was Sarah? But she certainly did know that Alice's only child was dead.

The conversation during dinner took a turn for the worse. In the middle of the summer of 1984, the campaign for the election of the next President of the United States was gradually moving into high gear. Thomas Crane announced that the advertising agency of which he was a partner would be handling the President's campaign throughout the entire Midwest. It came as something of a shock to the Cranes that the Coopers believed they would support Mondale against Reagan. The dialogue instantly dropped to the level of character assassination of the two politicians, thinly disguised with attempts at cavalier wit. But the coldness was forming between the two couples; the conversation slowed and sentences sharpened themselves against each other.

Stephen asked, "Why is it that in American political debates the issues no longer matter—only personalities?"

Tom replied with a laugh, "Because we were all brought up on beauty contests, we know that personality is more important than policy."

"Because it's more mysterious?" Alice asked.

Sarah offered: "Yes, the question is, who will be the better Mr. Nice Guy?"

"Not the better father?" Stephen asked.

It was Tom who said, "Nobody trusts fathers anymore."

Each time Stephen raised a bottle of champagne to refill the dinner glasses, Sarah refused any wine for Thomas as well as herself.

Back in the living room, after dessert and coffee, the atmosphere grew even worse. Alice withdrew into a corner of the sofa, cupping a glass of cognac. Sarah, sitting near her, continued to sip soda water. Stephen stood with his back against the mantelpiece, with a scotch on the rocks, while Tom slumped in one of the armchairs, gripping each arm with white-knuckled fingers, and continued to praise the fresh breeze that Ronald Reagan had allowed to blow through ideas of government in this country—without ever looking at the other three people in the room. His eyes moved in endless rounds through the bottles arrayed on the coffee table: from the vodka to the scotch to the bourbon to the sweet vermouth and the dry vermouth, the Campari, the sherry, the port, and back to the vodka.

Trying to make light of it, Stephen said, "It's so difficult to carry on a discussion with metaphors. For example, one man's fresh breeze is another's hot air."

It ended badly. The Cranes left much earlier than they might have otherwise. Sarah's last attempt to be flippant was her suggestion that they not get together again until after the next inauguration. But there was no humor in the remark. Both Tom and she looked crumpled by the end of the evening, exhausted by the strain.

When they were gone, Alice took the offending silver pomegranate and put it out of sight on the bottom shelf of a cabinet under one of Stephen's bookcases.

Stephen huffed and puffed in the living room, bemoaning the impossibility of political debate. "In most of the countries of the world you cannot express a word of opposition to an entrenched government. You'd be a dissenter; you'd be locked up in jail or more likely sent to a concentration camp; if not tortured and killed.

"Every party in power in this country swears its allegiance to the principle of free speech and open debate. But what happens? Each of us takes everything personally, and you can't possibly go on having a friendship with someone who doesn't believe exactly the same thing you do."

Alice said, "Of course not. You can't feel safe with someone whose belief is radically different from your own."

"Safe?" Stephen laughed. "When there are no radical differences? The same thing happens every four years. Why must our friendships be at stake over such slight differences of ideas? We're talking about the political middle. Reagan is four feet to the right of the middle and Mondale is three feet to the left—on a spectrum that's as wide as one mile. Do the differences between Carter and Reagan matter today? Can you remember the differences between Lyndon Johnson and, and—who the hell did Johnson run against?"

Alice said, "We're afraid of any differences being made public, being made explicit. Maybe we're under too heavy a lid and we're afraid of exploding. We have to be tolerant of everything that's different from ourselves: other people's religions, other people's color, other people's cultures. You tell me even within your own department no two of the professors of philosophy discuss anything of importance with each other because no two of them agree on anything—especially what's important. But every four years we think we *ought* to talk about political choices, and then it frightens us to discover how different other people's beliefs are from ours."

"Is that what makes Sarah look so beady-eyed and nervous and Tom so uptight and pulled back into himself?"

"Oh, no, you've got that one all wrong." Alice pointed to the display of colorless and colorful bottles of liquid. "I've just figured it out. They're both ex-alcoholics, reformed alcoholics. I suppose it's easy enough to understand, given the pressures of the newspaper and of the advertising business."

"No. I'm sorry," he said. "I didn't see."

Alice took a deep sigh. "I have the feeling she must watch him like a hawk. She must watch him day in and day out, never knowing when or whether he might slide back, might go off on a bender. Or maybe she's even more worried about herself if he leads her astray. She can never let down her guard."

"Good God," he exclaimed. "It's enough to drive you to drink."

"Can't you be serious about anything?"

"I don't have what it takes—anymore."

Difficulty over renting a post-office box started in the middle of July when Stephen Cooper thought—rather grandly—that he should sign up for one in the central post office that stood at the heart of the mail system for

Chicago, imagining that it would somehow give greater status to have such "an address" and probably increase the speed of delivery. Therefore, he took the train one day from Evanston to the south end of the Loop and walked along Congress Parkway toward the huge post-office building, which straddles the highway like a fifteen-story square colossus. He found his way up to the central public hall, larger than an airplane hangar, as if one of Piranesi's fantasies of a prison had been wedded to the idea of a clean, well-lighted place. It was somewhat crowded—although people were not milling about, as each of them appeared to be familiar with what they had come to do there. He found the information desk, was directed to the cage at which he received an application form, and filled it in, standing up at a glass-topped table. The glass was bolted to the brass legs which were bolted to the marble floor.

The form—which he filled in with the name of Leslie Egmont—asked for his permanent address, for which he used the rural free delivery number of his grandfather's farm in Ohio—a tract of land that had been converted into a suburban shopping center in the late 1940s. It also required that he swear, affirm, or attest that he would break none of the laws governing the use of the United States postal system, such as trafficking in illegal weapons, drugs, pornography, or attempting to overthrow the government by violence. He smiled to himself as he printed Leslie Egmont's name and then wrote as his signature those words in a clearly legible upright autograph unlike his own script, which slanted heavily to the right.

He held the application card firmly in one hand as he stood in the appropriate line for the request to be processed, assuring himself that his wallet was in the breast pocket of the lightweight summer suit he was wearing. He was calm and confident until it suddenly occurred to him that a photograph might be taken for an identification card, such as is used now for drivers' licenses or bank identification cards. He was not wearing the disguise of Leslie Egmont. That unnerved him momentarily; but he decided, on the spur of the moment, that if a photograph was required he would casually wave it away with some remark like "I don't feel photogenic today," or "Well, I'll have to give some more thought to whether I really want this box." And then he would walk out of the building, only to return another day in disguise.

To his surprise he walked out of the building without having rented the box because, when it came his turn at the cage, he was bluntly told that no box was available.

"We're all full up," the black clerk stated.

"How soon will you have an opening?"

The man who looked at him straight in the eye shrugged his shoulders and then added, "A month? Two months? Hard to tell. Can't know who'll renew and who won't renew." Then he softened his tone, became informative, friendly if not avuncular. "Listen, fella. We got eight million people in this city. Seems to me about half of them don't want their mail delivered at home. If they got homes. Now, it seems to me this central office gets the greatest demands of all for use of our private boxes. But we ain't the only post office in town. Lots of branches, oh, yes, *lots* of branches, all over town. I ain't got no way of knowin' which ones are all full up and which one has openings. You could tramp all over the city, take 'em in one by one, until you find a branch that has one you can rent there and then. Or"—he became confidential, if not conspiratorial—"you could go to one of those private agencies."

Stephen echoed the last phrase as a question.

"Sure. There's a whole handful of private companies, here and there around town, who'll hold your mail for you or even forward it for you." He winked.

Stephen paused, heard the irritated clearing of the throat of the woman who stood in line behind him, and then asked, "Any of those—agencies—around here?"

The obliging clerk spoke the name of a company and then put a small pad of white paper in front of him, wrote on it the address 26 South Franklin Street, and handed that piece of paper to Stephen.

Stephen thanked him, genuinely feeling that his luck was holding. Surely a private mail drop would never require a photograph on an identification card.

The walk from the central post office to 26 South Franklin Street was hardly longer than a stone's throw. The building at that address, nearly across the street from the gigantic Sears Tower, was a five- or six-story dilapidated structure, a rabbit warren of fly-by-night offices. The mail-drop company occupied a space about the size of the second bedroom in Stephen's apartment. It had two large windows and on this bright summer day was filled with sunlight, but everything about it was makeshift. There was a gray steel desk behind which one person sat, a nondescript young man in a sport shirt and blue jeans whom Stephen pegged as a college student holding down the only summer job he could find. But everything else in the room was made of raw wood. An unpainted pine door laid across two carpenters' horses made a table around which were set up four old-fashioned bridge chairs; and along two walls and coming into the office as an island were a series of wooden fruit and vegetable crates, along with a number of empty wine cases. A three-by-five filing card was tacked to the upper edge of each crate—one letter of the alphabet per card. Packages, manila envelopes, printed matter, and personal letters were piled in higher or lower stacks in most of the crates, lower more often than higher.

There was only one client present when Stephen walked in; he was going through the stack under the letter "T." But he left the office empty-handed.

The clerk behind the desk stood up and handed Stephen an application, which he read sitting on one of the bridge chairs at the door-table. It was more elaborate than the form required by the United States Postal Service. It asked not only for a permanent address and an additional forwarding address but for two personal references with their permanent addresses, as well as an affirmation that nothing immoral as well as nothing illegal would take place through an abuse of this middleman service.

Stephen realized how easy it would be to fill out the form with phony information, but he could not easily imagine himself returning to this sleazy room and fingering through the illicit correspondence of emotional derelicts who were hoping to find satisfaction for some polymorphous longing. It was all too risky. The place smacked of a kind of borderline operation ripe for a police bust at any moment: tawdry and possibly criminal.

Stephen stood up and asked the clerk how much it would cost to have "the service" for a month or three months, and when he heard the answer he grunted, said he'd have to think it over, and handed the application form back to the young man.

The experience had made him feel unclean, but when he described it to Alice that evening he made a joke of it, caricaturing the situation in amusing exaggerations, and she agreed that he had done the right thing. They would of course have to find a proper post-office box. That condition suddenly took on an enormous advantage to them, as if such an address would indicate that their "business" was given official sanction by the federal government.

They fell asleep that night mellowed by the humor of the thought.

The next morning Stephen was determined to rise to a higher level of enjoyment.

He drove Alice to work—on the highway along the lake, which was calm as a sheet of apple-green glass—and parked in the underground lot near the Art Institute. Then he walked north up Michigan Avenue to the splendid small shop that is Tiffany's outpost in the Midwest.

He wore the disguise, in which he was not entirely easy because of the slight probability of running into someone with whom he was acquainted in his hometown —although the degree of probability was greatly lowered as soon as he entered Tiffany's. However, he was growing accustomed to it, the way a man who has been clean-shaven all his life gradually grows accustomed to the beard that he puts forth in his fifties.

The wig fitted over Stephen's own hair tightly as a swimming cap; he was now more than comfortable with the silver-gray lock that fell over onto his forehead; he was fond of it. The bristly mustache and the three moles were in place, and the square-shaped blue-tinted sunglasses were perched on his nose.

In any case, for all the years that Tiffany's had been located on Michigan Avenue—surely for the past fifteen or sixteen years—he had had rare enough occasions to enter the shop, going there only to buy a gift for some unusual event or some ceremonial occasion for which the "trademark" would be as important as the gift itself.

Here again nothing seemed changed: the first room, in which precious jewels were presented for sale, was as usual heavily guarded; the second, much larger room, walled with glass cases displaying porcelain and silver and crystal, was populated by three salesladies each dealing with a female customer, one of each generation, equally overprivileged, with too many cosmetics and too short a fuse. The air they created about them was not one of *noblesse oblige* or even that of genuine good manners; rather, there was the aura of petulance held just in check, as though any one of these spoiled women might stamp a foot at a moment's notice, throw back an arrogant head, and sweep out of the shop. It was not because none of the salesladies was treating them properly—with appropriate deference, respect, solicitude; rather, it was because of their assumption that they could not be satisfied here, that their standards or expectations were so high that they could rarely be satisfied anywhere. Perhaps, Stephen thought, these are women who shop every day, not so much to purchase things as to reconfirm the altitude of their standards and the rarity with which those Mount Everests are ever scaled.

Stephen went to the back of the room, where there were trays that held modest objects such as he had bought as gifts in the past: painted pottery salt and pepper shakers made for Tiffany's in France or Italy, crystal paperweights, silver letter openers. When one of the customers left, a saleslady presented herself to him, her face and hands wrinkled as pink prunes, and her suit a stiff black jacket and skirt with a pearl-white ruffled blouse, and asked how she could help him.

He said that he wanted stationery and a calling card engraved, that the name should read "Leslie Egmont," and that while that was being prepared he would return as soon as he could with further information that might be added regarding an address.

They then sat down opposite each other across a small table on which a sample book was placed, and while he turned the pages he realized he would have to choose the size of the card, the quality of paper, and the typeface for the lettering. He ended by selecting a particularly dignified, perfectly legible typeface. Had she called it Bembo? He was told that it would take two weeks for the preparation of the engraving stamp—during which time he'd be able to supply her with the additional information, and that once "all the pieces were in place" the printing should not take more than an additional week.

When asked how many he wished to have printed, Stephen felt enormously extravagant in saying, "Two hundred and fifty." After the costs were calculated, he left as a deposit fifty percent of what the total charge would be.

He felt thoroughly at ease at Tiffany's; he was in no hurry to leave. He judged that he had been taken care of by a professional, one who not only took pride in what she had to sell but, by identifying with it, enjoyed the status that came with being gilt-edged by association. The implication was perfectly clear: if you cannot afford to buy at Tiffany's, then the next best thing is to be someone who sells for Tiffany's. Experiencing this friendly, helpful professional manner on the part of the saleslady, Stephen found himself casually asking if she could tell him where the nearest branch of the post office was.

She responded by explaining that Tiffany's would be happy to take care of shipping through the mail or through United Parcel or even through a personal messenger service anything that he would like to send from the shop. But he countered by explaining that he simply had some letters in his pocket that he'd like to register and repeated his question. Her answer made matters even more convenient than he had hoped for. She told him there was a post office practically around the corner: on Ontario Street, about two blocks east of Michigan Avenue. He thanked her courteously and sauntered out of the shop, nodding to the other salesladies and even to the security guard as if he were a well-recognized habitué.

He found the building with no difficulty at all: there it was, a neat red-brick WPA-type post office—the Fort Dearborn branch—now squeezed between the concrete and glass Museum of Contemporary Art on one side and a glass and steel office building on the other. It looked like any one of a hundred small-town post offices he'd seen in the Midwest, but for the fact that here all of the civil servants were black. Of the rows of post-office boxes that lined two walls near the entrance as he came in, he noticed that some were opened by keys and others by combination locks.

This time, before asking for an application to rent one, he tried to find out if there was one available immediately, only to be told, "No." But then the clerk reassured him that there was a high rate of turnover and in all likelihood at the end of the month—within a day or two after the first of August—he could be pretty sure of having one assigned to him. So then he did fill out the application form with its fantasy information in place and received a waiting-list number, just as he would have at a popular bakery. He promised to return as soon as possible after the beginning of the new month and the clerk, agreeing with him, smiled, "Sure. See ya then."

Things were looking up.

But the next time he drove Alice to work wearing his Egmont disguise, he was much less sure of himself and therefore decided not to give Alice any hint of his plan. He parked the car near the Art Institute and agreed to meet her there at the end of the afternoon. Then he walked slowly away toward the group of tall black glass and steel buildings of government offices that surround the bright orange metal sculpture made by Alexander Calder—great arches off center in that concrete plaza, looking like an ostrich with its head in the sand.

In the Everett Dirksen Building, housing numerous bureaus of the federal government, he found his way to the Passport Office, where dozens of people stood in queues of varying lengths. He got into the line to wait for an application to fill out. But when he began filling out some of the information that was "true to" Leslie Egmont he wondered: How could he hope to supply a birth certificate? Or two character witnesses from years of professional or personal acquaintanceship? Or other evidence of place and property?

He folded the application and placed it inside his jacket pocket as he began to walk out of the large room. But he nearly froze, and then he nearly became entangled in his own feet, as he saw Professor Johnson, the chairman of his department, coming directly toward him down the corridor as he was about to leave the Passport Office. He remembered that Professor Johnson had said he would be in Japan for the second half of the summer vacation. Then he remembered that he was wearing a disguise. He lightly touched the mustache on his upper lip and then the moles on the left side of his face.

Professor Johnson came toward him, looked at him, and walked straight past him. There was no flicker of recognition.

Stephen found the nearest men's room; he saw his ashen look in the mirror over the sink; then, suddenly, cooled off, calmed down, having regained his poise, he felt more determined than ever to brazen it out.

Across Jackson from the two stark federal buildings on the north side of the street are a few buildings on both sides of Plymouth Court with neat modern shops on the ground floor where passport photographs are taken and printed "while you wait"—for a price. There were a few other such establishments on the floors above those, and the price comes down the higher up you are willing to go. Stephen started on the second floor, wandering around the hall, peering into different establishments, asking for prices, noticing that there were usually two or three people in each office: one to handle the cash and the bill of sale, another to make use of the camera, and a third who was some kind of handyman, who rested on a broom or occasionally ran a dustcloth over a radiator cover, a vibrating air-conditioner, or the clean-topped desk.

Using the stairs, Stephen wandered upward from one floor to the next. On the fifth floor he found an office with only one man in it. The door was open, the room was small, the light was dim. A man sat behind a small table staring at a camera or beyond it to a silvery blank backdrop. He was bald and narrow-shouldered but with a potbelly; he wore a faded red polo shirt, Bermuda shorts, and leather sandals. He smoked a long thin cigar very slowly and flicked the ashes on the floor behind him.

Stephen Cooper sidled in and sat down on the hard wooden chair across from the bald-headed man. There was no air-conditioner in this room, and the open window let the summer noises of traffic come in from the street below. "Hi," he said nervously, and asked how much . . .

Three passport photographs for twelve dollars was the cheapest price he had been quoted so far.

"I really wish I could do it."

The slender man with the potbelly snorted. "Well, if

you can't do twelve bucks for the passport pictures you can't afford to go anyplace where you'd need a passport."

"No, I don't mean I can't afford the twelve bucks." Stephen looked at the door and then lowered his voice. "They just won't . . ." Without finishing the sentence, he pulled out of his pocket the passport application form and shrugged his shoulders.

The man across the table finished the thought for him: "You don't qualify for a passport."

"Well, it's not my fault. I was an orphan and I ran away from an orphanage when I was sixteen. I don't have a birth certificate. I don't even live here. I'm just passing through. I was on my way from Buffalo out west. But I got wind of a great job that I could have—I can have— if only I can get to Venezuela. But I don't have a passport. I've never had a passport. I don't know anybody here who could vouch for me. I just wondered—if there's any chance . . ."

The man behind the table stood up and leaned forward, ominously resting both fists on the rough tabletop between them. "If you're fuzz," he said, "and trying to trap me—I'll knock your block off." He spoke through the cigar clenched between his teeth.

Stephen stood up and stumbled back behind him; then, boldly, took the knob of the door and closed it onto the hallway so that they were alone in the small room together. "I'm not fuzz," he said. "I'm not here to trap you. I really need a passport. I can make it worth your while."

Behind the door was a white Styrofoam cooler speckled with blue spots. The man behind the table bent over, lifted the lid, and brought out two cans of beer, handing one to Stephen; they both sat down again.

The beer was weak but the cool wetness of it made Stephen realize how parched his throat had felt and how profusely he was sweating. Beads of perspiration formed along the tight hairline of his white-haired wig and slipped down along his cheekbones. One heavy drop teetered on a mole near his jaw and then dropped onto the back of his hand, which rested on his left leg.

After sipping his beer, the man behind the desk asked, "What made you think I could do anything for you?"

"Just a hunch," Stephen risked saying, and then added—more honestly—"Just a hope."

"Lemme see that application form." The man's hand reached beyond the edge of the table and Stephen laid on it the white printed form, which he had filled out with make-believe information about Leslie Egmont.

The man read through both sides. His only comment was, "Looks phony as a three-dollar bill to me."

Stephen ventured a brief laugh, a kind of nervous throaty chuckle. "Could I get a passport for a three-dollar bill?"

"I just take passport pictures," the man said. "They're cheap. Passports cost a lot of money. I wouldn't know, myself," he added, "strictly speaking. But I get around. I know people"—he waved, with the beer can in his hand, vaguely toward the northwest, saying, "—elsewhere."

Stephen tried: "I thought you might have some connection . . ."

"No connections! I just know people . . . you might say skilled artists." He smiled, but then quickly wiped the expression off his face. "What's it worth to you?" he asked.

"How's two thousand?"

"How's six thousand?"

Not wanting to appear overeager, Stephen was silent for a moment, after which he said quietly, "Three thousand."

"Five thousand."

"Four."

"No." The man behind the table was surly now. He dropped the empty beer can into a wastebasket by his side. "Five," he said, "or nothing."

Stephen began, "How can I be sure—"

He was interrupted by the declaration "You can't be sure of anything." But then the man continued, "But then you could be half sure if you left a deposit of twenty-five hundred."

"I don't have that much on me."

"What do you have on you?"

Stephen thought for a second, then answered quickly, "Five hundred."

"That's no deposit. That's what the pictures will cost you today."

"But the sign says . . ."

"These are extra-special pictures for a special purpose, right?"

"Right. And how long will—"

"How much of a hurry—"

"One week!" His own vehemence amazed Stephen. But of course in one week's time the bald-headed man with the narrow shoulders and the heavy belly could have taken his camera and moved. He heard himself say, "In a week's time you could pack up your camera and be in Topeka or St. Louis or . . ."

"I could be in Key West, Florida, in twenty-four hours; but you wouldn't be in Venezuela, would you?"

"Here's the five hundred dollars," Stephen said as he withdrew the bills from the wallet and handed them over.

"Let's see how photogenic you are."

The pictures he took remained with the photographer along with the passport application form. Stephen Cooper left the seedy office with the promise to come back in one week even as he imagined that, when he returned, the office would be empty. He rode in the elevator down to the lobby of the building, equally amazed by his nerve and his naïveté. He decided to say nothing about the adventure to Alice.

During the last week in July, the last week of the lease on Alice's old apartment, they transported to his apartment on Hinman in Evanston—now their home together, for "both of them"—the few possessions she chose to keep. She had sold her furniture to the landlady. Her clothes fit into three large pieces of luggage. There were two cartons of books, a few scrapbooks and albums of photographs, and one box of mementoes of her dead son.

Theirs was a three-bedroom apartment, so that while they shared the master bedroom and one of them had always been Stephen's study, the third bedroom, which Stephen thought of as the guest room, although he had only on very rare occasions housed a guest there, became Alice's study. Her books occupied no more than half of one bookcase in the room; the box of mementoes and family albums went into a closet as though down a memory hole; the only obvious touch of her personal presence was a snapshot of her late son in a thick clear plastic frame, which magnified it slightly. She set that on the night table next to the head of the bed.

Stephen thought of her clothes sharing the closet in their bedroom and sharing the drawers in the dresser as a comfort to him, especially when he wandered into her study during the day while she was away at her work, measuring how modestly her belongings impinged upon his small realm. He thought of himself as poverty-stricken, and wondered if it wouldn't have been much

171

better for her to have kept all her old furniture, brought it along with her, filled up the rooms that were so spare with the paraphernalia of another life. This was only an additional instance in which Stephen realized how desperately he had wished to be joined with the life of someone else.

He knew that soon enough, during the month of August, he would have to begin to prepare his classes for the fall semester; but he could barely think beyond the next week or ten days as a waiting period during which so much preparation had to be made. He would wait for the post-office box number and then for the calling card and the stationery to be engraved at Tiffany's; wait for a passport, and for the arrival of the leather from Spain.

In the meantime there was one thing he had been planning to do that he would now turn his attention to. He must find a particular model of Olivetti typewriter.

It took eleven telephone calls. Sitting in his office in the Department of Philosophy building, with the university telephone directory on his desk, Stephen began to ring up one departmental secretary after another to ask if she happened to have—or knew where he could find—an Olivetti electric typewriter, model 15, about ten years old. The first ten secretaries he was able to reach, in the course of a little more than one hour, each said "No," along with a greatly varied range of emotional charges. There were those who felt deprived and only wished they could have a machine as elegant as that sounded; there were those who had moved up to the world of high tech and worked only on word processors with ample memories and print-out attachments that made the letters of every word appear as though they had been stippled with black pinpricks; there were those who were either dismayed or dismissive because they knew nothing of such a machine.

But on the eleventh attempt the prospector's luck panned out.

The secretary to the Department of Economics answered "Yes." That was the typewriter she had; it was the typewriter she liked; and, yes, he could use it for a half hour or so during her lunch break that day.

It was then eleven-thirty in the morning. Stephen took the little bottle of white-out from his office desk, placed it in his nearly empty briefcase, and went down to the Xerox room, where he removed from the envelope inside his briefcase the letter signed by Reginald Carver on Sotheby stationery and made three Xerox copies of it. In addition to that, his briefcase contained only a handful of blank bond typewriter sheets.

He reached the office of the secretary in the Economics Building precisely at twelve noon.

Miss Annie Finn, whom he did not recognize, said that they had met once seven or eight years before at a university-wide reception; she shook his hand in a businesslike fashion but with a demure but distinct twinkle to her eyes and a shake of her head which said, "Charmed, I'm sure." Her eyes were cheerful and she had a large smile but otherwise could be described only as ugly. Hers was a short, dumpy body inappropriately dressed in black gaucho pants and a large blouse on which were printed thousands of miniature Michaelmas daisies. Her moon face was topped with innumerable small, tight gray curls —permanent!—that made her look like a sheep. Under her eyes innumerable horizontal lines glowed with a sheen of some optimistic application, which made Stephen think of a rumor he had heard that some women use a preparation meant to shrink hemorrhoids as a treatment to minimize wrinkles on their faces.

Miss Finn nicely introduced Professor Cooper to her

Olivetti electric typewriter. The original baby-blue color of the case had aged to a nearly gunmetal gray, but it had been cleaned and oiled frequently over the years and she was proud of its efficiency. She demonstrated the margin controls, the tabs for underlining, for superscript, for italics, and even a few diacritical marks. She thought he would be undisturbed from twelve to one and she wished him good luck with whatever his project required while she was gone.

Professor Cooper thanked her appropriately but, with caution, not excessively and promised to reward her, if there was something he could do as a favor.

When he was alone in the office, he brought a Xerox copy of the Sotheby letter out of his briefcase and laid it on the clean desk. Then he put a blank sheet of typing paper into the machine. Suppressing all his fears of disappointment, he typed out the first sentence of the letter, which began: "Regarding the decorated leather wall hanging . . ." With a feeling of joy rising steadily through him, by comparing it with Mr. Carver's declaration, he had the absolute reassurance that the typeface and size of each letter was identical with what appeared under the Sotheby letterhead.

With cheerful self-indulgence he typed over and over again the two words, first "As" and then "If."

He then laid one of the Xerox copies on the desk and unscrewed the cap of the bottle of white-out. He wiped the excess drop of whiteness from the brush in the cap along the rim of the little bottle and eliminated the word "If" at the beginning of the second paragraph of the letter. The word disappeared as under a magic spell, but the amount of whiteness was thicker than it should have been, and so he experimented again with the second and then with the third Xerox until he could make the word disappear without leaving a lump of whiteness elevated on the paper.

For the sake of practice he put the first Xerox into the typewriter to get the alignment exactly correct for super-imposing the substitute two-letter word in the space where the "If" had been eliminated. Over it he typed the word "As." When he was satisfied with the experiment on all three Xeroxes, Stephen brought the original of the Sotheby letter out of his briefcase as carefully as if he were dealing with the genuine Declaration of Independence. He licked his lips; he dried his palms with a Klee-nex from his back pocket; he brought the tiny brush of white-out with its minimum amount of magic down onto the stationery and brushed that "If" away forever. When he was satisfied that it had dried, as if woven in with the rest of the fine stationery, he rolled the paper into the typewriter and adjusted it for proper location and spacing, took a deep breath, and typed the word "As." It was not dark enough. He reversed the spaces and made a second impression. That satisfied him and he carefully rolled the letter out of the machine.

With these strokes of legerdemain he had turned an all-important cautious hypothetical sentence into a de-clarative statement. The full sentence now read:

As all the necessary documents of authentication
and ownership are properly, legitimately certified,
Sotheby's would be happy to undertake
representation for a public auction of that valuable
object . . .

It amazed him that, having gathered all of his things together in his briefcase and zipped them up, ready to leave, the door of the office opened and Miss Finn returned, for it was one o'clock, whereas he might have guessed that only ten minutes had passed.

Miss Finn mopped her brow and complained about how swelteringly hot it was out of doors, asking him if he hadn't especially appreciated the air-conditioning in her office. He was full of smiles and gratitude, although he had been unaware of the fact that he was in an air-conditioned room. Stephen realized he was conscious of nothing at all but the exultant sense of accomplishment in the thought "I've done it! I planned to do it. I did it. It is done!"

He wanted to telephone Alice at work to announce his triumph immediately; but, of course, he restrained himself from doing that. They had been in good spirits, behaving as if they were contented, trouble-free people, but it struck Stephen—as he walked into the university bookstore to buy some clear plastic file folders to keep the letters safe and yet see them at the same time—that there would be changes of moods, low points, blue periods or depressions and that he ought to save the good news of the successfully doctored Sotheby letter to present to Alice when she would need a lift to her spirits, when it could be of double use. So, after making a number of Xerox copies of the "corrected" version, he locked all of them away in a drawer of his office desk.

Therefore, a week later, on Thursday morning, August 2, the day after the unpleasant evening with Tom and Sarah Crane—which left Alice sullen and withdrawn—Stephen decided to retrieve the Sotheby surprise from his office and have it waiting for her when she arrived at home that evening.

By that fluke, he was in his office at 10:30 A.M. when a telephone call came through to him from London.

It made him feel that he was on a roll, so that by the

time he had walked home and placed the plastic file folders with the Sotheby letter in the center of the dining-room table and brought a large Chinese pewter bowl out of the buffet to use as a paperweight on it, it no longer seemed enough. He wanted more—even more—to cheer her up with.

Stephen made ready for the trip to the Loop and the Near North Side by withdrawing $5,000, in five crisp $1,000 bills, from his Evanston bank and then walked on to the train station. He appeared dapper in a blue blazer with brass buttons and an open-necked sport shirt. All the elements of his disguise were carried in his pockets.

He found his way to a men's room in the Everett Dirksen Federal Building, where he carefully arranged the wig, the mustache, the moles, and the glasses in the privacy of a stall and then checked it well in the mirror over the sink. He told himself to be prepared for disappointment across the street, where he expected that the office in which Leslie Egmont's passport picture had been taken would now be an empty room, or it would be manned by someone else, who had no knowledge of a passport prepared for him, or that he would have been betrayed and a federal officer of some sort would be waiting to arrest him.

He was trying to think of a plausible explanation for wanting a false passport if he should be arrested, as he walked across the street and then took the elevator upward in the old building; but none came to mind. He would simply have to remain silent and demand his right to call a lawyer. Then he realized he didn't have a lawyer. He couldn't remember the name of the law firm that had drawn up his last will and testament; he must have had that done about fifteen years ago. He wondered if Alice had a lawyer.

These were the thoughts which made his heart beat rapidly as he walked the short distance from the elevator to the office where the only photograph in the world of Leslie Egmont had been taken.

The door was open. A warm breeze came through from the open window. Behind the desk sat the bald-headed man with the narrow shoulders and the potbelly wearing a white T-shirt, Bermuda shorts, and leather sandals. He smoked a cigarette and flicked the ashes over his shoulder onto the floor. "I wondered whether you'd show up" was his greeting to Stephen.

"I wondered whether you'd be here."

"I'm pretty permanent. You're the one who wants to travel."

"There are some places I can't get to without . . ."

"Money. Money can take you just about anywhere. Right?"

Stephen closed the door behind him and sat in the chair across the desk from the man, who leaned forward on his elbows. It was then that Stephen said, "I have the money."

"I don't," said the man behind the desk, with a smile.

Stephen cleared his throat and then said, "I don't have a passport."

Still looking Stephen straight in the eyes, the man unbuttoned a back pocket in his Bermuda shorts, brought out a passport, which he laid on the table between them, and suddenly freed his hand of it.

Stephen looked at the thin passbook of navy blue stamped with the seal and the name of the United States of America. He reached out to take it, half expecting the man to stop him before he raised it in both hands, but he was not interfered with. All of the information that mattered appeared on the inside front cover running vertically from top to bottom. He turned the passport around slowly in his hands to see the colored photograph of Leslie Egmont with the typed-in reference to his imagined birth date and birth place, with the date of issue and the date of expiration—ten years later—all under a plastic coating. He was amazed by the appearance of authenticity. The man pointed to the page opposite the picture where under a line read the phrase "Signature of Bearer," and said, "You have to sign it there."

Stephen flicked through the remaining blank pages, the twenty-four pages decorated with a faint watercolor-cool impression of red, white, and blue shields of stars and stripes. All he could say was "It looks like the real thing."

"Who's to say it isn't?"

Stephen brought out of the inner pocket of his blazer his wallet with the Evanston bank envelope in the middle of it; he laid the envelope on the table, slipped the passport into the wallet, and replaced that in his jacket pocket; then he opened the white envelope and spread out on the table the five one-thousand-dollar bills, one at a time. The man scooped them up, returned them to the white envelope, folded it, placed it in the back pocket of his shorts, and rebuttoned the pocket.

Stephen concluded: "Beautiful work."

The man said, "I'll give your compliments to the chef."

Out on the street again, Stephen waved for a taxi. Not only was he on a roll, he could barely believe his good luck and he certainly would not question it. Moreover, appearing in public as he was doing now disguised as Leslie Egmont, he felt free from the burden of his identity as Stephen Cooper. It was the freedom of becoming a man without a history, a man who had made no mistakes and suffered no disappointments. He was pure potentiality for which all things are possible. He had no responsibilities, which made him feel that he was freedom itself.

A cab pulled up to the curb and he got in, asking to be taken to the Fort Dearborn post office on Ontario a block and a half east of Michigan Avenue.

His luck held and he was assigned a post-office box, which he rented for six months, paying cash for it in advance, box number 307. Then he was given the sequence of combination-lock numbers on a piece of paper, which he stuck into his wallet opposite the passport.

The moment he left the post office he began walking toward Michigan Avenue. He felt that he might jump into the air and click his heels, he might run wild for joy—but he restrained himself. He knew he was smiling broadly. People looked at him as though he were talking out loud to himself; but he was too happy to give a damn. He had a passport! He had an address! And now he would have printed calling cards and stationery: evidence of identification. He laughed at the thought that he was going from an imagined possibility to an almost legal entity. Or, better still, he was becoming a work of art.

He entered Tiffany's with the easy familiarity of a regular customer. Seeking out the saleslady who was taking care of the engraving for him, he spoke to her as "My dear." He informed her of the address to be engraved under his name:

Box 307
Fort Dearborn Post Office
Chicago, Illinois 60610

The stationery, however, was to carry only the name of Leslie Egmont. He offered to pay twice the price if the work could be completed in a week to ten days. The saleslady offered to see when it might be done for his "satisfaction."

Everything was falling into place.

When Stephen Cooper came out of Tiffany's, he discovered that a swift summer shower had rained upon the sidewalk and the street, suddenly washing it clean, leaving black reflecting puddles along the gutter. The storm had obviously moved south. Looking toward the Loop through the clear sunlit air where he stood, Stephen saw the black and blue clouds in the sky over the southern half of the city, heavy rain clouds moving east toward the lake. But in the foreground the skyscrapers of Michigan Avenue, heavy with gray stone carved into imitations of Gothic pinnacles like the Tribune Tower or seemingly weightless like the glass and steel buildings of Illinois Center, were all gilded by the sun moving toward the west. Those imperious buildings, splattering golden light against the ominous heavy sky of rain clouds beyond them, offered one of those dramatic moments of urban life in which nature reasserts itself, as if to remind a person that for all the intricate and complex creations of mankind they are still only transient in a natural world independent of him and vastly more all-encompassing.

The huge arc of a rainbow suddenly appeared—apparently arising from somewhere in the south, perhaps near the Museum of Science and Industry, up over many of the skyscrapers, out toward the center of the lake. Stephen did not think of it only as a gift of beauty but as an event that creates merely another illusion. What is a rainbow, he asked himself? An accidental arrangement of drops of water reflecting light, which in turn create an impression of a semicircle of bright colors for the unnamable delight of human beings who enjoy colors and arches. One of nature's luxuries to cheer up human beings. I am trying to rescue myself from the shambles of my life, Stephen told himself, and at the same time bring some measure of delight to Alice. I am gathering fragments together out of which to make a bouquet to lift her spirits. I should buy her some new phonograph records, he told himself. I should buy her perfume and a jar of French chestnuts in syrup, which she loves on vanilla ice cream. I will cheer her up with luxuries.

So it was that, by the time Alice entered their apartment in Evanston, a new recording of Prokofiev's Third Symphony sounded from the stereo, and there were all the elements of a ready-made meal in the refrigerator, from shrimp salad to the *marrons glacés* for dessert, and marinating in soy sauce two salmon steaks waiting to be broiled.

But the dining-room table had not been set. Instead, Stephen had spread out, for their cumulative effect, the bill of sale for the leather wall hanging from Salamanca, the declaration of authenticity on the stationery of the Prado in Madrid, and the "corrected" letter of approval and support on the stationery of Sotheby's in London. On a blank sheet of typing paper he had written the number of the post-office box that was now the mailing address for Leslie Egmont, and next to it he propped up for admiration the key "card of identity" for Leslie Egmont—a United States passport. He had written on one sheet of blank paper the date on which Tiffany's expected to deliver the stationery and calling cards; and on another blank sheet he wrote the telephone number of the U.S. Customs Service at O'Hare Airport, with a question mark for the date of arrival of the leather wall hanging.

Alice arrived to gradually revel in the sounds of the music and take enthusiasm from all that the display on the dining room table promised for the future.

Then she took a long, refreshing shower, and returned to Stephen scrubbed clean and reinvigorated, wearing only a white terrycloth bathrobe, casual as summer itself.

While she was changing, he had cleared away the invaluable papers in their protective clear plastic folders, set the table for dinner, and placed the gift-wrapped bottle of perfume next to her plate with the shrimp salad.

Alice stared at the ribbon-decorated gift box in silence for a moment and then slowly unwrapped it, took out the glass bottle, sniffed at the fragrance, and then held it against her heart. "Sometimes," she said, "I believe that you truly do love me."

Stephen realized that he hadn't thought about love at all, but only of how to make her feel better at the moment. Perhaps they were the same thing. He knew that some partners in married couples spoke of how the other tried to bribe or buy affection with gifts, with presents, with "things." He supposed that it was just a matter of timing: there are times when things are necessary; and times when nothing that money can buy will satisfy the need.

He felt pleased with himself.

When dinner was over, he took her by the hand and led her into the living room, seated her in an armchair, put a different record on the stereo set, and then filled the meerschaum pipe—which he was trying to cultivate—and stood before the fireplace looking down at her benignly. Between puffs at trying to get the pipe tobacco going, he announced: "I saved the best for last."

"You mean there's even more?" she asked. "What a day for fulfillments!"

"While I was in my office, first thing this morning, I received a phone call from London."

"Really? It must have been the end of the afternoon there."

"Yes, I suppose so." He used two more matches to help get the tobacco lighted.

"Aren't you ever going to tell me?" she urged him along.

"I think," Stephen began, more modest than hesitant, "that there is a potential buyer for our rare piece of sixteenth-century Spanish leather . . . a possible buyer hovering somewhere in the wings."

Alice leaned forward in the armchair, straight-backed, her hands clasped on her knees. "Do I have to pry it out of you?"

"No. I'll spill it all out before you like a shower of gold coins. It was a call from the managing director of Sotheby's, Mr. Reginald Carver. He wondered if I could put him in touch with Mr. Leslie Egmont."

Alice said softly, "Oh, my God."

"Of course, I had to say that I didn't know anyone by that name. He explained that Egmont had called on him in London about a month ago and he'd been expecting to hear again from him—at least to receive an address at which he could put someone in touch with him. Now, surely," he went on, "that can mean only one thing: he's been passing the word around in appropriate places and must have at least one possible buyer on the hook and so he is eager to move the process along."

"But why, in heaven's name, did he call *you?*"

"I asked him. And he replied quite openly that he had called up James Crow—old Professor Crow in Cambridge —who couldn't remember anything about a man named Egmont, but by association with Chicago and someone who had studied philosophy with him years ago and now taught at Northwestern, he gave Carver my name."

Alice now sat coldly rigid in the chair, spoke very softly, controlling all expression of emotion. "You mean to say that even before we have the leather in our hands you have undercut our cover story by giving someone reason to make a connection between you and Leslie Egmont?"

"Undercut? But I denied knowing him."

"Why did you give Carver any point of contact—any reason to make any connection—between you and Leslie Egmont?"

"I didn't do anything of the sort. I merely used the name of James Crow in order to get in to see Reginald Carver."

"That's the stupidest thing I have ever heard in my life."

The meerschaum pipe dropped from between Stephen's teeth. He caught it in both hands at his waist. He felt instantly more degraded than if she had spanked him like a child. Almost inaudibly, he asked her, "How dare you?"

She looked up and faced him, coldly stating: "I don't want to get caught."

"But you do want to pull this off, don't you?"

"Tell me again . . . how this happened. When you were in London you said that you had tried Professor Crow but that he was too old to talk to you on the phone."

"That's right. I talked to some kind of housekeeper or nurse."

"You told me he was senile."

"Well, he didn't recognize my name while I was on the phone."

"You didn't offer him the name of Leslie Egmont as well?"

"Certainly not."

"But when you went to see Carver at Sotheby's did you say you were a friend of Crow?"

"I said I had been a student of his decades ago."

"So when Carver got restless about not hearing from Egmont he called Crow to ask how to get in touch with him."

"Apparently. And, naturally, the name Egmont didn't mean anything to Crow, but the associations of Chicago, and a philosophy student, and maybe Northwestern, triggered a memory in Crow so that he gave Carver my name. That must be how senility works: memories come and go."

"How it works to our disadvantage," she said, tight-lipped. "So you're telling me that before we have got this project off the ground there is someone who could indicate to the police that there may be a connection between Stephen Cooper and Leslie Egmont."

"A very old, senile man."

"I don't mean him at all." Alice's voice had become high and shrill. "I am thinking of the managing director of Sotheby's. He's neither doddering nor senile. And if he has anything to do with the sale of the leather and anything goes wrong, later—when it comes to the point of an inquiry, later—he will be right there to supply every bit of information that might come to mind. And *his* mind sounds just fine."

Stephen sucked on the pipe as he tried to relight it and remained silent. Finally, he replied, "I told Mr. Carver that I did *not* know of anyone by that name. I don't see that the coincidence created by James Crow as a point of contact carries with it any fatal implications. But I do see something very strange. If, even before we have something to sell, let alone *have made* a sale, you should already be imagining how something might go wrong with it and boomerang to—"

"Explode in our faces."

"Isn't that taking such a grim view of what might

happen that we'd be smarter never to try carrying this out at all?"

"Oh, yes," she said rapidly. "We'd be much smarter not to do it."

"But then what would we have to look forward to?" It was at that moment, he imagined, both of them realized what overwhelming truth was carried in the remark he had uttered so unthinkingly. It was this scheme alone they held in common. It was only this plan of subterfuge and felony that was true of "both of them." And, while each came to it compelled by a different motivation, it alone gave them common cause.

Stephen then went to the crux of the matter. "I don't want to get caught, either," he said. "I see what you mean about any possible association between Egmont and me."

Alice interrupted by adding quickly, "And *me*, too."

Stephen continued, "But I think it a very remote, a very attenuated association. And since I told Carver pointblank that I don't know the man—and since he *will* be receiving something in the mail fairly soon from Leslie Egmont—I can easily believe that he will lose from memory any reference to a Stephen Cooper he may have spoken with for three minutes once on the telephone."

Alice appeared implacable. She stared at him and said, "Sometimes I think you don't love me at all." Then she commanded: "You must never do or say anything ever again that could connect you or me with this business."

"Readily," Stephen said, "I swear it."

She looked up at him from the corners of her eyes, a gaze filled with doubt, suspicion, the uncertainty of whether her accusation of stupidity might be justified again in the future. And then she looked away with contempt.

I have lost her respect, Stephen told himself. Or am I

reading too much meaning into that gesture, that looking away, which is the opposite of re-spect, the desire to look at again? He pretended that he had not seen the gesture and, instead, forced himself to move toward where she sat, lean forward, kiss her on the forehead, and say only, "Believe me."

She tried to smile. She looked up at him and asked, "If I believe in you, will I be saved?"

"At least for another day."

CHAPTER NINE

Then, every day became more oppressive than the day before. The heat of August in 1984 belied Stephen's expectations of the pleasures of midsummer weather in Chicago. It was as if the heat wave that might be anticipated in the first week of September had begun a month early. He discovered that the heat and the humidity undermined the very fiber of Alice's personality. First she behaved like a wounded animal who could only fearfully skulk from the air-conditioning in their bedroom or her study to the air-conditioning of the office in which she worked, having to steel herself against the torture of the scorching, heavy, wet air between those enclosed places of refuge. Increasingly lengthening periods for recovery were required in making the transition from one to the other. She seemed to melt like wax, to lose her character, under the pressure. She could pull herself together only gradually and only in isolation. As the torture continued, she began to behave like a maddened beast suffering from a cruel and unbearable personal torment. She could not stand the touch of his fingertips even in a gentle stroke of sympathy or kindness on her cheek or on her upper arm. She cringed from any touch.

They began to see less of each other as she spent more time by herself in the guest room. It was smaller than their bedroom and she explained that, because the air-conditioning unit in the window there was more effective, she'd prefer to sleep in it alone during the heat wave. She was gathering together materials to be used in the "treatment" of the leather wall hanging when it arrived, but she would not talk with him about any of the materials she was buying, a little at a time, rather like an author who's afraid of talking about a work he's writing for fear that the thoughts and feelings he wants to impart to it can be spent only once, and if he gives voice to them they will evaporate before he has fixed them by written words into just the sentences that will last.

At that point, Stephen also discovered to his surprise that Alice did not read. For him, reading was so ingrained a habit, so profoundly a necessity of his nature, that he barely recognized at first how different her behavior was from his. During the days of the sweltering summer, he became aware that Alice would notice the publications that came in with the daily mail or the books or journals that he brought into the apartment with him but did not actually pick up any of them to finger through or let her attention be caught by anything in print; and she brought home none of her own. As for himself, he began Sunday morning by reading through the *New York Times* and ended Sunday evening by looking at some text that he would be using in one of his courses. During the week there were the daily newspaper, *The New Yorker* magazine, *Time*, *The New Republic*, *T.L.S.*, and the occasional monthly or quarterly journals in philosophy, *The Public Interest*, *The American Scholar*. He bought three or four books that were published each month.

The fact that Alice did not read made him focus attention on the question of what did actually take place in her mind when she was not working, when she was alone in the guest room, when they were not making small talk over a meal or sitting silently in each other's presence watching a program on television. Stephen felt it as a lack of understanding on his part that he was unable to imagine how she could be alone with her own thoughts so much of the time. And yet he could not ask her point-blank: What are you thinking about? or he would find himself doing it every half hour. By the same token, he would suddenly become aware of her standing in the entranceway to the living room while he sat in an armchair reading, and when he looked up would see on her face an expression which asked, "What are you doing?" To which he gave no answer. He knew that he had disappointed her, that she suffered from the festering of doubts about whether he could be counted on not to make a mistake again in the future. As a result, it seemed to him, the oppressive heat and humidity became the excuse for the silences between them.

On the landfill that jutted out into Lake Michigan, at the east end of the university's campus, was a fine white sand beach, with a long view south to the skyscrapers at the center of Chicago and a long view east across the gray-blue water. On a Sunday afternoon Stephen made a picnic and urged Alice to walk the few blocks from their home so that they might swim in the lake. He carried a beach blanket and she held his large, colorful golf umbrella over her head in place of a parasol. Stretched out on the beach sand like a stranded fish, gasping for whatever breeze might come off the surface of the water, Alice twisted and turned in discomfort, detesting the hot sand as much as the hot air, until she seemed to give up all fight entirely and lay limp, motionless, while he quietly, in proximity to students and faculty and university staff people and local inhabitants of Evanston, orally drafted for her hearing the letter that he was continually composing in his mind—the letter of Leslie Egmont to imagined museum officials, gallery owners, auction houses, indicating to them the possibility that their priceless object might be available under the right conditions.

Eventually Alice responded, even more quietly, by saying, "Not yet. Be calm. Let's wait till we have something to put up for sale before we try to sell it."

It seemed to him that she was defeated in advance and yet he knew that was not so; it was only that she was moving along into the future on her own timetable, which was different from his. She was more practical than he. It struck him that, if something went wrong with their scheme, she had more to lose than he had.

And yet he felt the lust to be able to do something, and the frustration of not knowing which way to move. Despite the fact that the engraved stationery was not yet available from Tiffany's, it suddenly struck him in this instant of lying on the beach beside Alice that there *was* something to do immediately. "We could cable to Salamanca!" he suddenly exclaimed.

"What for?" she asked.

"Look. We have an address now. Leslie Egmont could send a cable to the people who sold you the leather—asking for details about the shipment: the date of export, the export license number, the approximate date of arrival. Don't you think we could do that? I could give the post-office box number and ask for a response by cable as well."

Alice thought about it in silence for a little while, and then she said, "Yes, I think that will be all right. If—and only if—you don't send it on our telephone or even from a cable office here in Evanston. But if you go into Chicago to a place where nobody knows you and you pay for it then and there so that there's no way of tracing you. Yes, then I think it would be all right."

It made Stephen feel his dignity was beginning to be repaired.

His mind raced ahead to the prospect of potential buyers. "And you ought to be working on the list of people the letter will go to . . ."

"What letter?"

"The one about Something for Sale . . ."

"Wait," she said. "Please, wait. Be calm. All in good time." It was as if she had to be courted. They were married now; they had taken the great plunge together, and now it seemed to him that she regretted it, because what was missing was a period of being appealed to, lured, cajoled, seduced—in a word, courted. Courtship had been missing, and the lack of it had to be made up for somehow. He had not paid the proper price for what they appeared to have together by this time. A proper exchange has to take place for each significant accommodation in nature; and if it is not paid at the proper time then it has to be substituted for later on.

The next day—disguised as Leslie Egmont—he sent the cable to Salamanca and then wandered up Michigan Avenue to Tiffany's, where he was told that the stationery and calling cards were not ready yet but would be in just a few more days. He then looked over their collection of silver frames.

He had clearly in his mind's eye the recollection of the unadorned, the plain, not to say gross clear plastic frame in which Alice kept the photograph of her dead son on the night table in the guest room. He looked for something grander to replace it with. Most of what were offered for sale were silver rectangles in a variety of sizes. Stephen had almost decided on the one he'd figured was approximately the right size when a saleslady—*his* saleslady—

interrupted him; she commiserated with him on the weather outside; she asked about his health; she reassured him about the almost momentary arrival of his stationery and asked him if she could be of help.

When he described what he was looking for, she took him away from the cabinet of plain rectangles and brought his attention to a frame of the size he indicated; it stood on one of the display islands near the rear of the store. This frame was an elaborate imitation of a baroque design: a heavy encrustation of scrolls and pillars with a broken pediment at the top in the center of which stood a small urn.

"Yes," he said. "I think that would be wonderful. That's just what I want. How much is that?"

The saleslady stated an impressively exorbitant amount of money.

"I'm afraid I don't have that much on me."

"Well, to tell the truth, Mr. Egmont, you really shouldn't always pay in cash. You know, for your records, it's much better to have the bill and then a canceled check."

He realized that the credit cards in his pocket were all made out to Stephen Cooper. He said, "I don't have a charge account here."

"But you are a regular customer. I can arrange for that without any trouble. I'll send you the form along with the bill for this purchase. How will that be?"

"Actually," he began hesitantly, "you don't have my address."

"Well, then, let me take it down now."

He gave her the post-office box number, which she recorded without batting an eyelid. "Shall I have it gift-wrapped for you?"

"No, thanks very much just the same. It's . . . for me."

He was satisfied to have her simply wrap it in tissue paper and secure it with a robin's-egg-blue ribbon and bow. Then he slipped it into an inner jacket pocket.

She asked if she could telephone him when the stationery arrived, but he said he moved about so much of the time—he thought it would be better if he telephoned her.

And then he walked the few blocks to the Fort Dearborn post office. There was no relief in the weather. The thin cover of gauzy clouds did nothing to keep the intensity of the sun's heat from broiling the air. The view of Ontario Street as he walked east wavered before his eyes.

But the post office was cool by comparison and he then knew the exultation of unlocking *his* box to withdraw the first pieces of mail delivered to Mr. Leslie Egmont. First there was a picture postcard of Mount Fujiyama with a conventional tourist's message sent to him by his chairman, Professor Johnson, on one of the first days during his stay in Tokyo. Stephen had slipped the card into an envelope, stamped and addressed it to his alter ego at this post-office box number. The second piece of mail to come to him here was a letter he had written on stationery he'd brought back with him from the hotel on Russell Square where he had stayed last in London. There was only this brief, not to say elliptical, message, without salutation or signature: "By the time you receive this, almost all of the necessary pieces will have fallen into place. When you have been recreated, will you recognize yourself?"

Stephen was back in their apartment a good two hours before Alice could be expected to return. He unwrapped the silver frame and took it into the guest room. Removing the snapshot of her son from the thick plastic object, he then inserted it and secured it into the elaborate new frame he had bought and left both of them together on the night table.

In the bedroom, he put away his clothes and the disguise, took a shower, and then, dressed only in shorts and a sport shirt, he set the table in the dining room and checked the refrigerator for the soup and the cold cuts they would have for dinner. He made himself comfortable in the living room where he sat down to read for an hour or so. But he fell asleep.

He had no idea what time it was when he was awakened by Alice sitting opposite him dressed only in her bathrobe, holding the silver frame in her hands, shaking her head from side to side, and repeating the word "No" in a low, moanlike dirge.

Stephen sat up suddenly, saw that she was looking at him but hardly seeing him in the same instant that he saw the silver frame was empty. She had removed the snapshot.

She offered the frame back to him, saying softly, "You use it for something else."

"I meant it as a gift for you."

"You can't buy into my past life."

"I'm trying to make the present and future life better."

"It doesn't work that way. At least, not for me. I don't want to enshrine a memory. In any case, it's a memory you can't share with me."

"I thought it would make us feel closer."

She responded: "I think we're at about the right degree of closeness . . . considering that we each have our own limits. I try to respect yours; please respect mine."

What did he know of his own limits? he wondered. He knew that he had not shared with her his sense of loss of the value of his life. He could not risk letting her know that; it would be like inviting her to share his apartment and then never coming home to be with her. That is what he felt himself to be: a furnished apartment where no one any longer cares to make use of all the comforts or conveniences, or knows why any of the contents once mattered to someone.

Alice placed the silver frame face down on the table before her. She took a deep breath and rested back against the end of the sofa where she was sitting. "Let me tell you a story," she began.

"I had a visitor in my office this afternoon. She stayed for only about fifteen minutes but she upset me a lot and I didn't do very much work after she left.

"Her name is Louise, and she is about twenty-five years old. She was a secretary at the Art Institute during the past few years—until she got married and left. She is very pretty, intelligent, pleasant; she's what anyone would call a lovely person. She married a man named Lewis, just as good-natured and attractive and solid as she is. And everyone joked about their being the ideal representations of man and woman right down to how their names reflected those masculine and feminine forms.

"They've been married for about six months. She came by today to share her happiness in telling friends that she's just learned she's pregnant—how lucky she feels, and how grateful she is for her good fortune."

Stephen asked, "Why did that upset you?"

"She reminded me exactly of myself when I was two months pregnant. Life had not yet played any of its dirty tricks on me. When I was her age—no, even younger—I thought my husband and I were fulfilling the norms and expectations of our race, our class, our religious beliefs; we were realizing or fulfilling the ideal. I didn't count on being disappointed or frustrated or crippled or undermined by anything. I was then, as she is now, happily living a life as instinctual as any ant in an anthill, natural life. Nature's way—"

Stephen interrupted by intoning the lines: "Wise men in their bad hours envy the little people making merry like grasshoppers . . ." and wondered whether he was remembering those words of Robinson Jeffers correctly.

Alice continued as if she had heard nothing. "That kind of instinctual life—or the human, socially conditioned version of instinctual life: the perfect marriage—is the only one that a human being can feel is beautiful, is genuine, is authentic; that's what each of us aspires to. I have no idea how many people achieve it: live it out, the real thing. But, after Louise left me, for the rest of the afternoon, I felt that anything less than that—any accommodation to disappointment, any adjustment, any starting over with lower expectations, any second chance, is always second best, or third or fourth for that matter. Anything that only approximates the real thing is an imitation, a conscious make-believe, a substitute. There is only the genuine or the fake."

Stephen said, "In a dark mood, you are too hard on human beings who have to make do with bad luck."

She replied, "I don't think I'm being either hard or soft; just realistic, objective."

As a philosopher, Stephen almost began to expound his interpretation of objectivity as an illusion, but he thought better of it. Instead he said, "It is also received wisdom that human beings are never so old or so disappointed that they cannot share some things together that make for some degree of a good life."

"Respecting each other's limits?" she asked.

"And without sleeping every night in the procrustean bed of ideals."

Alice leveled her head to look at him clearly now, eye to eye. "We cannot share the past but we can do something together that will give us one great experience in common in the future." She stood up then, somehow reinvigorated, expressing her strong sense of determination, and said, "Let me show you what I've done so far—so that we'll be ready when we have the leather in hand." She stretched out her hand to him and gestured her fingers toward herself. "Come with me. It's all in the guest room."

The first thing Stephen saw on entering the chilly room was that the photograph of Alice's son had been replaced in the plain plastic frame. He did not feel unhappy to "learn limits"; he would be content to take what he could get.

From the drawers of the desk Alice withdrew boxes of various small sizes. But, before she opened any of them, she said, "First we start with the plan, namely, to replicate the pomegranate image on a large piece of sixteenth-century leather."

Stephen smiled sardonically. "I remember, I remember."

She continued: "When I was in Washington I made a tracing of the pomegranate pattern as it appeared in that wall display in the basement of the Freer."

"You traced it right on the wall?"

"Yes. There were very few people around; when, occasionally, someone went into or came out of the men's room around the corner, I'd appear to be reading the legend on the wall. But otherwise I was uninterrupted."

From the central desk drawer she drew out the original tracing paper of the pattern, showing the stem, the leaf, and the shape of a pomegranate opened partly to reveal eight pomegranate seeds. The whole design fit within a circular shape of no more than an inch in diameter.

"From that," Alice began to explain, "I made a master copy on a carbon paper in order to transfer it to the brass tool that will be used to cut the pattern in the leather." She then opened one of the boxes on the desk, not more than six inches long; and from it she brought out an object of wood and brass that looked like the handle of a gardening trowel. Stephen felt the heft of the wooden handle in his hand and then he examined the flat surface of its circular brass head.

Incised into the metal was an exact duplication of the pattern of the pomegranate opened to expose its seeds, the leaf, and the stem.

He marveled at it and asked, "How did you do it?"

Alice took out of the drawer the miniature triangular-shaped files she had used to cut into the brass. The pattern was no more than a sixteenth of an inch deep, a little deeper than old-fashioned foundry type. "This," she said, "will make it possible to engrave or incise the pattern into the leather."

He fondled the shank of the brass tool with admiration. It was the appreciation of a man who works only with words, whose work does not yield a product that can be held in the hand.

"And then," Alice continued with enthusiasm, "the fun begins. Once the design has been pressed to make the whole pattern, the process for decorating it and aging it can start. I'll need gold for the leaves and the stems." She opened another box to show some of the gold, which she explained would be broken down from the nugget in a mortar and pestle, as it was very soft and easily pulverized. Then it would have to be mixed with glue from the skins of animals or hooves of horses boiled in water. Alice quietly reassured him that the gelatinous substance came in little paper packets of dehydrated powder.

She showed him the fine-haired brush with which she would apply the gold to the leaves and the stems. "But for the pomegranate seeds I'll have to lay down a lot of preparation before the vermilion can be used to color them. First there'll be an egg-white treatment—called a 'glare'—to moisten the leather; and that has to evaporate. Then a second coat to fill the pores; as that's absorbed it primes the leather. It shouldn't become bone dry, so I'll use oil of clove or Vaseline or perhaps best would be body oil."

"Whose body?" Stephen asked.

"Mine. All I have to do is take a little swab of cotton and wipe it across my forehead. That's as much body oil as I meant. Then, both the gold leaf and the vermilion are bonded to the leather through that tiny amount of oil." She appeared lost in her own thoughts and said, "For the pure pigment of vermilion I'll need to add a glaze of madder lake. And after all of that is done there'll have to be a coat of either shellac or varnish and then a period of time for antiquing—in order to crack it all, to age it, probably with heating lamps. . . ."

"By then we'll need artificial heat, I suppose."

"It will take a little time. And a lot of effort."

"I want to help. I want us to do it together."

"We'll try to do it together."

Although Alice slept in the guest room and Stephen slept in the bedroom that night, he got into bed with her early the next morning and they made love for the first time in over a week. It was neither romantic nor athletically erotic; and they were not bonded together by the exchange of words that express any shared thought or feeling. At least, he felt that they were colleagues who were shoring each other up. Neither of them knew on this first occasion that it was the beginning of a pattern to be repeated in the future. They went their separate ways at night, but he would come to her bed early every other morning, or every third morning, and they would, wordlessly, challenge and restore each other.

CHAPTER TEN

At the end of that week, Leslie Egmont picked up his cards and stationery at Tiffany's and then, from his mailbox at the Fort Dearborn post office, he read a cable from Salamanca giving the freight identification number on the leather shipment along with the approximate date of arrival in Chicago—which turned out to be five days earlier than the day on which he received the information. He telephoned the imports customs office at O'Hare Airport and learned—to his glee—that the shipment had arrived and that, yes, the customs office would be open on Saturday, the next day, until noon.

He was able to greet Alice with this information that evening when she returned home. Before she arrived he had written a short friendly letter on his new stationery, informing Reginald Carver at Sotheby's in London how he could be reached in the future. He enclosed a number of his cards so that they might be used by Mr. Carver with appropriate people; and he drafted a short business letter informing the Zürich bank of his new post-office box number, to which statements should be mailed in the future. He felt especially responsible to Alice not to put either letter in the mail until she had read them and approved of them.

That Saturday morning brought the blessing of a break in the weather; it was sunny but dry with a balmy breeze. Stephen and Alice put on their disguises in the car as they drove toward the airport. It amazed him how her auburn-brunette curly wig, a darker lipstick, and a nose ring with an imitation diamond in it created a radically different appearance. He had grown accustomed to his own transformation by the white-haired wig, the moles, the square tinted glasses, and the mustache, but he was amazed by how unidentifiable Alice became with her few elements of transformation, which he had seen but rarely.

She, on the other hand, accustomed to seeing through the surface of things, appeared unaffected by his disguise, implying that it could have no influence on her.

He drove the car to O'Hare Airport and found his way through a labyrinth of one of the enormous self-parking garages, and then they walked through to the customs section at the international end of the terminal. Despite the large proportions of the rooms of glass and steel, it was oppressively warm, for there was no air-conditioning in that building. They were directed to the proper office and stood there waiting for an available customs inspector.

Alice brought a Kleenex out of her pocketbook and dabbed at the perspiration on her forehead.

"Body oil," Stephen said, as an example of the fact that he was a fast learner. Alice smiled, but was obviously tense and impatient.

When a heavy-set, middle-aged civil servant, comfortable in his tan short-sleeved shirt, turned his attention to them, he offered his services with the invitation: "Next?"

Stephen presented the cable addressed to Leslie Egmont with the freight identification number on it. The customs man took the cable into his hand to read it, and then, seemingly acknowledging recognition of the name, grunted, "Oh, yeah. It looks like a skinny coffin." He turned and walked back through a metal frame door in the mesh screen wall that separated the outer office from the storage bins piled high with packages of all sizes and shapes from briefcases to steamer trunks and roundish objects from India wrapped in white cloth and sewn shut. He returned with a helper at the other end of the long narrow pine box, more than six feet in length and a little more than a foot square. As they approached the outer office, Stephen whispered to Alice, "Looks more like the counter of a sushi bar."

Staring at them as they hefted the object onto the length of the counter before her, Alice expressed no emotion.

The customs inspector checked the name on the box itself and then riffled through the customs documents from an envelope that had been attached to it under a plastic cover. "Antique, huh," he said.

"Yes," Stephen supplied readily, "it's a very old piece of leather, a leather wall hanging." He had responded as if answering a question, whereas the customs inspector had made a statement.

"You Leslie Egmont?" he asked.

"Yes."

"Who's your friend?" the inspector asked, raising his eyebrows.

"My wife."

He said, "Pleased to meetcha," and then returned his gaze to Stephen's face. "Let's see your driver's license."

"I don't drive," but he quickly added, "so I brought some other identification with me." Nervously, out of one inside jacket pocket, he brought his passport and presented it to the customs inspector, at the same time that he fumbled in another jacket pocket for envelopes addressed to him at his post-office box number. He laid those on the counter and then drew out of his wallet one of the engraved calling cards. From the corner of his eye, he read in the expression on Alice's face the judgment that he was overdoing it.

The customs inspector was not particularly interested. He flicked through the passport, and said, "You haven't been doing much traveling."

Stephen rushed in with the explanation: "My old passport just expired. This is a brand-new one. I haven't been able to use it yet. But I will, I will."

Then it was necessary to open the carton and look to see whether the contents fit the description and nothing else was inside. Gradually, it became clear to Stephen that there was no customs problem with the large piece of old leather; what the customs officials concerned themselves with was whether something else was "included" in the package, something undeclared, something smuggled, illegal. Long brass screws were unwound from the neatly crafted pine box and the top removed. The inspector and his assistant unrolled the leather from between two sheets of thin, beige flannel.

Alice said quietly, "I do believe they used two bed sheets to wrap it in. How sweet of them."

The inspector examined the full length of the leather on both sides, shook out both sheets of flannel, and examined the empty box. Then, most unexpectedly, with a fierceness of voice he had not used up to that moment, he asked them harshly, "Where's the beef?"

Stephen flinched, and then looked with bewilderment at Alice. For all his worldliness, he was out of touch with American popular culture in the summer of 1984. That was the season in which an advertisement on television for a chain of hamburger restaurants made the question "Where's the beef?" the most popular three words in the country. They were identified with a little old lady who asked the question on television: old and demanding, crusty and determined, sort of "I'm from Missouri. Show me!"—a craggy crone who looked like an armchair decorated with antimacassars for collar and cuffs, wanting her fair share. That expression went across the country like wildfire and was made use of by everyone from nightclub stand-up comics, who made it into dirty jokes, to Walter Mondale, campaigning for the presidency of the United States, who used it to ask what had become of the government's sense of social responsibility.

But Stephen Cooper, preoccupied and distracted, had missed that cultural happening. He stared now from the face of the customs inspector to the face of his wife and back again, with the distress of one who imagines a code expression in espionage or in the language of imports and exports is being used—and, although he should be expected to know what it means, in fact, he does not.

Alice reached out and touched his arm.

The customs inspector and his assistant were both trying to recover from the laughter they enjoyed for the surprise appearance of the "beef" line. "Scared ya, didn't I."

Stephen felt the wetness of his shirt and jacket sleeves under the pressure of Alice's hand. Then, suddenly, he was aware of her pinching him through the fabric: a small, steady, needlelike pinch. He looked up to her face to be confronted by the suspicious look of the alcoholic's wife. More than an innuendo of accusation, it boldly communicated her anxiety over whether he would make some terrible slip, the kind of false step that would instantly give them away.

Stephen remembered the cold, clear way in which Alice had said to him, "I don't want to get caught." While the customs officials behind the counter rolled the leather back upon itself between the two sheets of flannel and prepared to replace it in its box, Stephen calmed himself and gathered his documents together on the counter and replaced them in his pocket. He did not slip a glance out of the corner of his eye but baldly looked at Alice now in profile—simply all business, no nonsense—in a cool navy-blue dress, showing no more feeling under the circumstances than a housewife would as she watched a grocer placing her bag of potatoes on a scale. We are cut from different cloths, he thought; we can only try not to rub each other the wrong way as much of the time as possible.

The customs men replaced the screws in the lid of the box, tightened them securely, and dismissed Mr. and Mrs. Egmont, saying, "No hard feelings . . ." for having played the "beef" trick on them. As a genuine antique, their leather wall hanging cleared customs without a duty charge.

With Stephen in front and Alice behind, they carried the long wooden box, under their left arms, out through the glass and steel building, through the underpass to the garage, marching along in silence, until they came to Stephen's old car. It was a 1975 four-door Chevrolet Impala. They rested the long box on the trunk, while Stephen unlocked the door of the driver's seat and then the door behind it. After he wound down the window in the left rear door, together they angled the box through the open window and rested the front end of the box on the dashboard. But the rear end of the box stuck out through the window by at least two feet.

"I'll drive," Stephen said, "if you'll sit in the back seat and anchor down the box. All right with you?"

Alice agreed. When she was seated, he checked to see that all of the doors were securely closed, set himself up behind the steering wheel, and cautiously drove out of the garage.

They were well on their way toward Evanston when Stephen, unable to bear the silence any longer, began to tell a story. "Once upon a time there was a president of the University of Chicago named Lawrence Kimpton. He succeeded Robert Maynard Hutchins about 1950. He was no Hutchins intellectual, but he did some good things for the university, like improved the neighborhood it's in."

Alice snorted.

"Don't laugh," Stephen said. "Well, not yet. The story I want to tell you has to do with the fact that he was a hard-drinking man and a man of other simple-minded pleasures. On a Sunday afternoon in summer he liked to relax on a sailboat. He and his wife would drive to the yacht club, take off in somebody's sailboat—maybe it was his own, I don't remember—and spend Sunday afternoon out on Lake Michigan sunbathing and drinking. Apparently he wasn't any kind of sailor; it was just a matter of relaxing by boozing.

"One late afternoon the sailboat came back to the yacht club with the good president in his dark blue suit, white shirt, and Sunday-school tie—drunk as a lord. When they docked, he fell off the gangplank and came up onto the marina soaking wet. His wife helped him stagger to their car in the parking lot.

"But then, as she was about to open the door, his wife, suddenly realizing that it was a brand-new car, said that she wouldn't have him get into it sopping wet as he was. So instead she opened the trunk and he crawled in like a baby, but an over-six-foot-tall baby—with his legs and feet protruding, trousered and shod; and they took off down Lake Shore Drive toward Hyde Park.

"There were police patrolling as usual on a sunny

Sunday afternoon and they were alert enough to notice an automobile with a pair of legs and feet sticking out of the trunk. They turned on their siren and chased the car for a while until it pulled to the side. When it was stopped, the lid of the trunk came up and Lawrence Kimpton emerged on both feet, addressing the police officers in a calming, a positively Olympian calming and reassuring tone, telling them that there was nothing to worry about, officers, because he was the president of the University of Chicago."

Sitting in back, with one arm draped over the raw wood box, Alice made no response.

Stephen asked, "Don't you think that's a funny story?"

"Not particularly."

"Why not?"

"It's just another put-down type story—even if it's true."

"It probably is true." Stephen felt himself becoming irritable. Is nothing I do ever going to please her? he wondered.

Alice explained, "It's just that I'm preoccupied. I want to get this bloody thing into our apartment safe and sound. Then I can relax. I can't think about whether your story is funny or not right now. Speaking of appearances —we must take off our disguises before we get into Evanston!"

As they drove along, Alice bent forward partly under the box to remove her wig and the nose ring. Then she brought a Kleenex out of her pocketbook and wiped the bright lipstick away.

At the next stoplight, where no pedestrian appeared anywhere in sight, Stephen leaned forward beside the steering wheel to remove his disguise as well.

It was noon when they drove through Evanston toward the lake. As they paused to turn onto Hinman, Stephen felt curiously aware of the brightness of the sunlit sky and of the apparent health of all he could see—the huge trees, the oak and elm and beeches and maples that created pools of cooling shade along the sidewalks; and bathers a block or so beyond, walking toward the beach. He was touched with a strange sense that in all of the neatness and well-being of the outer world, corruption was concealed within, breeding its own destruction. He felt the fear of wondering how soon the rot, the breakdown of moral rectitude, which he had always previously maintained, would come through onto the disintegrated surface of his life, or whether it could be concealed successfully forever.

Alice, unnerved by the long wait, suddenly asked, "Why don't you turn the corner?" He then drove around onto Hinman without a reply. He felt that a correlative of her uncertainty about his behavior, the continual suspicion that he might make a false move at any moment, was that she had to keep an eye on him, she had to ask questions like Why are you doing this? or Why don't you do that? Was she to become his policeman, his guardian?— not out of willful possessiveness—not that obsessive need —but out of fear that he would ruin the situation for both of them.

They found a parking space less than half a block away from their apartment house, and together carried the unusually long but unpretentious box with its potentially valuable contents along the street, flaunting it, as if reveling in the oddity—as if they had brought home for a house pet an adolescent giraffe.

It was a little awkward maneuvering the box through the outer vestibule and the front hall of their building.

They ran into only the janitor-handyman, who raised both eyebrows as a question.

Alice answered it by saying: "New floor lamps." And they proceeded to take it up into their apartment.

As a consequence of having the leather in their possession, through the rest of the month of August Stephen and Alice did not risk any social life. No one was invited to their apartment; and they did not go out evenings or weekends.

To accommodate the leather in the guest room, Alice bought dozens of one-inch-thick squares of cork, the sort that are used for bulletin boards, and Stephen helped her glue them to the wall over an area larger than the piece of leather. A sheet of foam rubber was then cut to size and fixed over the cork board. Finally the leather was placed on top of those two pads and fitted with snap clamps, which would leave no trace.

Alice measured her tracings from the wall display at the Freer and calculated the exact distance of each pomegranate image from the other and then together they laid out a grid across the entire piece of leather with lengths of string that ran both vertically and horizontally, attached to the wall securely with carpet tacks. The intaglio of the pomegranate image was to be placed in the upper right quadrant where the strings crossed.

But Alice hesitated to begin pressing the images into the leather, which she studied through various magnifying glasses and with the most sensitive touches of her fingers, as if she were reading Braille. She came to the conclusion that the leather was too cracked and too dry to take the impression from the dye she had prepared without treating it into a more supple condition. Even then, she explained to Stephen, she would have to warm the brass end of the tool before striking it into the leather. Meanwhile she decided on ethylene glycol—the main ingredient in anti-freeze—to soften the leather, and once she began to apply it, first with a sponge and then with cotton and water, moistening it and massaging it one inch at a time, Stephen ceased to be of help to her or, rather, she no longer wanted his help. The creation of this replica, this artifice, engaged all of her professional skill. She felt fully responsible, so that without becoming unpleasant about it—in fact, without becoming at all personal about it—she eased Stephen out of the activity as well as the responsibility of preparing the counterfeit gift of Catherine of Aragon.

Stephen felt himself more than ever a bachelor. During the evenings he would read or listen to music on his record player or watch a baseball game on television or follow the news of the presidential campaign. During the day he would shop for their food, take care of the laundry, do chores around the house, and then work over his notes in his office in preparation for the courses he would teach that fall. He was a man who had lost interest in his life and was unsure of whether he believed in the magic that might grant him a new life.

On the last working day before Labor Day weekend, Alice telephoned him at home from her studio in the Art Institute before the end of the afternoon and said in a dry, husky voice, "I just can't come home. I can't go through the same routine night after night. I'm so bored I could scream."

Stephen, who felt that he was no good at guessing other people's feelings and almost never tried to understand them, took only at face value what people told him they felt. It had not occurred to him until the moment of this telephone call that Alice was fed up—disappointed or dissatisfied, unhappy in any way.

"Well, we'll have to do something else," he responded rapidly. "Let's go out to dinner and take in a movie, or go visit some friends."

"We have no friends."

"What?"

"The people we know are even more boring than we are."

"I'll throw on some clothes and meet you in one hour. Want me to pick you up at your office?"

"No. I've got to get out of here. You can meet me somewhere around here in one hour, right? Well, then, I'll go to the Ritz. I'll go up to the lobby of the Ritz Hotel and sit in that lounge—what's it called? the Greenhouse, I think—and I'll order tea or a glass of sherry, and I'll pretend I'm being photographed for a page in *Vogue,* the way everybody else does."

It struck Stephen that he understood Alice no more than he'd ever understood anybody else—including himself.

When they met at the Ritz, they ordered tea and sat on a cushioned wicker sofa as the others about them did, trying to look decorous—imitating the ways they imagined English people took tea.

During the previous hour Stephen had heard repeated over and over in his mind only the word "bored" and through it the tone of Alice's voice, which seemed to him near desperation, near the end of her rope; whereas, previously he had not understood that she might even feel put upon. He was prepared with the first few words he offered her: "You've been working too hard. You've got to stop it. You need a vacation."

"No, I don't. I had a vacation in Italy. Remember?" Stephen realized her voice was no longer strained or upset.

"You sound much better than you did on the phone an hour ago," he said.

"Just getting it into words—just getting it off my chest —helped."

"Onto my chest?" He smiled. "Shouldn't I be the one to say, 'Let's stop this. Let's not go through with it'? Is that what you want to hear?"

"No. I want to see it through."

"Why do you want to do it?"

"For the money," she said. "And to prove that I can do it." Then she added: "And to get even." Then very quickly she turned to face him above the tea sandwiches and the doughy English cake and the British china and asked him sharply: "Why do you want to do it?"

"To become someone else," he answered.

"Who would you like to be?" she asked with a smile.

"A rich man."

"And what would you do with your money, Mr. Richman?"

Without a pause he said: "Live in a beautiful, ancient house on the Lago d'Orta."

Alice laughed, a snortlike laugh. Then she said, "I don't think you want to become someone else; it sounds to me as though you just want to be fossilized. Preserved in amber. You want to feel safe and sound. But it's as if you saw pressed flowers behind glass, and said to yourself, 'They're safe and sound. I'd like to feel that way, too. So I'd like to be pressed under glass.'"

Stephen told himself at that moment: Alice and he were not basically *simpático* with each other. But it did not break his heart; he wondered what would. But his heart didn't give him a hint. Therefore, it did not surprise him that when he saw the opportunity to begin a new love affair he reached out for it without a qualm.

In September Stephen was forced to meet with his colleagues on the faculty in anticipation of the opening of the fall semester and then with students once classes began. He felt remote from them all; a gap of some sort, which he could not name, was opening wider than ever between him and everyone else. He prepared to give his three core courses: in the history of philosophy, in aesthetics, and in logic. But, alone in his office during the day, he frequently found himself—instead of working on his class notes—writing letters to Leslie Egmont at his post-office box. One read:

> Perhaps the whole idea of the history of philosophy is a mistake. It is much more chronicle than it is history. First this happened, and then that happened, and then something else happened; because each great original thinker was reinventing the wheel. Just as each individual has constantly to reinvent himself. What one loves in history is to see the developing consequences of choices, making the sharpest distinction between those that were intentional and those that were coincidental but inescapable, especially if unanticipated—that's where the drama of discovery is! That's what makes plot in fiction thrilling. But we are now at a stage in Western culture where we barely believe in the consequences of actions or the effects of thoughts. If we live for the moment, who cares what effect that will have on the next moment? Tracing influences no longer excites the intellect. Was it always so? Was each great thinker imagining himself a Moses

coming down from the mountain with an entirely original decalogue? There would be no consequences, no influences then. Only pointless originality.

Despite the fact that Stephen thought more and more of each person's "high seriousness" as a condition of solitary confinement, he found himself under the pressure of the chairman of his department, Professor Johnson, who was pressing for what he took to be ever-greater impersonality of thought, personless objectivity. Johnson had come back from his trip to Japan without any interest whatever in Eastern or Oriental mystical thought. On the contrary, he returned crazy about computers and word processors. It was as if he'd hoped to eliminate the vagaries of individual personality by taking communications among members of his faculty one step beyond the typewriter into the word processor. A handwritten letter embodied the impression of the personality out of which it came; the typewriter eliminated those individual marks and offered the appearance of uniformity, such that any bloody fool might have written it; but a word processor, with its microscopic dots making up letters to make up words to make up messages, went a step beyond that and by its very appearance implied that no personal mind was necessary—a machine could have created the message by itself. It appeared to Stephen that Professor Johnson lusted for such impersonal assurances. "On the other hand," Stephen complained to Alice one evening, "Johnson is becoming more eccentric than ever. For the sake of economy he has stopped sending official notices through the mail in sealed envelopes. He's taken to sending them on postcards marked 'personal and confidential.' Imagine! On open-faced postcards . . ."

Alice shrugged her shoulders. He took it that she implied the world consists only of eccentrics, that each person sees himself or herself as the center of things and everybody else, by definition, must be somewhere off-center.

By the middle of the month she believed that her work on the leather had made it supple enough to begin hammering the impression of the pomegranate image and she calculated that it might take her about six weeks to impress the pattern over the whole of the space. In anticipation of the time when his letter of inquiry could be sent to appropriate "fences," Stephen drafted and redrafted the wording of his announcement and invitation, polishing phrases of ambiguous meanings, waiting for Alice to tell him the time was right for mailing them off.

In the meantime, classes had begun. Stephen left his apartment twenty minutes before his ten o'clock class started and walked up Hinman, slowly, with a sense of a lamb being led to slaughter. At the curve of Sheridan, from which he could see an array of pseudo-Gothic, pseudo-classical, and resolutely twentieth-century concrete and glass buildings—that hodgepodge of university eclecticism—he ran into Professor Winston Claiborne Hubbard. He was, of course, a man in his sixties; it was only professors over sixty who maintained the tradition of insisting on all three of their names being used.

Professor Hubbard was what used to be called a fine figure of a man: well over six feet tall and broad-shouldered, with wavy soft white hair and a white beard, dressed in tweeds with leather patches at the elbows of his jacket. He admitted that it amused him a little—but only very slightly—that he looked like photographs of Havelock Ellis. He was a professor of eighteenth-century literature, specializing in the writings of Samuel Johnson.

Dr. Johnson offered him full scope to enjoy the skepticism of a profound cynic at the same time he was enjoying a Pascalian gambling man's Christian orthodoxy. He thought of himself as an eighteenth-century pendulum; his swings were heroic. They would vary with his moods, his personal needs, the makeup of the class he was teaching at the moment, or the seducible nature of a favorite student. He was the author of five volumes of occasional essays, all of which shared the tone of a pedantic dogmatism charmingly seasoned with a worldly indifference to whether he was convincingly persuasive or not.

Professor Winston Claiborne Hubbard fell into step with Stephen Cooper and they headed toward the center of the campus.

"Am I right in thinking that you are a little *blue* today, my friend?" he asked.

Stephen replied, "As usual, sir, you are perfectly accurate."

"Well, it is the first day of classes; you are to be forgiven. Do you fear that today the fraud will be discovered?"

That stopped Stephen short; he turned and looked squarely at Professor Hubbard, nearly whispering: "I beg your pardon."

Hubbard suppressed his surprise at not having been perfectly understood; he was always surprised when he was not perfectly understood. Therefore, he explained, "You know the fear we all suffer from—those of us who think we know everything. The fear of the moment when a student or a colleague or an administrator or someone from Mars will stand up in our classroom and point a finger at us and say, 'The truth is that you do *not* know everything.' That is the fraud I was thinking of. Don't we all suffer from it?"

"Oh, that fraud . . ." Stephen replied with a smirk.

"Were you thinking of some other fraud?" A large smile opened in the ample silken white beard of Professor Hubbard's Olympian head.

"In this day and age," Stephen began, "there is so much that is likely to be fraudulent, it is very difficult to know when one might actually encounter something genuine."

Hubbard laid his heavy hand upon Stephen's shoulder and said patronizingly, "It is not only too early in the day but it is too early in the semester to attempt an epigram regarding fraudulence—if you don't mind my saying so."

"Not only do I not mind your saying so," Stephen responded in an attempt to be equally grandiosely gracious, "but I am most grateful to you for reminding me that the essence of a liberal education is to arrive at the point of spiritual humor that enables us to bear up despite everything we can see through."

"Well, then, you'll be all right, Cooper. You'll be able to get through the day without being discovered."

This kind of conversation, Stephen concluded with a certain sour appreciation, is the nature and, thus, the benefit of academic collegiality.

CHAPTER ELEVEN

A FTER THREE DAYS OF TEACHING, Stephen complained to Alice that he'd had a headache for three days. "It might be your glasses," she replied. "When was the last time you had your reading glasses checked?"

"How sensible you are!" he replied with admiration. "I haven't had them looked at in four or five years."

"Well, now you know what you have to do."

Stephen decided that, just for the hell of it, it would be Leslie Egmont rather than he who would have his eyes examined. He was taken by the idea of appearing in public in his disguise for a few hours, now and then, as a kind of mini-vacation from life.

He asked three or four of his acquaintances to recommend an eye specialist, saying that his old one had died. A Dr. Danilov was recommended twice; Stephen telephoned his office and made an appointment for the following Tuesday. The office was in the Pittsfield Building, that mecca of medical and dental practitioners on Washington Street just off Michigan Avenue. When the examination was complete and he had a new prescription in the breast pocket of his jacket, he came out of the elevator into the lobby and looked around until he found the coffee shop. He wanted only a late-morning cup of coffee but the restaurant was filling up with people taking an early lunch. Toward the far end of the room he saw a woman seated alone at a small table for two.

She was a petite brunette with rather long hair held back from her face somehow down the length of her neck.

Her complexion was peachy and radiant, her eyes dark. She stared rather intensely at the chicken-salad sandwich before her, or let her eyes roam about the restaurant inattentively. Her summer suit of blue-and-white-striped seersucker would have been mannish, but the cut of the jacket and the folds of her chiffon blouse pointed up her breasts. Stephen observed the wedding ring on her left hand, as he approached, rested his hands on the back of the chair opposite her, and asked with gallant politeness, "Would you be generous and kind enough to let me sit at this table with you?"

She looked up quickly with uncertainty but then smiled her acquiescence. Stephen remembered with pleasure that what she was seeing was a white-haired, mustached man with three warts on one cheek. He took off the blue-tinted glasses and introduced himself as Leslie Egmont.

"That's a very unusual name," she suggested, obviously willing to engage in conversation.

He brought the new prescription for eyeglasses out of his pocket and showed it to her, saying, "That's how it's spelled. *If* you want to remember me . . ." He then launched into a direct assault. "It's not that there is no other available seat in the restaurant, you know," he said. "It's just that you are the most attractive woman here. You drew me to you by your magnetism. You make me feel a very lucky man!"

The woman actually blushed—a delicate, rosy hue suffused her rounded cheeks. She put the chicken sandwich back onto its plate and dabbed her coral-colored lips with her napkin. Clearing her throat, she said, "My name is Nancy Waters."

He wanted to match her remark by saying, "What an ordinary name," but he prevented himself from making such a mistake. Instead he asked, "What are you suffering from?"

"What makes you think I'm suffering?"

"We meet here in the Pittsfield Building. Nobody comes here except to visit a doctor. It's like being on *The Magic Mountain.*"

"What magic mountain?" She was vaguely disturbed; but Stephen was all the more delighted to discover that she had never heard of the novel. He said, "I'm here just to get this new prescription for reading glasses. You?"

"Oh . . ." She began somewhat hesitantly, but then confessed. "I come here two days a week for relaxation sessions."

"It must be very successful. You look quite relaxed to me. What is it you have to relax from?"

"Stress," she said.

"Even you : . . I would have thought that a lady as beautiful as you, as neatly turned out, as happily married, probably with two young children, living in the suburbs, should be without a care in the world, should be the last person in the country to suffer from stress."

"Are you reading my fortune?"

"No. Counting my blessings."

The waitress interrupted them and took Stephen's order. He suddenly realized that he was ravenous and asked for ham and eggs, a side order of cole slaw, a pot of coffee. And then, to ingratiate himself with Mrs. Nancy Waters, he also asked for a diet Pepsi-Cola.

She asked, "Are you married?"

"Yes," he responded in a perfectly neutral tone of voice. "I live in Evanston and I have no children. I, too, suffer from stress, but I haven't thought of what to do about it. What happens in your relaxation sessions?"

"First of all, it's a group therapy. We do exercises. We

meditate. And we—how shall I put it?—share our worries."

"Confessionally? And is there a father confessor?"

"Not exactly. We just try to comment on each other's concerns and needs. It's very nondirective."

Swiftly Stephen suggested, "But it's directions that everyone longs for, isn't it? Don't we all want to be told what we should do?"

After a pause, Nancy Waters admitted, "I don't know. I think I've always done what I was supposed to do."

"And still you find that you aren't happy all the time."

"I'm amazed to be talking with you like this. Up to a few minutes ago I'd never seen you in my life, and here we are being, being . . ."

"Intimate."

"Yes. That's the word."

"Then you must feel very strongly that you can trust me."

"So it seems."

"By the same token, I, who rarely ever talk to a stranger, feel grateful to you for letting me speak so freely. I feel that we are drawn to each other."

"Oh, isn't that going a little too far?"

He stared at her eyes, at her slightly upturned nose, at her diminutive lips (was she without lipstick?), at the soft pink shells of earlobes. She indicated that he was making her feel self-conscious by turning her head aside and looking down at the floor and then up at the wall beside her. He noticed the two demure white ribbons that held her hair in bows behind her head.

Stephen Cooper thought of the old saying that if you get a bored housewife into your hotel room she turns into a sex fiend. He had been a successful seducer for so many years of irresponsible philandering that it came to him with considerable surprise that now, as a married man, he was not only planning her adultery but his infidelity as well. Having no previous experience of what fidelity was worth, it did not occur to him to imagine what this abuse of trust would mean to Alice if she were ever to find out about it.

"I think," he began, "we could come to mean a great deal to each other." He held out his hand across the table, offering it to her. She looked down at the inviting palm of his hand and then laid her moist hand in his. His fingers closed around hers.

"I know nothing about you," she said, and withdrew her hand. She took a sip of her tea and then both of her hands were concealed under the table.

"Well, what would you like to know?"

"What do you do?"

"About what?" He laughed. "That's an old joke. It was unfair of me." He had doubts about her sense of humor. "Actually, I inherited a great deal of money, and so I don't have to work for a living. My wife and I travel a good deal but we're here for the fall season. Especially because of the Chicago Symphony. Do you like music?"

"With two teenaged children I'm exposed to a great deal of rock and roll—if you call that music."

"I'd like to offer my help. I think I could help make you relax even more than therapy sessions twice a week. When is your next session here in the city?"

"Thursday."

"Let me take you out to lunch. Let us have a little time alone together—two kindred spirits trying to ease the stress of life away from each other's souls."

"I've never known anyone who speaks the way you do."

"If you are free at this hour on Thursday, I will come here and pick you up and take you away to someplace beautiful and comforting, and we will talk our hearts out."

"I just know I shouldn't . . ."

"I was afraid I would offend you. I know you're too good. . . . I'm so sorry I suggested—"

"No. No, it isn't that . . . the truth is I wouldn't mind."

"You will, then! You'll have lunch with me on Thursday." He clapped his hands and whispered, "Bravo! I knew we were kindred spirits the moment I saw you. God, you're so beautiful."

Driving home Stephen congratulated Leslie Egmont— a man without a past, without a well-established personality, responsibilities, or experience—for having benefited from years of association with Stephen Cooper. For a man with no character, no history, and nothing to lose, Leslie Egmont was making his way in the world.

Forty-eight hours later Leslie Egmont collected Mrs. Nancy Waters as she leaned against a heavy brass decoration in the lobby of the Pittsfield Building, squired her into a taxicab, and led her away to lunch at a remarkable restaurant, at the corner of Michigan Avenue and Oak Street inside a towering new skyscraper of rose-colored marble and glass.

The restaurant Spiaggia—the Italian word for beach— was designed on three levels in such a way that diners seated at any of the tables had their attention directed outward through the windows two stories high toward the Oak Street Beach across the street. In contrast to those restaurants that are oriented toward the bar at the entrance or the dance floor in the middle or the dessert wagon at the end of a central aisle, Spiaggia was constructed so as to lead the sight of every diner not only away from his companion but away from the restaurant out to the view of the sky and the lake. Stephen thought that his choice of this restaurant was a master stroke of cunning for it did not appear as though he were throwing himself at Nancy Waters; on the contrary, he was simply inviting her to share with him an aspect of the outer world. He felt certain that it would only reassure her of his intentions that when he said, "I've thought of nothing but you for the past two days," he was staring at the joggers or the bathers or the swimmers on the other side of the intersection below them. Similarly, staring away from him, she said, "I couldn't find your name in the Evanston telephone directory."

"Well, of course, I have an unlisted telephone number." His voice was calm, impersonal; but he felt a jolt of triumph, realizing that she had tried to make contact with him.

"I understand . . ." she consoled herself.

A waiter took their order for wine and then drew their attention to the menu. When they had chosen rich North Italian dishes, they looked about the restaurant itself, taking in the dusky rose and pale lime green, powerfully punctuated by black marble columns.

"I've never had lunch alone with a man I barely know in my whole life." Her voice was demure but her body seemed relaxed—unafraid.

"Tell me the story of your life," Stephen asked of her.

She described the world of Morton Grove—a western suburb—in which her husband was the most respected lawyer; her thirteen-year-old daughter and her eleven-year-old son were model children; where people performed only basic functions of society: they were merchants and professionals, builders and teachers, policemen and mailmen, grocers and bakers—and most of them knew each other.

Stephen said, "I had forgotten that communities like that existed."

"How could you?" she asked. "That's the way most of the people in the world live."

"I think of people living only in great cities where they believe happiness depends on not knowing anybody else."

"But that's the smallest percentage of people in the country," she said. "If by great cities you mean New York and Boston, Chicago and Los Angeles and half a dozen more—you're still talking about only some fifty million people."

"Only?" He stared at her so she could bask in the expression of surprise on his face—and feel appreciated as an original thinker. He felt confident she could not guess how much he doubted the thought was original to her.

"But that's about twenty percent of the population of the United States. The other eighty percent live in small cities or towns like Morton Grove, where I live."

"And believe that you are happy because you know everybody?"

"I'm not entirely happy. For example: I've never had a friendship with a man. I married my husband when I was nineteen years old—the day after I graduated from high school. I think I've had lunch alone with another man maybe four or five times in my life, but he was either a relative of mine or a relative of my husband. Is it true that in a big city like Chicago a married woman can be the friend of a man, meet with him alone socially—and that's really all right?"

"Better than all right. It's the way sophisticated people cultivate their best selves." It did not matter to Stephen what they were saying to each other; they could have been cooing and crowing. It mattered only that their voices intermingled, stroking each other's need for company, so that he could fire her imagination with fantasies of friendship and melt her assumptions about being a faithful wife in the warmth of his pseudo-solicitude. He did not touch her—did not hold her hand or even to try to kiss her. Now he must play hard to get.

He spoke of his world-wide travels, implying that he invested much of his unearned income in building up a vast art collection. He spoke of places in Europe and Asia and South America that were unknown to her.

"Imagine," she exclaimed. "To think that there's a place named São Paolo in Brazil where millions and millions of people live—and I have never heard of it before."

"That's all right," he counciled her, "they've never heard of you, either."

It was the first time that they laughed together.

Stephen calculated correctly that by the time they had finished eating, walked up the stairs and back out through the restaurant to the escalators down toward the exit from the building, it would be she who asked him, "Will we ever see each other again?"

"Would you do me the honor of having lunch with me again next Thursday?" He knew the word "honor" would make the invitation irresistible.

"You aren't bored with me?" she asked modestly.

"You're joking of course. What you offer me is the very opposite of boredom; what you offer me is the fresh air of purity." He proposed that on that next Thursday they have lunch in a private dining room.

After accepting his invitation she admitted that she had never been to "a private dining room" before.

What Stephen had meant by "a private dining room" was the sitting room of a suite in the Drake Hotel. Nancy

Waters showed no trepidation. She sat on the sofa and he in the large armchair opposite her. They selected lunch from the menus that were on the walnut desk and he phoned their order to Room Service. When the waiter had left, Stephen locked the door behind him. They drank champagne and left the food until later. He suggested that he supplement her relaxation sessions with a deep body massage, and she laughingly said she would "try anything once."

What he knew, from years of experience, was that she'd try anything three or four times. Because his interest would last for three or four times; and then she would want to see even more of him but he would break it off. It is one thing to escape from your wife occasionally; it's another to escape from the escape.

After the third time that they had taken lunch in "a private dining room" and then made love in the adjacent bedroom, and after seeing her off on the train to Morton Grove, Stephen returned to the garage to take his car out and withdrew the wallet from his jacket for the parking check. He found—wedged in between the laddered pockets containing his credit cards—a message on the notepaper from the Drake, which read: "Leslie—For when you want to call me—" and gave a telephone number. "Nancy."

He felt defiled to discover that she had intruded herself into his wallet, assuming she had done so in the bedroom while he washed up in the bathroom; and then he felt grimly appalled by the thought of her riffling through those cards, his driver's license, his bank identification card, all in the name of Stephen Cooper, whereas he had sedulously let her know him only as Leslie Egmont. What could she have thought if she looked at any of those cards? He knew at that moment that he would never choose to see her again. He tore her note into tiny squares and dropped the pieces of paper into a rubbish can of the parking-lot office while he waited for his car to be brought down.

Having forgotten that he'd written it to himself, Stephen was surprised when he stopped off at his post office and found the following remarks in a letter sent to Leslie Egmont:

The pleasure in seducing a suburban housewife like N. W. is not only in the sexual satisfaction that comes with a little "change of scene," a vacation from home, but also in a vacation from academic work. Academics are so concerned about whether their judgments are right and their arguments are persuasive—they have banked everything on the aggressive powers of their competitive minds—they become nothing but the powers their minds can exercise. Whereas a suburban housewife—and I suppose her lawyer husband—think of powers of the mind as only one of many means of entertaining themselves and others; a *power* on the level of singing in the shower, or turning over an omelet effectively, or quoting from a feature-story writer in some popular magazine. Their kind of thinking isn't constantly being called before the bar of accuracy and plausibility and verifiability. They are closer to understanding thought as a means of creating pleasure in personal relations rather than the academics' means of intellectual warfare.

Conclusion: therefore, my professorial colleagues are under the delusion that it is more important to win a scholarly argument than it is to make another human being feel good; whereas Nancy Waters, who has never imagined what it would feel like to win an intellectual battle, cares most of all about how to combine feeling good herself with making someone else feel good.

Now that I no longer see the point of the whole long "scholarly argument" that has been my teaching and writing career, I had better concentrate on good feelings.

Stephen read the letter as he strolled down Michigan Avenue and tossed it away into a litter basket at a nearby corner. He was on his way to take Alice out for dinner. She had asked him to meet her not at either entrance to the Art Institute but at the dock in the loading zone, an enormous barnlike stone annex to the museum on Monroe Street.

They were now at the end of October, and Stephen realized that work on the leather wall hanging was nearly completed. The impressions of the pattern were all in place. Alice had begun applying the colors. She had told him that in order to "age" the gold and the vermilion she would keep heat applied for a week or so.

They calculated that the "letter of inquiry" could be mailed out by the first of November. Alice had been gathering the names and addresses of curators, museum directors, gallery owners, and others to whom it would be sent. She had promised to bring the list home with her that evening. But why she had especially asked Stephen to meet her at the loading dock remained a mystery to him.

Arriving just before the five-o'clock rush hour began, Stephen walked up the ramp. A uniformed guard came out of the office on the platform to ask what he was doing there; he recognized Alice's name and said Mr. Cooper could wait for her there. Two other uniformed guards sat by the doors to the office building. There was no other bench or chair for anyone to sit on, so Stephen leaned against one of the concrete pillars, watching a truck pull out and the people on the sidewalk beyond stride purposefully toward the underground garage or to their cars parked along Columbus Drive. Members of the museum staff began to come out between the guards. When Alice appeared he was standing only about eight feet away from her. She nodded.

Alice then directed her attention to one of the uniformed guards, who reminded Stephen of the customs inspector at O'Hare. They were obviously familiar with each other. She opened her handbag and the guard looked into it casually. Then she pressed together the metal clasp, opening a manila envelope, and pulled about half an inch of blank bond stationery out of the envelope, running her thumb along the edge. The guard checked the list on the clipboard in his hand and then winked his approval. Alice linked her arm through Stephen's and they descended the ramp together.

Only when they were well away on the sidewalk toward Michigan Avenue did Stephen venture to ask, "Now, what was that all about?"

Alice turned to face him and whispered, "To show you why I can't go through with it."

Even as he bumbled out the question, "Can't go through with what?" did he imagine she had set the leather wall hanging to self-destruct before they could get home to their apartment that evening.

But she explained slowly, as they walked toward the steak restaurant in the Palmer House where they planned to have dinner, that she could not go along with the part of the plan to bring the leather wall hanging into the Art Institute, where it could be shown to potential buyers. Their original scheme was to keep it on the floor under one of the large work tables in her studio for the time when an interested party would make an appointment to see it. They would then rent one of the small dining rooms in the museum for an evening and set up the leather to be displayed there. The buyer would be asked to arrive at the Michigan Avenue entrance and be accompanied by one of them through the monumental halls and galleries all the way to the dining rooms in the new wing at the opposite end of the building. Such a person would arrive for the "unveiling" with his psychology already conditioned by the weight of authority of works of beauty—rare and glorious objects—if not literally priceless, then surely of enormous financial value, and, therefore, he would be in the most receptive frame of mind for considering the purchase of what would then be put on display before him.

Alice said, "I know you love the idea of showing it at the Art Institute because you thought that would outweigh even the documents or the leather itself, for that matter—as far as authentication goes. But you had to see for yourself that anything other than personal belongings in a handbag are inspected on leaving and checked against the guard's lists, so that if you take something out of the building a week or a month after you brought it in, you have to remember the date . . ."

"Well, yes, but I thought we could do that with a long pine box."

"And the contents would be recorded by the guard—'one large sixteenth-century leather wall hanging'—alongside my name. I don't want anything about this forgery identified with my name."

They had reached the restaurant when Stephen asked, "How long are those guards' reports kept?"

"They started doing this only a few years ago, after

the Cézannes had been stolen. But I imagine they'll have to keep the reports forever. What if the director brought in a bag of golf clubs a year ago and doesn't decide to take them home until five years from now? They'll still have to find the record of his having brought them in before they'll let him take them out."

"They literally kept a record of your having brought typing paper with you this morning?" Now seated in the steak house, he tapped his fingers on the manila envelope on the red tablecloth between them.

"Many valuable etchings or engravings or drawings would fit into a manila envelope this size. That's not to say," Alice continued slyly, "that the reports are more accurate than the guards themselves. For example, this morning I took into the office, in this envelope, about fifty pieces of blank typing paper that I brought with me from home. This evening I walked out with about the same number of sheets of Art Institute stationery."

Stephen quickly opened the envelope, pulled one sheet out. The letterhead was at the bottom end of the envelope. "How clever of you!" Stephen said.

"So, along with your 'invitation to the dance' proposal, you can include a letter signed by the chief financial officer of the Art Institute on this stationery authorizing you to negotiate on behalf of the museum, eh what?"

"You are brilliant." Then he asked, "How do we get the signature of your chief financial officer?"

"It's on my every salary check." Drawing the end-of-the-month envelope out of her pocket, she handed it to Stephen, saying, "Be my guest."

And then she handed to him her precious list of twenty-three names and addresses on three-by-five index cards.

"You are as methodical as you are brilliant."

"And beautiful?"

"And beautiful!"

"And hungry!"

"But *where* will we show a buyer? Not in our own apartment . . ."

"Of course not. In a hotel room. Don't you agree? Not just a bedroom, but a suite. We'd invite him into the sitting room. Have you ever rented a suite in a hotel in Chicago for the night?"

Stephen nodded and wondered whether he was blushing.

CHAPTER TWELVE

T<small>HE TWENTY-THREE LETTERS</small> went into the mail on the day that Ronald Reagan was reelected for a second term as President of the United States. They contained the letter of authorization on Art Institute stationery, an explicit description of the priceless object for sale, with polished ambiguous phrases referring to the death of Dr. Joachim and the necessity for the sale to be exclusively "private." There was an invitation to respond to Mr. Egmont at the Fort Dearborn post office along with the instruction to send a telephone number and a suggestion for the best time of day to be reached by phone.

That evening Alice and Stephen sat together on the sofa in the living room watching the returns of the national election on television. The electronic calculation of probable results projected from a minimal count of votes in the eastern half of the country undercut all of the uncertainty and therefore excitement of the results. From very early in the evening it appeared "statistically inevitable" that Ronald Reagan would win by a landslide. Numerous pictures of him taken through his long career flashed on the screen. The Hollywood actor turned politician, seen as governor of California, seen on horseback on his ranch, seen waving as he emerged from a swimming pool. Unexpectedly, Stephen heard his wife ask, "Why is he called an ideologue?"

"Well, all politicians are ideologues to some degree," Stephen began, warming to the invitation. "I mean, political leaders stand for certain ideals and propose certain policies to bring them about—and more often than not they stand for *ideals* without being specific about how they will put those hopes into practice. Reagan is a wishful thinker who gives us next to no idea of how he'd make his wishes work. He's an old-time actor who reads his lines as convincingly as he can, without making anybody believe he understands how all those incompatible wishes can be brought into being at the same time."

"I suppose all politicians are wishful thinkers."

"Yes, but some of them have read books. Reagan doesn't give the impression he's ever carefully thought through any ideas. It seems to me he never refers to having read anything. He goes back to a very ancient tradition." Stephen smiled. "He's really an old-fashioned warlord, like Genghis Khan or Attila the Hun—out of the oral tradition. They didn't need books. They had king's messengers and court councilors who would *talk* to the leader about what they might do and then he would make some grand strategic plan, and other people would have to figure out how to put it into practice."

Both of them laughed and then Alice suggested, "Since he's over seventy years old, you know, it may be he's like some of those outdoor statues that have to be removed for protection, and there's a substitute that appears for it in public. Years ago Michelangelo's sculpture of David was taken away from its place in front of the ducal palace in Florence. A replica was put in its place, and the original preserved indoors in a museum." She laughed out loud, and then continued: "And now the great equestrian statue of Marcus Aurelius that has been outdoors in a square in Rome for nearly two thousand years has been taken away to be restored. For all we know, Ronald Reagan is a kind of Dorian Gray moldering in the attic in the

White House while a reasonable facsimile appears on all public occasions."

He felt that they were becoming silly together—a release from tensions that they had hardly experienced since they were married. Only here and now, he reckoned, could the deadly seriousness of politics be thought of as a drawing room comedy.

Despite the rare occasions such as those moments of feeling silly together with Alice, Stephen reflected before he fell asleep that night, he continued to be aware of a gradually increasing distance from other people. There was no one he was close to, no one he shared human warmth with. His new reading glasses came to symbolize in the physical realm what he felt in his psychological world: only when the plastic lenses were in front of his eyes could he read anything within three feet of his eyes. Beyond that he could make things out clearly. But a sheet of typescript or a printed page was indecipherable—in effect a blank—when it was closest to him. In the end, he thought as he fell asleep, everything would become as invisible to him while awake as everything becomes unconscious to him when he sleeps.

The next morning Alice announced that she was turning off the space heaters and the heat lamps because she believed they had done all the good they could for the aging process; and that that evening they should enjoy a sort of unveiling.

After dinner they undertook to remove the leather from the wall in Alice's room: they disconnected each of the strings that had made up the grid and rolled the leather away from the foam rubber and the cork board. It was then that Alice expressed an unexpected romantic wish—she wanted them to look at the leather only by candlelight. Stephen and she searched the apartment and rounded up four pairs of candlesticks, two with long, fresh, white tallow candles in them, the others with half-burned remnants, placed them strategically about the living room, lit them, and then turned out all the electric lights.

They carried the warm "body" of the rolled-up leather between them, through the dark hallway, into the candlelit living room, and in the glow of those golden flickering tapers, they unrolled the leather so that part of it hung behind the back of the sofa, the rest fell down and across the seat onto the floor.

Stephen broke the silence by exclaiming, "My God, it really is beautiful!"

The rich faded chestnut color of the aged leather showed the warmth of time on its wearied surface; the endless pattern of pomegranates spotted it inconsistently with the muted glitter apparently cracked by the passage of time. The brilliant red of the vermilion appeared here and there as only the remnants of an antique legacy. Stephen felt the silk-smooth heftiness of it between his fingers and brought his nose down close to it to inhale what he thought of as the muskiness of its fragrance.

Alice ventured to express her critical judgment: "I think it can pass for the genuine article."

"Authenticity," Stephen said, "is in the eye of the beholder."

"Well, yes, if all the other signs are right. I've gone over this—every inch—with a magnifying glass, again and again, and I haven't found a single clue to give away the truth. This very object *might have been* the one carried by Catherine of Aragon in her luggage when she arrived in England."

They were seated in the armchairs opposite the sofa now and contemplated the beautiful forgery opposite them.

Stephen said, "Do you realize that the house of the Spanish Ambassador where Catherine of Aragon arrived on the day that her ship docked in London is still standing there on the south bank of the Thames River, more or less opposite St. Paul's Cathedral? There's still a plaque on that narrow house to commemorate the event."

"I had no idea. Really, you know the oddest facts."

He smiled. "I remember being shown the house when I was a tourist in London, in my student days. It's in that section of London near where Shakespeare's Globe Theatre stood. That's all gone now, of course. But it's also near where the only Gothic church remains in London."

"There's only one Gothic church in London?"

"All the others were destroyed by the Great Fire."

Still staring at the leather rather than Stephen, Alice said, "It's because there are people who care about such associations that our fortune will be made." And then she laughed nervously.

"There really are such collectors, aren't there?"

"Oh, yes! Of course, it isn't that they care so much about historical objects for their own sake, but they care to enhance their status by being identified with them. It's not an impersonal joy that such things still exist in the world, and there are people to protect and preserve them, as much as it is the possessors' satisfaction in saying to themselves, 'Now, this is mine!' That's what they care for most! It's as if the object is both a window into the past through which they see something marvelously rare and precious and, at the same time, a mirror that reflects them looking at it, so that they always see both the object and themselves possessing it."

Stephen said, "A kind of fantasy ego trip."

"By the way," Alice began, "speaking of mirrors, the longer I worked on this the less likely it seemed to me that this was a wall hanging. My bet is that this piece of leather was the inner lining for the ceiling of a canopy bed. Not exactly as sexy as a mirror on the ceiling over a bed, but serving a ritual function of invoking fertility."

Through the rest of the month of November, Stephen felt that he was treading water. One day dully succeeded the next while he waited for responses to the "fishing" letters he had sent out. He got into Alice's bed and made love with her every other morning; he conducted his classes at the university three days a week; he felt the pointlessness of his office-hours meetings with his graduate students—the blind and the hopeless leading the uneducable; he reduced his reading to nothing more than newspapers and magazines. He waited. He looked at overcast skies and watched the temperature drop at the beginning of what would be an unusually cold winter. He watched reruns of 1930s and 1940s movies on the television Late Show. One evening Alice and he killed three hours playing gin rummy, in silence.

When he stood at the open door of her bedroom and found her staring at the photograph of her dead son, he only half jokingly asked, "When we are rich—and infamous—should we buy a penthouse apartment on the Gold Coast, or would you rather have a mansion in Lake Bluff?"

She looked at him sadly and shook her head. "Neither."

At Thanksgiving time he received a joyous note from

his sister-in-law in Washington announcing the birth of her daughter's daughter, with statistics of her height and weight and the moment of her delivery. Stephen said, "The wedding was at the end of April. That makes it a seven-month baby, doesn't it?"

"Perhaps that's why they got married," Alice remarked.

"Perhaps that's why she looked so radiant at the marriage ceremony." The recollection that came vividly to his mind was the sight of the beautiful girl in the bikini diving into the swimming pool.

But immediately after Thanksgiving everything changed. In the course of four days, seven letters appeared in Leslie Egmont's post-office box: one each from London, San Francisco, and Washington, four from New York. Each of them was from a person representing himself as the appointed agent of "a private party" designated to open negotiations for the sale of the object that Mr. Egmont was authorized to arrange on behalf of the Art Institute of Chicago. Each supplied a telephone number and the most appropriate time to reach the party's agent. Five of them were during office hours; two were home numbers for use during the evening.

With a clean pad and a sharp pencil on the desk, his voice husky with self-confidence to disguise his uncertainties and anxieties, Stephen placed the calls from the telephone in his study, during the solitude of the following mornings, and then later in the evening.

Five of the seven representatives made it clear during the first few minutes of conversation that, while their principals' interest had been piqued by the description of the object, they did want to confirm that the asking price was negotiable downward. When Stephen insisted that the figure of a million dollars was the floor, not the ceiling price, they withdrew their expressions of interest. Stephen was not fazed; he was then still under the optimistic expectation that there would be many more responses in the mail.

The man who signed his letter "Mr. Peterson," reached at home during the evening in the Washington, D.C., area, raised no difficulty about the asking price and proposed that he fly into Chicago a week later to meet with Mr. Egmont about eleven in the morning.

Stephen suggested the Ambassador East Hotel. Mr. Peterson promised he would telephone from the lobby when he arrived.

Similarly, "Mr. Mahdi" in San Francisco expressed no reservations concerning the asking price. He was eager to come to Chicago as quickly as possible. Stephen suggested the Wednesday afternoon before Mr. Peterson arrived on Thursday morning. Mr. Mahdi was to telephone from the lobby when he arrived at the Ambassador East.

In both cases, Stephen said he would telephone again if there had to be any change in the plan, but when he called the Ambassador East he was assured there was no difficulty about a reservation for a suite the following Wednesday. He specifically asked for rooms on the second floor because he and his wife would be bringing with them a rather large object, which might not fit into the elevator but could be carried up at least a few flights of stairs.

The voice making the reservation asked, "What kind of object?"

Stephen surprised himself by his ingenuity in instantly lying, "An Oriental carpet."

In the course of the following days, Stephen continued to check the post-office mailbox, but no additional response to his letter arrived. Instead he discovered a let-

ter he had written from his office, on university stationery, which read:

I have just come out of a faculty colloquium in the
philosophy department here with the distinct
impression that the more than two-thousand-
year-old tradition of Western rational thought has
been so invaded and rotted out by Eastern
mysticism it will take another thousand years to
restore it. We now suffer from a kind of Buddhistic
sense of transformations: anything can become
something else; everything can be understood to
mean anything and everything else.

Not only young students but aging faculty
members appear to be taken in by the idea that we
do not use language in order to arrive at truth, to
refine truths, to try with ever-widening grasps to
incorporate more and more truth in harmonious
systems of thought. On the contrary, they believe
that language thinks us; language is reified to a
causative power, the way Marxist thinkers used the
idea of history, for the past hundred years.

It's enough to make you swear you'll never use
language again. Would it be possible to live only
through music and graphic and plastic images? They
never aspire to delimitations of truth. There has
always been the assumption that beauty contains
truth but within larger and more satisfying
arrangements. I'm sure that must be why I believe
the best thought I have read in any novel for the
past few years is in Umberto Eco's *The Name of the
Rose,* when he says: "We must make the truth
laugh."

I am so weary of the absence of laughter.

Wearing their disguises, Stephen and Alice registered
at the Ambassador East Hotel as Mr. and Mrs. Leslie
Egmont, while two uniformed porters carried their long

pine box away to a service elevator. Stephen gazed about the lobby with a jaded eye, regarding the green marble floor shot through with lightning strokes of white, the huge crystal chandelier, the folding Chinese screens, the gross pottery vases filled with elephantine bouquets of flowers, the heavy glass-topped tables—without any appreciation of the effort at elegance but rather with a question as to whether any of the objects was genuine in any sense.

When one of the managers, carrying their overnight luggage, showed them into the suite at the end of the corridor on the second floor, he declared, "Marlene Dietrich stayed here in 1936." After he'd gone, Stephen said, "I'd bet you anything they say that about every suite in this hotel." And then, more reflectively, he added, "I feel as though everything in the world we live in is an invitation to imitate something else."

Standing at one of the ample sitting-room windows, Alice looked out at the narrow street between State and Astor; from that angle she could see cars driving up to let passengers out under the marquee of the entrance to the hotel and, across the street, the quaint turn-of-the-century brownstone houses and their oddly green-toned stone façades or turn-of-the-century brick and plaster transformations of American gingerbread, with curved glass windows that created narrow turrets. "It makes me think of gremlins and gargoyles." She asked, "Did you know that at the corner of Astor Street, in the basement of an apartment house, there is a replica of Maxim's of Paris?"

"No. Is it open to the public—like Ripley's Believe It or Not?"

"It's a restaurant."

"Let's go there for dinner tonight."

They examined the rooms: from the foyer to the living room, bedroom, bath, closets; considering the size of the chintz-covered sofa, the armchairs, and the desk; taking in the color scheme, all hues of pastel blue and lavender, with large watercolors of flowers framed on the wall— irises color-coordinated with the upholstery. They decided to display the piece of leather on the king-size bed. Unscrewing the pine box in the bedroom, they withdrew the leather from between the sheets of flannel that had come with it from Salamanca and smoothed it out over the bedspread.

Stephen imagined that his wife and he gazed down upon it lying there before them with the joyous adoration of parents beholding a wondrous child they had produced. "Aren't you nervous?" he asked her.

"No. I'm a fatalist. We've done what we can; now, what will be will be."

He chuckled. "I'm a nervous fatalist."

Mr. Mahdi was forty-five minutes late for his appointment. By that time Stephen was standing sentinel at the window watching each taxi, passenger car, or livery that drew up under the marquee to let out men or women who entered the hotel. Therefore, he had seen the chauffeured limousine from which a passenger appeared when he announced to Alice, "This one is an Arab."

When Mr. Mahdi arrived in the room and introduced himself, he said merely as a statement of fact, not as an apology, "I hope I haven't kept you waiting." He appeared to be an Arab only from the shoulders up, in that his large head was covered by a burnous of white silk held in place by a black and gold cord like a laurel wreath encircling his head. The fabric concealed his hair, his ears, and his neck, revealing only his thick black eyebrows and dark eyes, a rubbery, bulbous nose, and strangely thin lips surrounded by a black mustache and goatee. But he was dressed in a Western business suit of Oxford gray and wore a pin-dotted navy-blue necktie on a white shirt. He was a man of medium height but barrel-chested. There were no rings on his fingers. He shook hands cordially with Mr. and then, to his surprise, Mrs. Egmont; he looked around the sitting room with approval and out the window from which, he was pleased to announce, he could see that his driver had most conveniently found a parking place directly across the street. He spoke a flawless American English with no identifiable accent.

"My master, the prince," he said, "is one of the great grandees of Saudi Arabia." He went on to explain. "He is in a position to entertain a whim—that is to say to indulge a wish—to express his admiration for many things British, even to the extent of building on his estate in Riyadh a reconstruction, as it were, of Hampton Court."

Stephen suppressed a laugh of ridicule.

"In fact, he has had all of the bricks baked in England, and they are being shipped to Saudi Arabia even now. The construction of the palace will commence in the spring. Since Hampton Court was a cardinal's palace given to King Henry VIII, it struck me that the leatherwork that you, Mr. Egmont, are in a position to sell on behalf of the Art Institute of Chicago would be a most appropriate decoration for the palace in Riyadh when it is completed. I suggested that to my master, the prince, and he allowed me to open negotiations with you for purchase of the object."

Mr. Mahdi sat in the middle of the sofa, with Stephen and Alice in armchairs facing him across the coffee table. Alice, apparently inclined to slow down the course of the interview, suggested that they order tea or sherry or cock-tails if Mr. Mahdi would enjoy something to drink; but he declined.

On the desk between the two windows lay the documents in their clear plastic folders, prepared to convince a potential buyer of the authenticity of the leatherwork. Mr. Mahdi, invited to examine them, stood for a few moments with his fists resting on the edge of that piece of furniture and lowered his head toward the pieces of paper, which he read in a cursory manner, showing no interest in pursuing further questions of provenance or proprietorship.

"But I would like to see the leatherwork!" he said. Stephen led the way into the bedroom.

While Alice remained in the doorway between the two rooms, Stephen went to the head of the bed and stretched out his arm toward the leather lying there like a virgin princess about to be inspected by representatives of a royal suitor. Mr. Mahdi walked around the bed with his head lowered, his eyes piercing to the golden and vermilion pattern on the chestnut-colored leather. He leaned close enough to smell it. He reached out and felt the edge of it between his thumb and forefinger. The inspection took no more than three minutes.

When they were seated again in the living room, Mr. Mahdi, with his arms crossed over his ample chest, stated, "My master, the prince, is like a great gourmet who, when he hears of a restaurant that offers meals of exquisite delicacy, is not in a position to dine in public but sends a representative to see if such food might be prepared for him in private. I am in that sense his 'taster.' "

Stephen and Alice smiled understandingly.

"My master," he continued, "will accept my judgment in such matters as these. But as the buyer he does not consider that my services are worth a great deal and I am not compensated by him more than to a token extent. He considers that my services are of very much greater value to the seller—since, without my recommendation, the seller will not have the benefit of his making the purchase."

Now it was only Mr. Mahdi who smiled broadly.

Alice pronounced: "You are not objecting to the asking price, however, I take it."

"Not at all. It seems quite fair for such a rare and beautiful object—and one so appropriate for the new Hampton Court in Riyadh."

Stephen asked, "Well, then, won't you tell us what token of appreciation you have come to expect on behalf of the seller?"

"Gladly. In my relation to those who sell objects or services to my master, the prince, I am accustomed to receive twenty-five percent of the list price."

Stephen laughed and then cut his laugh short.

Alice, in a level voice, asked, "And you have experience of receiving that percentage?"

"Indeed."

"Therefore," Stephen said, "in this instance, where the price is one million dollars, you would expect our commission to you to be a quarter of a million dollars."

"Correct."

Alice suggested, "But if the asking price were one million two hundred and fifty thousand dollars then, perhaps, you would accept the two hundred and fifty thousand dollars."

"No," Mr. Mahdi sighed with a gesture of resignation, "you see the figure of one million dollars has already been approved of by my master. I could not return to him with an altered figure that is higher." He paused to add, "It would be *infra dig*"—and then translated the Latin for their benefit: "beneath his dignity."

The three of them sat in a mutually awkward silence.

Eventually, Stephen was able to clear his throat and say, "I'll have to discuss your proposition with my principals."

"Naturally. It is understood—just as the fact that all of these discussions are in the strictest confidence."

Stephen agreed, " 'Confidence' is just the word for it."

"Then I will expect—or shall I say, merely, hope"—Mr. Mahdi concluded on a note of polished modesty—"to hear from you in the near future. You have my telephone number."

"Yes."

"I'm sure that everything can be arranged amicably." With that, the three of them rose from their seats and said goodbye at the door in the foyer.

"Ingrate," Alice muttered a moment later.

Stephen, who opened the door to see if Mr. Mahdi was lurking in the corridor, returned with the word that "He's gone."

"Rip-off artist!"

"You feel unappreciated," he realized. Without personal sympathy but with the cool intelligence of surprised recognition, he said, "You want your skill, your artistry, to be acknowledged."

"He couldn't tell an original from a replica if he had one in each hand. He knows nothing. He's nothing but a swindler."

They stood together at the window now and watched Mr. Mahdi cross the street. His driver opened the car door for him.

"If he's an Arab, I'm an Eskimo," Stephen said. "Do

you think, if he actually represented 'my master, the prince,' he would have said a single word about him or Riyadh or a reconstruction of Hampton Court? Preposterous!"

Alice had turned away from the window when Stephen caught her elbow to pull her back. "Look!" he nearly shouted. As the chauffeur started up the car, "Mr. Mahdi," seated in the depths of the limousine, could be seen in profile through the rear window along his side, vigorously tearing the bulbous rubbery nose away from his face. As his car merged into traffic toward Astor Street, he was removing the black mustache and goatee.

Stephen laughed. "We haven't the faintest idea what he looks like. He's as phony—"

"As we are!" Alice concluded for him.

But they had survived a shared ordeal and, for a while, they were ebullient. They laughed at the absurdity of one deception confronting another. They appreciated the fact that the replica could be palmed off as an original—if they were willing to give up a sizable percentage of the sale price. Neither of them had admitted to the other their fears in anticipation of carrying off the interview, and so it was a great relief to both of them to discover they had done it, as Stephen suggested, "in a professional manner."

They took a long, slow shower together in the bathroom and began dressing for dinner at Maxim's or at the Pump Room off the lobby in the hotel, when it struck Alice that they should not leave the leather in this suite without either of them to guard it. They had rolled it up off the bed and laid it down in the pine box without screwing on the lid.

"No one is going to slip it into his vest pocket and walk out."

"Not likely," she agreed. "But *I* won't run the risk, anyway. I'll stay here. You go out to dinner."

"We could take turns. You go first. I'll wait. I'm not that hungry. I can eat later."

"This is foolish," Alice concluded. "Why go out separately? We can order dinner sent up from the Pump Room. I'd like that, wouldn't you? The way Marlene Dietrich did in 1936."

Their wake-up call was set for 9 A.M. and the prearranged-for coffee arrived at the moment the telephone rang. A good two hours were available for them to make all of their preparations before Mr. Peterson's appointment. They spoke little. Stephen felt a residue of resentment and irritation he imagined Alice shared with him over the frustrations of the previous evening because of the presumptuous proposal of "Mr. Mahdi." They had not talked it out between them. It remained like a bruise beneath the skin.

Not waiting for maid service, they straightened up the bed to be the display platform for the leatherwork. They dressed neatly and unpretentiously and ordered more coffee and an additional cup in anticipation of Mr. Peterson's arrival. Their disguises were in place. But they were on edge, as if sulky in advance of events that might disappoint. Once burned they felt twice shy. Alice broke a silence by saying, "Let's not be impatient."

"I'm not impatient. Just eager."

"Please stop trying to smoke that pipe."

He put the meerschaum down in an ashtray on an end table, and opened a window a few inches. "It's colder today," he said.

Mr. Peterson was only a few minutes late. He apologized sincerely and at length, for which Stephen was grateful because he felt instantly disconcerted by the impression that he had met this man somewhere before; his uncertainty made him reluctant to speak. But Alice—as Mrs. Leslie Egmont—was most cordial. They all shook hands.

Mr. Peterson had no distinguishing features: a nondescript "nice-looking" middle-aged man in a chesterfield coat with a black velvet collar; he wore no hat. When his topcoat was hung in the foyer closet he appeared ill at ease, buttoned up tight in a dark-blue suit, uneasily warming his hands against each other. He gladly accepted the invitation to drink a cup of coffee. "I've been up since dawn," he said, smiling.

It was then that Stephen recalled him distinctly: the suave solicitude, the restorative cup of coffee, the vaguely seductive smiles. Stephen nearly tripped over his own feet in his anxiety to take Alice away and whisper to her. As she handed Mr. Peterson his coffee, Stephen stammered, "Would you excuse us for a moment?"—gesturing for Alice to follow him to the bedroom.

When he had made her follow him to the bathroom beyond the bed and closed the second door behind them, he said, "I know that man. Name's Peter Brewster. He's a curator at the Freer Gallery in Washington. I talked with him when I was there."

"Are you sure?"

"Certainly!"

"Do you think he recognized you?"

Stephen turned to the mirror over the sink to stare at his white wig, the pepper-and-salt mustache, the moles, the tinted spectacles, thinking: I don't even recognize myself. How could he? "No. I can't believe . . ."

"Well, then, calm down. Let's brazen it out. He's more nervous than we are!"

After deep breaths, slowly they returned to the sitting room.

Yes, Stephen thought, Alice is right. He's more nervous than we. And what a simple-minded pseudonym: Peter B. becomes Peter's son. Not much imagination there. What he said out loud was "Mr. Peterson, please forgive us. I suffer from gout. Needed some medicine. Only my wife knew where it was. She's saved my life, *again.*" He chuckled in a hollow way.

A gesture of Alice's hand told him to back off and leave the conversation to her. She was more accustomed to dealing with weak men than he was.

They sat together on the sofa and talked of the late Harold Joachim. "I knew him," Peterson said. "Not well, mind you. But I respected him greatly. I know how these private arrangements come about sometimes."

Stephen observed them from his armchair. The man, he told himself, is not simply without character; there is a blandness about him that is not worldly polish, merely the smoothness of the All-American Boy: the determination to be decent and proper and polite, as if no situation could possibly arise that would be too difficult for good manners to handle. No conflict of wills—no matter how perverse—was beyond the competence of a Boy Scout's training to resolve satisfactorily. Still, Stephen could not suppress the feeling that Peterson was a boy sent on a man's errand.

Alice proffered their caller the documents displayed on the surface of the hotel desk. Unlike "Mr. Mahdi"— a man sent on a boy's errand—Peterson studied each piece of paper with determined seriousness, reading every word, examining the letterheads, the stationery, the signatures. "Most impressive," he concluded.

When the time came for them to move into the bedroom and consider the leather canopy lining itself, Peterson brought a magnifying glass out of his breast pocket and went over the length and breadth of it; he sniffed the surface, fingered the material, tilted it to see the play of light on the intaglio pattern at different angles. He made all the gestures and grimaces, and grunted all the monosyllabic comments of an expert, a connoisseur. No time limit seemed to restrain him. In the end, he said, "It could be the real thing."

"*Could* be?" Alice asked. She was offended. "Have you any reason to suggest it isn't?"

Peterson straightened up and put away his magnifying glass. "Well, yes. You see, I know where the original is."

"I'll be damned!" Stephen blurted out. He felt suddenly eviscerated.

Alice looked at him severely. She said only, "Wait," and turned back to Peterson. "One thing at a time," she began. "You say this could be . . ."

"Could pass . . ."

"As the genuine—missing—leather gift Catherine of Aragon brought with her to England."

"Yes, it could. It is a superb piece of work!"

Stephen was afraid Alice would say, "Thank you." But she grunted and said only, "If you believe—or imagine—the true gift is elsewhere, why did you even bother to consider this as a possible purchase for your . . ."

"Master, the prince," Stephen said half under his breath.

"For your boss," Alice continued, "whoever he is?"

"He's not my boss in any ordinary sense. He's a sort of friend; I'm sort of his agent on this one-shot affair. Really, I can't tell you more than that."

"You amaze me!" Alice declared. "If you had any reason to 'sort of' imagine this is not *the genuine article,* why should you have bothered to come here, to examine it— and the documents of authentication—at all?" She did not conceal her indignation. She was aglow with righteousness. She actually added, in a pique worthy of Queen Elizabeth the First, "You try my patience, sir."

"I'm here because my 'boss' hopes I'll confirm the authenticity, and that he'll have the pleasure—and the honor—of buying it."

Then there was silence.

"Despite your reservations," Alice said defiantly.

Now it was Peterson's turn to chuckle, mildly. "Yes. Despite what I know. That's why I came. And I think we can do business."

On that note they returned to the other room, and telephoned Room Service to order sandwiches and beer for lunch. But Mr. Peterson was somewhat ill at ease; he had yet to make his pitch.

Almost sharply, Alice asked, "What sort of business?"

Mr. Peterson studied his black wing-tipped shoes. When he finally brought his eyes up to look toward her face if not directly at it, he said—barely audibly, "If my word to my boss gets you a million dollars . . . will you give me ten percent of it?"

Stephen smiled broadly to himself at the thought of how it discomfited Peter Brewster to make this double-dealing "request." Stephen considered him a Mr. Clean, whose experience of depravity in the past was likely to have been limited to smoking a cigarette. Mr. Clean had evidently never placed such a "request" before anyone else in his life. This simply must have been a unique opportunity he could not resist taking—if, in fact, he did know what had become of the original.

Echoing Stephen's response to "Mr. Mahdi," it was Alice who now said, "This will have to be discussed with our principals, the officers of the Art Institute of Chicago."

"Yes, of course, I understand. But these documents"— he gestured cautiously toward the surface of the desk— "these are Xerox copies, are they not?"

Both Stephen and Alice nodded affirmatively.

"Then you have the originals carefully preserved elsewhere. In that case, would you let me take these copies with me?"

Alice and Stephen conferred silently and nodded again, in agreement.

Mr. Peterson then drew in a breath that seemed to give him more confidence and he announced: "If your principals will accept my proposition, then I'll see to it that my boss accepts my word for the 'genuine article.' "

Stephen said, "It might take a little time."

Peterson replied, "It hasn't changed hands often in four hundred years."

Stephen broke the silence in the room by saying, "We ought to leave. It's already beyond checkout time."

Alice laughed. "You mean that after just being asked to give up a hundred thousand dollars you're worried about being charged for another night in this suite?"

"Well, that does put it in perspective."

Nevertheless, within fifteen minutes Stephen had brought his car up to the entrance of the hotel, the pine box was angled into it, and they drove away onto Lake Shore Drive and north to Evanston.

It was during the drive that Alice offered the opinion that "It's unlikely anyone will come forward as an agent who isn't going to ask us for something between ten percent and twenty-five percent of the price."

Stephen said, "And that's what we learned on our summer vacation or, in other words, if you lie down with dogs you'll get up with fleas."

"Spare me . . ."

"How many more times do we want to go through this?"

"Let's accept his proposal and give him a hundred thousand dollars."

"And keep nine hundred thousand!" Stephen agreed triumphantly.

CHAPTER THIRTEEN

ALL THE SUBSEQUENT ARRANGEMENTS were made by telephone, after working hours, to Mr. Peterson's home number. Following the basic agreement on terms, he was given
information regarding the numbered account in the Bank
of Zürich to which the million dollars was to be transferred. When notification of that deposit had been
confirmed, Stephen requested that a bank teller's check be
made out in the name of "Mr. B. Peterson" and held by
him with the original documents of authentication.

Alice agreed to Stephen's suggestion for a particularly
operatic touch to the actual transference of the property.
She telephoned the Art Institute to say that she had
twisted her ankle and to ask whether the car that would
drive her to work that day might be allowed to park in the
loading zone of the Art Institute. A station wagon was
rented for the day so that no one could trace their own
license plate. She was then in her office by ten in the
morning, while Stephen remained in the station wagon
awaiting the arrival of a hearse. Perhaps Mr. Peterson had
a sense of humor after all; he had arranged for the large
pine box to be transported in a rented hearse by a driver
who would deliver it in Washington, D.C. Stephen helped
the driver take the long box out of the station wagon and
place it in the hearse. He turned over to him the manila
envelope containing the documents and the bank check
and even made the driver sign a receipt for them, in a most
professional manner. He then went off to celebrate.

For many days now since the beginning of December

he had tried to convince himself that, in fact, he was a rich man; but actual belief in that truth depends on the joy of spending money lavishly. He had recklessly—without consulting Alice—transferred $200,000 dollars from the numbered account in the bank at Zürich to his checking account in Evanston. Now he strode along Michigan Avenue from the Art Institute north to the Drake Hotel with his checkbook in one of the pockets of his trousers. The sobriquet "The Million Dollar Mile" for this stretch of thoroughfare took on a new meaning for him and brought a smile to his lips, despite the clouded sky and the frigid wind blowing off the lake against his right side as he walked north. If he was a rich man he would buy the things that rich men buy. He would lavish gifts upon his wife.

He walked into the extravagance of Neiman Marcus under the layered marble archway as if coming into his birthright. He asked at an information desk for the location of the fur department and took the escalator to an upper floor. There was something bizarre about the department of fur coats, which he could not immediately identify. There was no customer in the room at that late morning hour; only a handsome black saleswoman sat behind a kidney-shaped desk, its surface covered with deep red morocco leather. Soon enough, he realized what the oddity consisted of: there was a metal chain around each rack of fur coats and each coat was individually chained to it. The saleslady remained seated behind the desk. He wondered whether the chain was attached to her as well.

Sitting in the chair opposite her, he said, "I'm interested in a full-length mink coat. Or maybe a sable."

The saleslady became vivacious. They discussed the size of the lady for whom the coat was intended; they discussed the range of prices—basically between forty and ninety thousand dollars; they discussed the range of hues and lengths of pelts. She gladly disattached certain coats and laid them out on the thick pile of the white carpet.

Stephen Cooper enjoyed the exquisite pleasure of choosing a ranch mink coat with a shawl collar, "coachman cut," selling for $42,000—plus tax, of course—and asked the saleslady to try it on so that he might see how it would look "in motion."

He then withdrew his checkbook and asked how she wanted the check to be made out. She said she would need two forms of identification and she would have to telephone for a credit check. He waited while she did that, after making sure his wife could return or exchange the coat if it did not please her in any way. Then he waited while she had the large box gift-wrapped. The wrapping was a metallic silver and black paper, and he was able to hold the box by a clear black plastic handle. He took the escalator further up to the restaurant, where he had a long, slow, expensive lunch, while feeling the heft of the boxed coat secure on the floor between his legs.

He had spent an hour in the fur department and he had written a check for one gift for Alice amounting to more than he had ever earned in one year as a professor of philosophy. It did make him begin to feel that he was a man who could have all that money can buy.

By midafternoon back on the chilly street he walked along with his precious package in hand, past Water Tower Place, toward the Drake, where he thought he would find at Spaulding's Jewelry Store in the hotel another gift that he had in mind for his wife.

The soft carpeting was like velvet under the leather soles of his shoes. He almost glided toward the glass counters of bracelets, rings, necklaces, and earrings. He did not know what he wanted and he explained to the elderly salesman behind the counter that he would have to look around for a while by himself. But when he saw a marquise-cut diamond he knew *it* was what he was looking for. He had no idea of what experience earlier in life this particular ring echoed and reinforced—and he did not need to know; it was enough for him to sense that this was exactly what he had been looking for. He asked, first of all, to hold it in his hand, to try it on his own little finger for a moment; and then he asked the cost. It was priced at $35,000. Stephen brought out his checkbook, wrote the check out, and waited while the salesman telephoned his bank. This is a certain kind of waiting that a rich man—he told himself—becomes accustomed to. He was assured that his wife could return it or exchange it if there was any dissatisfaction on her part, and that in any case they would be happy to adjust the size to fit whichever finger she chose to wear it on. The diamond ring fit into a very small maroon velvet box, which he placed in his pants pocket warmly close to his genitals.

He was seated in the station wagon, at the loading dock of the Art Institute, when Alice came out, moving slowly, with her false sprained ankle strapped in gauze. They drove through rush-hour traffic, listening to a Brahms symphony on the radio in the rented station wagon; returned it to the Hertz station in Evanston; picked up their own old car; and drove home.

Stephen said that he had a surprise for her, but Alice was not curious about the large package in its shiny wrapping paper. She seemed only tired, withdrawn, and sad. The early darkness of this cold December evening pushed them to walking rapidly toward their building and taking refuge in their apartment. As soon as they closed the door behind them, Alice started a bath running and stripped off her clothes. "I have to get rid of this bandage." Dropping it into a wastepaper basket, she said, "I felt hateful about it all day—while I thought of you getting rid of the leather."

"We are very well rid of it," he replied. For the first time, it struck him that the absence from their apartment of that large piece of leather, which had been with them nearly since they married, could be felt as the disappearance of a third partner.

"It's not so much gone," he said, "as beginning to be transformed. It will return in different shapes." At the doorway he was smiling now as she lowered herself into the bath. He nearly sang the lines: " 'Nothing of it that doth fade but doth suffer a sea change into something rich and strange.' "

"Enough. Thanks." Alice gestured him to leave her alone.

When she reemerged, wearing a thick plaid bathrobe and fuzzy slippers, Alice's face glistened in its paleness. She had removed all of her makeup with a cold cream that left it shiny and she had pulled her hair back in a ponytail and held it in place with a bandana, a circle of kelly green tied in a knot under the ponytail on the nape of her neck. "Well," she said, "it's gone. We've done it. It's over."

"Now the rest can begin." He stood with his back to the fireplace, his hands in his pockets. "You are the magician who has turned leather into gold. Now you must be rewarded."

"Having done it successfully is reward enough."

"Nonsense. I have here something I can only say I wish I had given you when we became engaged."

"Were we ever engaged?" Alice asked, trying to smile.

Stephen ignored the question and brought the velvet

box out of his pocket. She had seated herself in the center of the sofa and he bent forward pressing it into her palm, asking: "Will you marry me?"

Alice snapped open the box and stared at the diamond ring with a kind of dumb disbelief. Finally she asked, "Why?"

"For you! For us. For celebration; for flaunting it; for doing with a lot of money what a lot of money can do."

She removed the ring from the box and slipped it onto the finger with her wedding ring. It was only slightly loose. She said: "It's very beautiful," studying it at arm's length and then close up. "But it isn't me."

"I don't see how you can tell whether it's *you* until you've worn it for a while, made friends with it. Give it some time; say, twenty-five years."

"I'll try," Alice said. "I'm really very touched." But she removed the ring from her finger and put it back in the box, leaving it open, facing her on the coffee table. "It was kind of you to think of me that way."

"Kind?" Stephen exclaimed. "I think of you all the time. This is what it means to be loving."

"Or, at least, to show the world what you think of me." She laughed, briefly.

Unfazed, Stephen fetched the Neiman Marcus gift box from the hall. He placed it on the sofa beside her. "This will wrap you in my affection," he said.

Warily, she edged the tough string with its plastic handle off the box and broke through the metallic paper. Stephen helped her to unwedge the flanges of the container, but it was she who drew away the tissue paper to uncover the mink coat. For a long moment she was silent and then—still staring at it, not at him—she asked, "Where could I wear it?"

"First I'd suggest in the bedroom. Then at the supermarket. But mostly, I imagine, to the theater, the symphony, and the opera."

"We don't go to the opera."

"Won't you try it on?"

Alice stood up and drew the full length of the massive but lightweight coat from the box and laid it back against the sofa. She then untied the belt of her bathrobe and dropped it off her shoulders down to the floor. She stood naked before Stephen, who held up the coat so that she could slip her arms through the sleeves and pull it around her body. Barefoot, she paraded through the living room, down the hall to the full-length mirror in his bedroom and then back again.

"What a fabulous feeling" was her only comment.

He said, "You look superb in it."

"They'll love me at the supermarket."

"Why do you knock it?"

She leveled her gaze at him and said simply, "I no more ever expected to wear a mink coat than to own my own private plane. Don't you see—this coat and I are light-years apart."

"No. I don't see anything of the sort. I think the two of you deserve each other. At least you ought to give it a try."

They sat down side by side on the sofa and Stephen stroked the luxurious fur from the collar, along the sleeve, down the length of her legs.

"The truth is," Alice began, "we've never talked about what we would do with the money. The ring and the fur coat are too much of a surprise for me. Too much, too soon. I don't know what to make of them. Let me think about it. Give me a little time."

"But will you respect me in the morning?" he asked.

Both of them laughed—the only cheerful release they

shared that evening; and then they tried seriously to consider what they would do with the money.

"I'd thought of it only as a kind of insurance for later on," Alice said.

"Well, then, there are other surprises to come. Why don't we go off on a marvelous winter vacation? I have two weeks coming between Christmas and New Year's."

"I don't," she said. "Besides, you're supposed to go to the American Philosophical Association convention."

"To hell with that. Why don't we fly down to Rio? Or Tahiti? Or Marrakesh?"

"Because I don't have two weeks between Christmas and New Year's. I took off time in June. . . ."

"Why don't we go to Italy and buy a house at Lago d'Orta? A house in the village overlooking the lake and the island. Or maybe a house on the island, in the town of San Giulio. We could think of it as our vacation house and go there whenever we want to take time off."

"I don't know, I don't know." Alice was obviously discomfited and confused. All she said was, again, "Too much, too soon. It's embarrassing." But she clutched the mink coat close against her nude body.

Stephen said, "Maybe you'll come to love it all."

"I understand that you're trying to be wonderful. You *are* being wonderful! It's just that I don't know what's best for me. I'll have to think about it for a while. It won't take twenty-five years."

It took less than twenty-four hours. The next day was Saturday and both Alice and Stephen slept late, but he had made an arrangement for 1 P.M. and by noon he was itchy with anticipation and eager to see that they had finished their coffee and were fully dressed, so they would be ready at the appointed hour.

"Will you wear the mink coat?"

Reluctantly she pulled it on over her wool suit, saying, "I don't even know where we're going. Why the mystery?"

"We're going for a drive."

"I'd better take my bag and a hat."

Together they moved briskly down the stairway toward the front entrance of their building. Just as Stephen put a hand on the knob of the large glass door he felt Alice's body go rigid next to him, immobilized as a flagpole. She was staring at the large car double-parked in the street opposite them. Glittering in the cold sunlight stood a magnificent Rolls-Royce with a uniformed chauffeur in the driver's seat. It stood there like a monumental work of sculpture: the lower half of the side swept back in curves of perfect smoothness over both wheels and was painted jet black. The upper part of the body and the roof were dark gray; the square radiator gleamed like sterling silver. Alice had difficulty finding her voice. Finally she said, "Don't tell me you've bought a Rolls-Royce."

"No, I haven't *bought* it yet. I haven't even driven it myself yet. But this is a demonstration and while we're out with the driver we can take turns driving it ourselves."

"How did this come about?"

He said that on the previous Wednesday afternoon when he was in the city he'd gone to the Hanley Dawson agency on Rush Street and spent the afternoon with their salespeople looking over the different models they had on the floor, pricing them; he made the arrangement for Saturday at that time.

"How much does it cost?" she asked.

"Oh . . . around a hundred thousand."

Alice opened her pocketbook to search for her apartment key while saying, "I'm not getting into that car." She turned on her heels where she stood and began to walk to the stairs.

"But wait. Maybe I should tell him to come back in a little while—if you change your mind."

Over her shoulder she said, "I don't care what you tell him. But I'm not changing my mind."

Stephen returned half an hour later. "I didn't want the driver to feel he'd come out for nothing," he said.

Alice sat at the dining room table with a cup of coffee before her. Stephen put his overcoat away and came back to sit opposite her.

"I really don't understand you." Her voice was level, she was clear-eyed if sorrowful-looking. "You just can't do these things."

"Why not? We have the money now."

"We can't change our way of life so obviously as to make us objects of suspicion. Of course, maybe I could wear a diamond ring in some private places, or even get away with pretending that it's only costume jewelry. Maybe we can go away occasionally to places like Rio or Marrakesh. That's not flaunting it. But for me to wear a mink coat and you to suddenly own a Rolls-Royce . . . !" She seemed to gag with the difficulty of continuing. Then she added, "How soon would it be before someone reported us to the IRS and the tax spies start investigating?"

"Who would report us?"

"Our neighbors."

"You're paranoid."

"On the contrary. When I first came to Chicago I lived in an apartment in Hyde Park and when I found a better apartment on the North Side I asked one of the guards at the Art Institute if he could help me move. He arranged for two young friends to come with him on a Sunday morning. They were all black. Within five minutes of their starting to carry my furniture out of the building to the beaten-up old van that they had brought with them, the police appeared. A kind neighbor had telephoned to say that three black men appeared to be robbing my apartment."

"But that was to protect you."

"The telephones are just as available for the neighbor who will call out of spite or envy. If we're going to enjoy this money, the only way we can do it is secretly."

"That's hardly like doing it at all."

"Well, I don't want the diamond ring and I don't want the mink coat anymore than I want to be seen in a Rolls-Royce. They'll have to be returned. We can get the money back, can't we?"

Stephen moaned softly. "I wanted them for you."

"I can't believe it," she said. "You never asked me whether I wanted them."

"I thought we wanted the same things."

"Why? We never talked about them. It's all in your own imagination."

"I wanted to make you happy. You've had such lousy luck in your life."

"You feel sorry for me!" she spat out, her voice increasing in volume and furious with contempt. "How dare you? How dare you feel sorry for me? I don't feel sorry for myself. I'm not just a victim. I'm no patsy. I can be angry about things that have happened; and you can be angry about them with me. But I'm not *sorry* for myself. And I'll be damned if I'll suffer you to patronize me. I don't sit around moaning and groaning about my life. I do something worthwhile, and I'm respected for it."

Stephen looked forlorn and remorseful. In a whisper he said, "I don't."

Unrelenting, Alice persisted. "You don't even know what's good for yourself; how do you presume to know what would be good for me? You really never gave a thought to how being ostentatious would put us at risk." Her shrillness was spent now. Calmly she asked, "Do you want me to lose all feeling for you?"

Flippantly, Stephen said, "At least our sex life is good."

"Really? Every other morning? Like clockwork. Rather mechanical, isn't it? Where's the romance?"

"So I disappoint you even in that." Stephen was more shocked than he would admit; was there no straw of his self-respect that he could cling to?

Alice was pursuing her own line of thought. "I should have anticipated it months ago. You're not taking me into consideration. Not asking me what I want. It started when you bought me that fancy frame for my son's picture. It's always been like that. You're not involved in the give and take of a real life." She went on staring at him directly, while he would occasionally catch her eye, but otherwise kept his gaze away from her.

"You just want to get away from life," she continued. "All that talk about a penthouse apartment or flying down to Rio—those are just symptoms. What you truly want—I see it now!—for all those times you brought it up, it's clear to me now. You want to retire, but in a very special way. To escape from life. You want a house on Lago d'Orta. You want a house in the thirteenth century. You want to escape into a fixed pattern that's all ritual and no freedom. No need for choices. It was all established long, long ago. It's your death wish. If you could have it, you could be at rest. No more proving yourself. No more tests, no more compromises. No more give and take. Just repeat your paces: become nothing but a twirling prayer wheel."

Stephen sarcastically asked, "When did you get to be so smart?"

"I've had to take care of myself for a long time now."

"I wanted to try taking care of you."

"You'll have to try a lot harder."

During the following week they met as combatants in a period of armed truce. The diamond ring was returned to Spaulding's and the mink coat was returned to Neiman Marcus. They filled their evenings with receptions for the end of the semester at the university—at the homes of professors and at the faculty club. Or they went out to movies. Stephen always asked what Alice would prefer to do. Even that began to irritate her. "Don't treat me like your mother," she said. "It's not that you have to do only what I want; it's that we have to agree—like equals."

He felt both possessed by her and, at the same time, conscious that the separation between himself and everyone else was growing wider. He was surrounded by a moat.

They ignored Christmas. They did not bring home a tree to decorate, they did not exchange gifts, they did not have a celebratory dinner. On Christmas night Stephen packed his bag for the few days in Washington at the philosophical convention. He was booked into a room at the Hilton Hotel, where all of the sessions were scheduled to take place. The program bored him; the old acquaintances he encountered seemed either drab and dull or arrested in earlier stages of narcissistic enthusiasms. But he barely ventured out of the excessively modern building; the weather was too cold. It was even rumored that Mr.

Reagan would cancel the Inaugural Parade if the weather did not warm up. Washington had rarely experienced such arctic frigidity. Stephen thought it was depressing to overhear the majority of self-selected elite of the philosophical profession in America discussing the weather more than any other topic.

Alone in his hotel room the night before the last day of the conference, he sat at the desk with a bottle of vodka and the blank hotel stationery before him. He drank the vodka and took up the hotel ballpoint pen to address an envelope to Leslie Egmont at his post-office box. Then on the letter paper he wrote:

> I think of the hills around Lago d'Orta covered with vineyards and woods, of the pastel-colored houses on the island in the center of the lake, of the rhythm of seasons, of old men playing boccie, of the carillon sounding from the campanile.
>
> Is it possible that I have drawn the picture of my death wish and not recognized it for what it is? Perhaps. It may be. All things are provisionally true until proven false.

The thought of wishing to be dead brought to his mind the evidence of new life. He remembered that his sister-in-law, Lillian, had sent him a message about their daughter's having given birth to a child. He was in Washington and he thought he ought to phone and speak with her or his brother Mark. It was only ten-thirty in the evening; surely they wouldn't be asleep that early. He placed the call.

The voice that answered the phone was too youthful and cheerful to be Lillian's but Stephen asked if it was she and gave his name.

It was his niece Katherine who spoke and at the same

time that she apologized for her mother's being out for the evening and her father's being somewhere in Iowa or Idaho—she couldn't get them straight—buying or selling the state, she couldn't remember which, she was enormously enthusiastic about inviting him to come and see her baby. "You do know about the baby, don't you?" she asked.

"Yes, as a matter of fact I do. You have my warmest congratulations. I suppose you're visiting between Christmas and New Year's."

"No. I've come home," Katherine said.

"With your husband?"

Katherine laughed. "No. Six months was quite enough. He's gone his way and I'll go mine. But I have the baby to show for it! You really must come and see her. Will you be here through tomorrow?"

"Yes."

"Well, then, come for dinner."

"No, I can't do that. There's a banquet here at the hotel—it's the end of the convention."

"Can you come for drinks?"

Stephen thought about it suddenly as a pleasurable break from the tedium of the professional conference. "Yes," he said. "I'd be delighted to."

"About five?"

"Yes, that will be fine. I'm really looking forward to it."

Mercifully, the baby was asleep when she was shown to Stephen.

The taxi ride to Georgetown had been chilly and the minute's waiting on the doorstep to be admitted into his brother's house was enough to make him feel frozen, so the warmth of the interior filled him with the comforting sense of hearth and home. A maid had opened the door but Katherine followed behind her immediately. She was so grateful for his coming to visit. He barely had his coat off before she took him by the hand and led him up the great stairway to the second floor.

He was taken into a bedroom evidently just redecorated as a nursery. At the center of the room a hooded bassinet was surrounded by a skirt of white satin flounces that would have made a ball gown for Scarlett O'Hara. Only the baby's face and clenched fists were visible above a white crib blanket.

"Her face is like a great big peach," Stephen whispered.

"Isn't she darling!"

Stephen straightened up and regarded his niece. He did not restrain himself from saying, "But you're still a child yourself."

She took no offense. Showing she accepted it as an affectionate remark, she said, "That way I have the best of both worlds. Come now, and I'll take you down to Mother. She's in the living room. We already have drinks. What would you like?"

They were halfway down the stairs when Stephen asked for a dry martini on the rocks. The maid standing in the hallway overheard and nodded to indicate she was off to arrange it.

Passing through the foyer in the hallway Stephen noticed empty pedestals and the nearly empty shelves of display cases.

"Ah, there you are," Lillian welcomed him. She stood up from her armchair close to the large fire burning in the fireplace, approached him with both arms outstretched, and greeted him with a kiss on his cheek. He was aware of how handsome she looked in a North African caftan.

He took the large tumbler of martini from the silver tray offered by the maid. Lillian and Katherine were drinking sherry.

"So you've already seen the baby," Lillian said.

"First things first" was Katherine's comment.

Lillian apologized for Mark's absence and then urged Stephen to tell them his news. What had happened to him since last spring?

This was his only family; they were trying to reach out to him; and he tried to reach back.

They were flabbergasted to discover that he had been married for six months without having told them. Each of them asked numerous specific questions about Alice—what she looked like, where she came from, how she dressed, what she worked at—which Stephen answered at length and with enthusiasm. While he felt that he was acting a role unaccustomed to him, nevertheless it was a recognizable part in a social play: partly the scene of return of the black sheep, partly the intimate gossip in a family comedy. It was a role he had rarely played in all his adulthood and yet he felt he knew just what was expected and could carry it off.

Then, during a pause in the conversation, he heard himself saying, "The house looks somehow different to me. Have you changed things around or is there something missing?"

Lillian said, "Yes, indeed, there's a great deal missing. The whole collection of Middle Eastern ceramics."

"All of it?" he asked. "What's become—"

"Mark tells me it's called 'trading up.' We've made a gift of the whole collection to the Smithsonian—that is, to the Freer Gallery." She explained: "It's one of the museums of the Smithsonian."

Stephen took a long sip of his cocktail. Then he cautiously asked, "What did you trade up to?"

"Oh, something unique! Something quite extraordinary. You must come and see it." The three of them rose from their seats and carried their drinks with them.

As they walked down the hall, Lillian continued, "I haven't decided exactly how to describe it. I think of it like a tapestry but of course it isn't woven. It's an exquisitely decorated piece of sixteenth-century leather. There's something of a mystery about it; we have to keep its source a secret for about ten years." Then she added: "And it has marvelous historical associations."

"What are they?" At that moment Stephen could see it glistening in the soft lamplight of the walnut-paneled library, hanging above the mantelpiece.

"Catherine of Aragon took it with her when she was sent to England to marry the heir to the throne. So you see, it once belonged to Henry VIII. Isn't that incredible? When I touch it I feel I've touched the fingerprints of Henry VIII!"

They entered the room as Lillian continued to talk, dropping phrases like "symbolic of dynastic fertility." Stephen stood near the center of the room with his sister-in-law and niece on either side. Staring at the leather wall hanging he felt himself go waxen and clammy. His hands began to tremble. The sound of the ice clinking in his drink glass was ominous. The two ladies looked at the rattling ice and then at his pallid face. He did not so much step back and sit down on the sofa behind him as he caved into it.

Katherine took the drink out of his hand and placed it on a table. Lillian sat down next to him and held his other hand. "Are you feeling faint?" she asked.

He nodded yes.

"Then put your head down between your knees. Just relax. Lower your head and be calm. Katherine, go and get me a cold compress."

Lillian continued to hold his hand and to pat it. She looked up at the gift of Catherine of Aragon to Henry VIII and then down to the back of Stephen's head and said quietly, "I had no idea you were so emotional."

In the hollowness of his being Stephen felt the idea of an ironic chuckle. This was the moment at which he felt drained of all possible emotion. He had defrauded his own brother: inadvertently, yes; but absolutely.

Katherine appeared with two washcloths soaked in ice water. She applied one to the nape of his neck and one to his forehead. In a few moments he felt better, straightened up, took a deep breath, and sighed.

"I can't imagine what came over me," he lied. "Must have been the drink. Very strong. Haven't had a martini in quite a while . . ."

Lillian said, "Now, now, you'll be yourself in a few minutes."

Stephen tried to smile at her even while thinking: I will never be myself again. I have lost my integrity. I have lost my own soul.

They were all standing then and Stephen grimaced the good actor's smile, conspiratorially saying to Lillian, "You won't tell Mark, will you?" trying to make light of the incident.

"But it was really quite moving," Lillian said.

He felt that she was truly sympathetic with him for the first time—and for the worst possible reasons, which, at least, were unknown to her.

It was then the doorbell rang and, in a minute, the maid came to say that the taxi Mr. Cooper had ordered to pick him up at six-thirty was waiting for him now. Even as his niece and sister-in-law helped him into his overcoat they continued to urge him to change his mind and stay for dinner.

"No, no. You must forgive me, but I am perfectly all right now and so sorry to have . . ."

"Nothing to be sorry for."

"You must come again soon, Uncle Stephen."

"And next time do *please* bring Alice with you."

Throughout the drive back to the city, solitary in a rear corner of the taxi, Stephen felt hot tears gliding down his cold face.

He arrived at the Hilton to find the lobby filled with his colleague-conventioneers dressed for the evening, on their way to the elevators to the ballroom for the banquet at the end of their annual meeting. Stephen was filled with self-disgust; he went directly to his own room. He took off all of his clothes, covered himself in his bathrobe, and turned his attention to the bottle of vodka.

He put both pillows together at the head of the bed and sat back up against them, with the vodka bottle stationed between his outstretched legs. Only the lamp on the night table next to him was lighted. There was no sound but that of his shallow breathing.

He tried to face the sense of guilt he felt for having defrauded his own brother. No consolation came from the fact that he had not planned it that way, he had not wished it so, and he had not done anything to bring it about. He had not thought of the person who might buy the fake leather wall hanging as another human being, a person who could suffer from being defrauded; he had imagined the purchaser only in the most abstract sense as someone who wanted an object that he shouldn't have and therefore would be willing to buy it under conditions that would require him to keep it as a secret to himself.

That psychology had allowed him to deny understanding the purchaser would be a victim, and that he—the perpetrator—would be guilty: would suffer guilt.

But now, as Stephen gulped down one vodka after another, he reckoned that the range of his capacity for feeling had been constricted to nothing but being held in the vise of guilt.

And yet he did not feel alone in that appalling responsibility. "Mr. Peterson" appeared in his reflections. Mr. Peter Brewster, that is. Mr. Curator at the Freer Gallery of Art. How much of a villainous role did that Mr. Clean play? Certainly the connection with Stephen's brother would never have come about without the intervention of Peter Brewster. Was there any truth in his having said that he knew where the original was? If anyone else was as guilty as he, it was Peter Brewster. If anyone else had cause to be ashamed of defrauding another human being —let alone his own brother—it was Peter Brewster. If it hadn't been for him, Stephen would not be alone in his misery filled with self-contempt and the corrosive of self-loathing. He knew that he must confront Peter Brewster. Sooner or later . . .

Stephen Cooper awoke at dawn to find himself lying on top of his bed with the lamp light on, next to him on the night table, and the wetness of vodka on the blanket as if he had urinated during the night.

He turned off the light, moved away from the wet spot on the bed, and fell asleep again for another hour, his head throbbing. Then he got up to shave and shower and dress and check out of the hotel. He left his luggage in the cloakroom, took breakfast in the cafeteria. Aspirins cleared his head, but between nine-thirty and ten o'clock he decided to ride in a taxi to the Freer Gallery, rather than walk.

When he asked a girlish receptionist if Professor Cooper from Northwestern University could see Peter Brewster, she came away from the telephone with the message that he could go directly down to his office. Stephen said, "Thank God."

The girl's southern accent lilted, "You must want to see him real bad."

"Ain't it the truth."

Stephen barely remembered Peter Brewster's office in the basement, with its high window through which the bright cold sunlight fell against the wall behind the desk. Brewster greeted him with a handshake and a thin smile. Dressed in a dark suit, he looked smaller than Stephen remembered him from the Ambassador East Hotel. They sat in worn chairs across from each other but this time Stephen refused the cup of coffee.

"I suppose you're here for the philosophy convention."

"Yes, but also for a family reunion." Stephen had no taste for small talk.

"I wasn't aware that you have family here in Washington."

"Mark Halsey is my brother."

Peter Brewster stared wide-eyed. "But how can he be?"

"Same mother; different fathers."

"Of course." Then he admitted: "I'm acquainted with him."

"I should think so. You were instrumental, I understand, in arranging for him to trade up in the art market. In fact, I take it that you were the key instrument."

Brewster asked, "Trade up? Yes, that's one way to put it."

"Well, it seems very suspicious to me. Mark's turning

over his collection of ceramics—a very valuable collection —and ending up with a piece of leather that cost him a million dollars. All this smacks to me of a swindle!" Stephen was agitated, and moved toward Peter Brewster. "A rather mysterious piece of leather at that—maybe even a forgery, for all I know. Of course, I haven't said anything to my brother about this yet. I thought I ought to clear the air with you first."

Brewster held up one hand to arrest the flow of Stephen's attack. "Hold on. Wait just a minute. You are confusing two completely separate transactions. Your brother's *gift* of his ceramic collection has nothing whatsoever to do with his *purchase* of the leather wall hanging. You've mistaken a coincidence for being connected in some way, when they're not."

"Why not?"

Brewster leaned back in his chair, folded his hands together, and started by saying, "I can give you the chronology of events. The Freer has a superb collection of ceramics from Japan, China, and India; but very thin holdings in ceramics from the Middle East. Mark Halsey began his collection twenty or twenty-five years ago; and during the past half dozen years, since it became known to us, the director has been cultivating your brother as a future patron of the museum.

"You must realize that the certified value of a noncash gift to a nonprofit institution such as this one becomes an income tax deduction.

"Now, by the middle of the past summer, about five months ago, your brother—I mean your half-brother—realized that he would make another fortune in real estate this tax year and he decided to make the gift to the museum then. Our director was away at the time; therefore,

I became involved with negotiations, the evaluation, and the legal transfer of the collection."

Stephen asked, "What was it worth?"

Brewster took a breath and paused. "You may think that is a simple question, but I'll have to tell you how it came about. Over the years, buying mainly at auctions, your brother spent between four and five hundred thousand dollars building up his collection. By now—considering the inflation of the art market, the competition among museums and other private collectors—if that collection were auctioned in the public market currently, it would fetch approximately two million dollars."

"So that's what it was valued at?"

"No, there's another wrinkle. The estimate was made on the value that the collection can be expected to have by the time of the donor's death. For this reason, your brother's gift came to be valued at three million dollars."

Stephen let out a short, shrill whistle.

"You really can't let yourself think of your brother as having been swindled in any sense. For the purposes of his income tax—because he's in the fifty percent marginal bracket—he is able to keep a million and a half in his own pocket." Then Brewster grunted, adding, "If anyone was swindled it was the Internal Revenue Service or, rather, all of us taxpayers."

Stephen stood up uncomfortably and stretched. He walked around to the back of the chair where he had been seated, rested his hands on it, and asked, "Where does the leather wall hanging come in?"

"As I told you, the two things are unrelated—except by the coincidence that I was involved with both. I knew that your brother had money to burn, or rather that he wanted to invest in other purchases on the art market, and

I happened to be informed about the leather wall hanging."

"By whom?"

"Someone on the staff of the Wildenstein Gallery in New York."

Stephen remembered the name among the twenty-three letters of inquiry he had sent out. "And you told Mark about it."

"Well, he asked me to act as his agent."

"And you confirmed its authenticity and told him it was worth the money."

"All in good faith." Brewster smiled.

"But there's something fishy about it, something that makes me very suspicious. The business about keeping it secret for ten years. And then the delivery of it in a black hearse."

"What hearse?"

"The hearse that took the pine box from Chicago."

"Who told you about that?"

"My sister-in-law. Mark's wife."

"That's impossible. She knows nothing about it."

"Then maybe it was Mark himself."

Slowly Brewster repeated the same statement: "That's impossible. He knows nothing about it. The hearse was used to deliver the pine box to my house in Chevy Chase. I delivered it in my own car to the Halseys." He stared steadily at Stephen and slowly announced, "Other than myself, the only people who know I made use of a hearse are the man I rented it from, the man who drove it here, and a Mr. Leslie Egmont." Then he burst into a short, high-pitched laugh. "Well . . . you aren't the man who rented it to me and you aren't the driver." He slapped his hands together gleefully. "So you are Leslie Egmont. I knew it."

"You knew no such thing."

"Well, yes, you're right. I didn't know it was you but I knew the man who wore the disguise was someone I had seen before. It's the nose, and the ears. I have a very good visual memory. I felt certain it was someone I had seen before. Surprisingly, I didn't recognize the voice."

Stephen found himself backing away from the chair until he stood against the far wall.

"It's like finding an old friend."

Stephen said hoarsely, "We're not old friends."

"But now we are permanent co-conspirators. I wonder why you came to see me."

"I don't know. I think I wanted to make you feel as guilty as I do."

Brewster waved away the thought. Full of aplomb, he said, "Oh, no. Not guilty. Rich people who buy up works of art as financial investments deserve . . . to be taken. To be taken unfair advantage of. To be screwed, right?" That must be the way Alice feels, Stephen thought.

"And you took an agent's fee both from him and from me, right?"

"Nothing I have done this time or in other arrangements that I have helped to facilitate makes me feel guilty. And you are not going to do so."

Stephen shook his head. "No more Mr. Clean."

"I beg your pardon?"

"I'm just dumbstruck by how wrong my guesses are about people."

"Could you really have wanted to find out if I share your guilty conscience?"

"I'm not sure. Do you know why you do what you do?"

"Maybe you wanted to find out where the real wall hanging is."

Stephen thought he saw Brewster licking his lips. He quoted the man's earlier remark back to him: "All in good faith.' Does it actually exist? Do you know where it is?"

In a stage whisper Brewster replied: "Right where it belongs. In the Peacock Room, behind the painting of 'The Princess from the Land of Porcelain.' "

"You must be joking. There were the signs on the wall just a few feet from this office . . ."

"Well, when those statements were put up they were true. But to everybody's surprise the original wall hanging was discovered in Germany at the end of the Second World War at one of those great depots for collecting works of art stolen throughout Europe by the Nazis. It was in Wiesbaden. It took years for the legitimate owner to be identified, but by 1948 the leather was returned to the Freer and it was installed where it belongs; and it was decided by the then officers of the museum that it would remain a secret. Why risk its being stolen again?"

"My brother must never know this."

"Never is more time than I expect to have."

"Then speak for as much time as you'll have."

"It would be as much a disservice to me as it would to you if he ever found out. You can trust me."

Stephen wanted to laugh but he felt paralyzed.

Brewster brightly asked, "Won't you tell me how you came by such a superb counterfeit of it?"

"I really can't go into that now."

Stephen asked the taxi driver who picked him up near the Freer to wait at the Hilton while he retrieved his luggage and then to drive him to National Airport. The great monuments he could see from the window of the taxi—the Capitol, the Washington Monument, the Lincoln Memorial, the White House—challenged him to wonder where real life ends and make-believe begins; to wonder how wrong he might be about all the guesses he had made about all the people he knew. Alice had told him, "It's all in your imagination."

However, throughout the flight to Chicago, only one question obsessed him: how could he tell Alice both of the discovery in his brother's home and of the fact that he'd given himself away to Peter Brewster?

CHAPTER FOURTEEN

No LIGHT SHONE in his apartment when Stephen entered and closed the door behind him. All was silent. He peered through the late-afternoon darkness to see Alice seated at one end of the sofa in the living room, a silhouette against the pale twilight beyond the window. He stepped beyond the archway to switch on the nearest table lamp. Her hat and coat were next to her and a suitcase stood on the floor between the sofa and the coffee table.

"What are you doing?"

She raised her eyes and stared at him coldly for a long moment before saying, "You betray me. You are a betrayer."

"It sounds like you've been planning that statement for a while."

"I had a whole day."

Stephen was relieved to interpret that to mean Peter Brewster had not telephoned her since he left his office before noon. Something else had happened.

"You are never to be trusted."

"Oh, well, then." He heard the bitterness rather than the fear in his voice when he asked, "Would you like a drink?"

She merely looked away from him.

"In that case, I'll take a vodka, thank you."

"That dulls your feelings *too*," Alice commented. "But you don't have a lot of feelings to turn off, do you?"

Stephen sipped the alcohol as if it would line him with

a protective coating; but he knew it would not be enough.

"Still waters run deep," she said.

He nodded. If she continued to be enigmatic, this might become a lengthy conversation, he thought, sitting down at the other end of the sofa. She wore her gray wool suit. It was then that he also noticed her wedding ring on the coffee table between them.

"One risks drowning in deep, still waters."

He could not yet estimate where the onslaught would come from.

Calmly and softly he asked, "Will you please tell me what you're talking about?"

Just as quietly she replied, "While you were in Washington, there was a telephone call from Nancy Waters. A Mrs. Nancy Waters."

Stephen felt that, if his soul was a balloon, it had been pricked and all of the air in it was doomed to seep away in a matter of minutes.

"She had hoped to talk with Stephen Cooper, but then she was willing to speak with Mrs. Cooper. Girl talk, you know."

He was not looking at her; he focused on the farthest point he could see in the hallway. But he heard the sneer in her voice.

"Mrs. Waters had a 'personal' request to make. She was trying to locate Leslie Egmont. Could I give her his phone number? It's an unlisted number, she knew. And he's been traveling a lot. But she thought he might be back and she *so* wished to be in touch with him again.

"I asked why she thought either my husband or I knew a Mr. Leslie Egmont—and that flustered the poor dear. She really couldn't say. It was a 'personal' connection she had made, somehow.

"It's painful for a woman to listen to the voice of

another woman who's been spurned. You know the sound: the post-adultery blues, when the lady *can't believe* it's over."

Stephen offered: "It was over a long time ago—before we were married."

"Don't be ridiculous. Leslie Egmont didn't exist before we were married. He exists now, though, doesn't he? And he leaves a trail of crumbs to Stephen Cooper, wherever he goes. Doesn't he?"

Stephen put his drink down on the table, crossed his arms over his chest for warmth, and said, "It was an insignificant little fling. I don't think I saw her more than three times. It meant nothing to me."

"Too bad," Alice snapped. "It means a lot to me. It means you're a fraud. A betrayer and a fraud. It means you endanger my life! Not only do you batter my self-respect—it's *infra dig*, but let's not care about my self-esteem—you run the risk of getting, and giving me, a disease—but, of course, let's not wallow in anticipation of *that*. You drop the clues that can put both of us in jail!"

Abjectly, he raised both empty hands before him. "What do you want me to do?"

"Leave me alone. That's what I want. Get out of my life!"

He looked at her abandoned wedding ring. "You can't be serious. You wouldn't leave me, would you?"

Now she looked him straight in the eye with a silent glare of incomprehension. "Can you actually be so totally selfish as to imagine I'd still stay with you? Yes. Selfish is all you are. Thoughtless and self-centered. Self-pleasing: any and every superficial whim of momentary pleasure has to be satisfied. And the devil take the hindmost. That means: let Satan grab your ass."

She went on: "The three men I've been closest to in my life—my first husband, my son, and you—turned out to be monsters of selfishness."

"Maybe that shows that if you get very close to anyone, you discover just how selfish he is."

"That's a smart guy's wisecrack. I'm not that cynical."

"You told me you are a fatalist."

"You think that means I'm a willing victim? Not on your life. I may have been taken in by you for a while—but I'll get out of it. Unlike you, I know how to protect myself."

"What will you do?"

"I'll change my name and become a nuclear physicist at Los Alamos."

"That's a smart guy's wisecrack."

"True."

Looking from her to the suitcase on the floor between them, he said, "I mean, what are you planning to do right now?"

"I'm taking the long New Year's weekend in Minnesota. I'll breathe clean, cold air and look at pine trees. I'm taking the car." She stood up and put on her hat and coat. "I don't know what you're going to do, but I hope I never see you again."

He stood up; his arms hung down at his sides, his hands like heavy weights.

Vehemently she said, "You must really understand how much I hate you."

"Alice," he began to plead, as she carried the suitcase through the hall and opened the door. "Please, listen to me. *I can't go on without you!*"

"Fake it," she said over her shoulder, and closed the hall door behind her. He heard the heavy catch snap closed, like the blow of a metal hammer, as if locking him in.

The balloon was as flat as an empty pillow case.

Stephen stood still, balanced on his feet wide apart, a hollow statue in the silent hallway.

He realized that he had not told Alice about either who bought the leather wall hanging or what Peter Brewster had found out. It didn't matter. Nothing mattered. Nothing at all. There were no more possible consequences to worry about. The worst of all consequences had been arrived at: Alice was lost to him. It did not matter if he lived or died. It may never have mattered to anyone else; but now it did not matter to him.

The thought occurred to him that perhaps Alice and he should seek the help of a marriage counselor. That idea struck him as inanely inappropriate and he burst into howls of laughter. "At least one aspirin for terminal cancer," he told himself. And then the bellows of laughing were transformed into an onslaught of tears. He wept uncontrollably. His sides heaved with the torrent of his weeping. The face he held in his hands was drenched with his weeping. He cried for the pitiful end of his life.

He staggered to the bathroom and bathed his face in cool water. He regained his composure. He caught sight of his reflection in the mirror above the sink and realized that he could not go on living as Stephen Cooper. He no longer had any sense of what could be *expected* of Stephen Cooper in the future to enable him to continue performing that role. He could not be a husband, a lover, a brother, a teacher, ʋr a writer. He had failed at everything.

This feeling of not being able to go on performing was experienced as a kind of stage fright—without any dependence upon an audience at all. He was not afraid of making a fool of himself before strangers—the remote audience. But, before the intimate audience of personal relations, he was incapable of performing because there was no author and no director who left him with any further instructions. He had used up all the directions he had come to be equipped with, self-contradicting as they may have been. All of the lines he had learned by heart—self-destructive as they had proved to be—were all used up.

He was afraid to leave the bathroom. Afraid of leaving the painful reflection in the mirror. He suffered the immobilizing arrest of absolute stage fright. If there was no longer a part for him to play called "Stephen Cooper," what was to become of him?

It dawned on him with the certainty of a revelation that he had been mistaken in the impression he had suffered during recent months of a feeling of remoteness from other people, of distance, as if a moat surrounded him. The flattening out of all content from his soul suddenly made him realize that the separateness was entirely within himself—not between him and other people. There was now so great a distance between what he was and what he appeared to be, between what he actually experienced and how he wanted what he did or said to be apprehended by others, that he had lost contact with his reality as a whole. There was no wholeness; he was a scattering of enemy fragments. His existence might appear to have the unity of his body; but the disparate parts of his thoughts, acts, and feelings had no coherence. He had fallen apart.

Alice, he concluded, had been wrong. He did not wish

to escape from life. He truly wanted to live somebody else's life.

The next morning, disguised as Leslie Egmont, carrying his passport and one piece of luggage, he boarded the Swissair flight on the last day of calendar 1984 from O'Hare International Airport for Geneva. No one who knew him as Stephen Cooper has seen him since.

In the middle of January, alone in the apartment on Hinman, Alice read a singularly practical letter from Stephen, written on the stationery of a hotel in Zürich. It recommended that she declare him "disappeared" to the State Bureau of Missing Persons. He was not sure, but he believed it would take a year or more before he could be declared legally dead. Despite the fact that he had not revised his will since they were married, he assumed that, as his wife, she would come into possession of all of his property. He advised her to inform the Provost of Northwestern University that he was gone. The previous September he had signed papers making her beneficiary of both his insurance and his pension from the university. There was approximately two hundred thousand dollars in their joint bank account in Evanston. He had added that to what remained in the numbered bank account in Zürich, subtracted the two hundred thousand she had received from her son's insurance, which was hers alone, subtracted their "investment expenses" during the past seven months, divided what remained by two—and taken his half out of the account. She knew how to transfer the remaining funds.

He added that she might well be one of the few people in the world who get exactly what they wish for, as she would not see him again. Nor could she expect to see him as Leslie Egmont. He had taken to alternating a variety of disguises. "It is," he explained with some enthusiasm, "the most liberating of experiences, if one can afford it. Now, at last, I understand the ultimate power of a great deal of money: dispensable identities." The letter was devoid of any expression of affection.

At the end of April 1985 Alice arranged for one week's vacation from her job at the Art Institute, adding two weekends to give her nine days in Europe. She told those who asked that she'd spend all of the time in Paris. But she took the flight from Chicago to Milan. She booked into a hotel at the airport, telling the concierge that she'd like to have a car with a driver who spoke English.

When that arrangement was made, she informed the man wearing a chauffeur's black cap that she wished to make a day's excursion to Lago d'Orta. He could not have been more agreeable. He had tape cassettes of the latest American rock music for the stereo set in his automobile; but she preferred silence. They drove north on the highway through the early-spring greening of the countryside, without incident and without conversation. But, when they arrived at the town of Orta, she wanted him to accompany her and act as her interpreter.

Alice could barely remember having visited there some ten months before. All of that visit seemed a blur to her. And yet the views were vaguely familiar. There was the orientation of the town toward the lake with its island in the middle. They walked slowly around the main square: the American woman peering at the faces of the people as they passed each other, as if expecting to recognize someone.

When they stopped at a table of an outdoor café, for sandwiches and fruit juice, the driver read aloud from the

Michelin guidebook he'd taken out of the glove compartment of his car:

> San Giulio Island is reached from Orta by motor boat (5,000 lire for up to four passengers) or by a small motor boat (3,000 lire per hour without the boatman or 5,000 lire return with the boatman and up to five people).
>
> The island is a jewel. The terraces, clumps of trees and flower gardens, which make it up, are circled by a pleasant road. The Romanesque Basilica of San Giulio is said to date from the 4th century, when St. Julius arrived and rid the island of a dragon and the snakes which infested it. The basilica was rebuilt in the 9th and 10th centuries (see: bas-reliefs, columns) and in the 12th century (when the campanile was constructed). Inside, between walls covered with interesting frescoes, you will see the curious 12th century pulpit in black Oira marble, adorned with relief sculptures and motifs, and in the crypt a sarcophagus containing the relics of St. Julius.

The driver asked if she'd like to make the journey: take a motor boat and tour the island. Alice looked at her wristwatch and then said, No, she would rather go to the townhall or wherever the town's records were kept. She wanted the driver to ask if someone had bought a house here during the past few months.

They crossed the nearly empty square in the clear, mild air of early afternoon, noticing the ornamental wrought iron on the old houses, walked through an arcade and up a flight of stairs to the offices of the townhall.

A plump secretary in a red polka-dot dress sat at a table behind a dark wooden altarlike railing, which Alice leaned against.

The driver asked—in the staccato but lyrical notes of

Northern Italian—whether anyone had bought a house in Orta since the first of the year.

The woman simply replied, "No."

"A Signor Egmont?"

"No."

"Mr. Cooper?"

"No."

"Mr. Richman?"

"No."

"Or, if not in Orta, then on Isola San Giulio? Or on the wooded hills above the town—from where one can view the lake?"

"No."

Alice complained that the woman hadn't consulted any document. Could she trust her memory without checking the records?

The driver translated, diplomatically.

With body language and much hand gesturing, the woman explained that no house in Orta or on the island or in the hills had been bought since the beginning of the year. The last house in the surroundings to be sold was a villa on the board of the lake that a Signor Ernesto Ferraro of Milano bought last October. He had been using it for a weekend retreat. Incidentally, his youngest child was born on the day after he purchased the house. A beautiful girl, growing nicely. But there was no real-estate boom in Orta. Not yet. Houses were sold infrequently. The lake and the town had not yet been discovered by developers, who would make it an international resort. Not yet. Maybe the Americans would come. The towns-people expected it—sooner or later.

Walking back through the square to the car, Alice said out loud but to no one in particular, "Then I did ruin it for him." On the plane flight from Milan to Paris, Alice read a day-old copy of the *Herald Tribune*. Oddly enough, she came upon an item on the back page, in the column of News in Brief, that read:

> Prince Philip, the Duke of Edinburgh, will represent the United Kingdom at a ceremony on the first of May in Riyadh. A cornerstone will be laid for the building of a replica of Hampton Court. Some seven hundred thousand bricks, produced according to the methods of the sixteenth century, at the Walmsley Kiln in Reading, have already been shipped by freighter. The construction of the imitation of the palace is under the sponsorship of a prince of the Saudi royal family. When completed and opened to the public as a luxury resort, it will be operated by the Hilton hotel chain.

Morris Philipson is the author of five novels: *Bourgeois Anonymous, The Wallpaper Fox, A Man in Charge, Secret Understandings,* and *Somebody Else's Life.* Born in New Haven, Connecticut, he holds degrees from the Universities of Paris, and Chicago, as well as Columbia University. After working in trade publishing in New York, he became Director of the University of Chicago Press in 1967, a post he has held for some thirty-odd years. Philipson has written short stories, articles, and reviews, and has edited a number of books, including a volume on Leonardo da Vinci. He has also published a biography of Tolstoy and a study of Jung. His numerous awards include a PEN "Publisher Citation"; in 1984 he was made a Commander of the Order of Arts and Letters by the French Minister of Culture.